LOLA WANTS— LOLA GETS

JENS T. CARSTENSEN

Outskirts Press, Inc.
Denver, Colorado

This is a work of fiction. The events and characters described here are imaginary and are not intended to refer to specific places or living persons. The opinions expressed in this manuscript are solely the opinions of the author and do not represent the opinions or thoughts of the publisher. The author represents and warrants that s/he either owns or has the legal right to publish all material in this book. If you believe this to be incorrect, contact the publisher through its website at www.outskirtspress.com.

LOLA wants - LOLA gets
All Rights Reserved
Copyright © 2006 Jens T. Carstensen

This book may not be reproduced, transmitted, or stored in whole or in part by any means, including graphic, electronic, or mechanical without the express written consent of the publisher except in the case of brief quotations embodied in critical articles and reviews.

Outskirts Press
http://www.outskirtspress.com

ISBN-10: 1-59800-281-3
ISBN-13: 978-1-59800-281-2

Library of Congress Control Number: 2006920227

Outskirts Press and the "OP" logo are trademarks belonging to
Outskirts Press, Inc.

Printed in the United States of America

DEDICATION

This book is dedicated to my wife, Catherine Gene Karr and to Stevie Andersson, Gerda Neal, and Knud Christensen; with warm thanks for their help and encouragement.

FOREWORD

"Alpha children wear grey. They work much harder than we do, because they're so frightfully clever. I'm really awfully glad I'm a Beta, because I don't work so hard. And then we are much better than the Gammas and the Deltas. Gammas are stupid. They all wear green and Delta children wear khaki. Oh no, I don't want to play with Delta children. And Epsilons are still worse. They're too stupid…

The Director pushed back the switch. The voice was silent. Only its thin ghost continued to mutter from beneath the eighty pillows.

"They'll have that repeated forty or fifty times more before they wake; then again on Thursday, and again on Saturday. A hundred and twenty times three times a week for thirty months. After which they go on to a more advanced lesson."

Aldous Huxley. Brave New World

PROLOGUE

I saw a movie many years ago - back in the fifties - called something like 'The Order of the Bell'. It fascinated me to some degree, but left me wondering what the purpose of such secret societies could rationally be. Why would people be fascinated by and belong to 'secret societies'?

I have in my life been concerned with women's rights - and have put my money where my mouth is in many instances and fought for equality. The book you'll read deals with male domination being one of the cornerstones of such a secret organization. The more enlightened aspect of the organization is that it fights for ecology, but then associates ecology with overpopulation. Reduction in the world's population, it deems, may to some degrees be accomplished by drastic means.

The book, however, is first of all a love story. A love between a woman who has been in a marriage with a high executive of such an organization (LOLA) and a man she meets, a man who helps her escape the confines of this extremely male-chauvinistic society.

This love, as the reader will learn, has its ups and downs and realistically - in a short time period - manages to go through most of the phases, usually associated with marriages.

CHAPTER 1

...we are the children of God...
Romans, 8:16

It was dark and it was raining.
     The patrol car had stopped at the corner of Countryside and Callew. The policewoman was eating a donut, chewing while looking out at the intersection.
It was three ayem.
A car pulled up on the other side of the intersection and stopped for the red light. The policewoman noticed the front door on the passenger's side open a bit, then close and then open full length.
A shape emerged and started moving fast. The door on the driver's side opened wide and another shape followed. A man running after a woman. The woman had high heels and they clapped against the Macadam in a strange rhythm. Like a Maruichi band.
The man was catching up with her when he stumbled and fell. You could see the water splash as he hit the pavement, then he got up and pursued the woman.
You could hear the man breathe heavily from the running. The woman started screaming and was running towards the patrol car.
The policewoman put on the flashing lights, and got out of the car. The woman was now in the middle of the intersection

and the man right on her heels.

The police woman lit a flashlight and yelled, "Get out of the intersection you two. Come over here."

They stopped and the man grabbed the woman. The police woman took out her pistol and said, "Let go of her, and both of you come over here."

They didn't move, and then the woman started screaming. "He's kidnapping me." She was wearing an expensive, sheer dress, and the wetness of the night made the shape of her nipples show through. The breasts were small and refined. She looked as if she had just come from a cocktail party. She could be a socialite. Or maybe a call girl.

The man said, "I'm a psychiatrist, this is my patient. She's mentally deranged." He, too, was expensively and well dressed, but his clothing was soiled from the fall. The policewoman thought his raincoat looked like an abstract painting she had once seen.

He produced some documentation, while the woman kept on screaming, "He's going to kill me."

The policewoman said to the man, "I'll take her in the patrol car. Maybe we should go down to the station. Or, I'll take you where you are going."

The man made hesitant movements. He obviously didn't like it, but said, "OK, I'll lead the way."

The woman said, "They're going to kill me. I know too much." She repeated it after a while. "Yes, I know," said the policewoman.

"It's the LOLA. You know the LOLA?"

The policewoman said, "Yes, dear."

"He wants to take me to the clinic, and let me die there."

"He's your doctor," said the policewoman.

"He's LOLA's doctor,"

What was this LOLA she was talking about? She was obviously deranged, as the man had said.

The doctor's car stopped at a dark, austere building. The surfaces were smooth and shiny from the rain. The policewoman got out and went around the car and opened the front door. The woman started to scream again. The policewoman grabbed the arm of the woman, and she was kicking and screaming, "Take me to the station, don't take me in here."

The doctor took the other arm of the woman and they lifted her up so her feet were off the ground. One of her shoes fell off.

"We can pick that up later," said the doctor. A nurse opened the door, and a couple of attendants appeared. One was a big burly woman, the other a wrestler type man with a shaven head.

"I'll sedate her," he said to the policewoman. "That is the only thing to do. She is hysterical. She is in her manic phase."

The policewoman nodded. The doctor was a nice man, cultured, well spoken.

"They are gong to kill me, can't you see?" The woman wiggled like a fish on a line, but the two attendants held her steady. Someone brought the doctor a syringe and he administered it.

The woman calmed down, and started looking apathetic, resigned. Her wet hair that had given her face rage before now looked raggedy. She started looking like a sick child.

The attendants took the woman away and the policewoman started taking notes from the doctor. He apologized for the incident. He was quite nice.

Sad with people who lose their sanity.

A detective rang the doorbell and the woman's father was told about the death of his daughter. His mouth tightened as he tried to withhold a tear. His wife came in; she had heard what was said. She first looked frozen in space, then she started sobbing loudly.

"My child," she said. "My beautiful child. She was God's child, you know."

The detective was visibly uncomfortable.

"Can we see her?" asked the mother.

"Are you sure you want to. I mean right now?" asked the detective.

"I'll go," said the man, "maybe you'd better stay home."

"I don't believe she did away with herself," said the mother, "I just don't believe it."

The detective showed the father the suicide note.

"It is her handwriting," he said. "See." He held the document out for the mother to see. She just turned her head away.

"My beautiful child," she said. Then she collapsed into a sofa and covered her head with her hands. You could see her shoulders shake in rhythm with her sobs.

The officer left.

That was the 13th of January of the year 1999.

CHAPTER 2

...the angel of the Lord appeared to Joseph in a dream, saying, Arise and flee into Egypt and be thou there until I bring thee word...
St. Matthew 3.13

John Jantzen drove over to the East Side of Madison and parked two blocks from where Neville lived. Correction, had lived. He still had the flat but was in the process of moving out.

It was late November and the last leaves were being swept off the trees. The trunks and branches were black from the rain, and the grayness of the late afternoon was fading into evening, into night. He felt as if his life was simply an imitation of the somber mood.

Some events can stay with you for decades, others fade away after a good nights sleep. What makes an event stay with you is not easy to come by - relative insignificant happenings may linger, while rather significant occurrences disappear from the memory bank.

But there are significant events that take place - events that form mileposts in your life. You know that when, at some future date, you think back, there will be a period before and a period after and nothing will ever be quite the same.

And for John Jantzen a milepost had been reached.

Was fate so that your trespasses were accumulated and that retribution came as an accounting of the sum of your sins of the past?

He had thought back all day on the past, thought of the things he had been guilty of. The affair with Helen - she was another man's wife. The fact that he had been cheating on his own wife, Hannah, was of less importance. The marriage was on the rocks, anyway. Had been so from five minutes after he said 'I do'. Then the money. Not a sin really. Half of it was his, but he was taking it all for the time being. He would return the rest at a later time.

But add to this what surrounded Neville's trial. He thought he was telling the truth when he testified on behalf of Neville. Celli was Neville's defense lawyer. They weren't an item then - at least he didn't think so. Neville had talked about the lawyer with the big jugs, as he called her breasts. That was the point in her appearance that drew your attention at first glance, and then in the next moment, it was her eyes. They were gray and they were so, so cold. Even when she smiled or laughed the eyes glared out in a chilly, almost god-like superiority.

She defended Neville well, and he, John, did well on the stand.

"I show you the appointment book the defense offered as exhibit 10. On the page I have indicated, the 10th of October, is that your entry?" The assistant district attorney's voice was confident.

"Yes."

"When did you make the entry?"

"When we made the appointment for his job interview."

"You didn't make it at a later time?"

"No."

"Why were you interested in hiring Mr. Schott?"

Sitting there in the witness box his thoughts wandered for a short spell. He had never thought of it - Neville Schott. Close to Neville Shute. Then he answered, "He knew about automated cash register systems, and he knew about sports equipment." Mistake, John thought, Celli had told him to keep the answers short and not to volunteer information. He didn't need to have said the bit about sports equipment. Oh well, what harm could it do?

"So Mr. Schott was a computer expert?"

"I wouldn't know that."

"But aren't automated cash register systems based on computers?"

"I wouldn't know that. All I know about computers is to open them up so I can use them as a word processor."

The lawyer leafed through some documents, then said,

"What kind of sports equipment constituted his expertise?"

"I didn't say expertise. He hunted and went fishing. Many of our customers buy guns. We sell anything from bait and hooks to rifles. We advertise that. In exactly those words."

"Do you go hunting?"

Celli's voice rang out, "Objection."

"Trying to establish that Mr. Jantzen was an expert in weaponry."

"Objection overruled, you may answer the question." The judge seemed competent.

"Yes, I go hunting."

"Are you an expert marksman?"

"Objection"

"Overruled."

"I don't know what qualifications an expert marksman needs to have."

"Can you hit a deer behind the eyes at 200 feet."

"Objection."

"Overruled."

Why overruled? It had nothing to do with the case.

"Yes."

"So you really didn't need Mr. Schott for the purpose of providing expertise."

Celli again: "That's not a question."

"Did you need Mr. Schott for the purpose of providing expertise?"

"He could handle the store in my absence."

"Were you and Mr. Schott good friends at the time you hired him?"

"I had never seen him before at the time I hired him."

"But you are good friends now?"

"Yes"

"And wouldn't that influence your testimony?"

Before he could answer Celli was on her feet,

"Question withdrawn." But the assistant DA had got his point across to the jury. It was not impossible that John would perjure himself. He was to learn later at what the assistant district attorney was driving at that time, but the relevance at the time escaped him. When he asked Celli later, she simply said, "We won the case; let's just leave it at that."

Nev was found not guilty. And Celli made no bones about the fact that it was John's testimony that made the case for her. "You're the best fact witness I've ever had," she said. Her smile showed her satisfaction. However, the eyes were still unemotional.

Yet, John now realized his mistake - just a couple of weeks ago. He was mistaken about the date; the alibi he had established for Nev was incorrect. Nev had not been with him for three hours at the date in question.

John was torn. What to do? He rationalized that no one had been hurt. Neville had been accused of obtaining false papers for an illegal immigrant. So what? It happened all the time. Yet, what about the not so many that bothered to go about immigrating the legal way? What about the impact, eventually, of illegal immigration on the country as a whole? Furthermore, what did Nev know about obtaining false papers?

Well, he, John, was not a crusader; he could live with the part that dealt with the impact on the country. It was the false testimony that had bothered him when he realized his mistake. He was in a quandary; he didn't know what to do. He could - in theory - go to Celli and tell her about it. He could see, in his mind's eye, the cold anger of the woman. Maybe the eyes would then show sparks. Who knows? But he lacked the courage, and he really didn't know if it was the right thing to do, anyway.

And then his own troubles started, and the perjury - not morally, because he had told what he at the time believed to be the truth - but, nevertheless, the perjury seemed of little importance.

And the help Celli and Nev were now offering was probably linked to their owing him a debt. Did they *both* feel they owed him a debt? He wondered, had they been romantically involved at the time of Neville's trial? That would hardly be ethical. Of course, after the trial it would be OK to get involved if they wanted to. But why did they marry?

He thought of Celli's cold eyes. Did their tying the knot have to do with marital immunity? That they could now never be forced to testify against one another. Was that it? Because it was an unholy union, he thought. This cold, professional, good-looking woman, and Neville, the drifter, who for a while worked for John.

And now John's fate was completely in their hands.

He sat in Nev's old flat and waited. He was no longer in control of his life. Here he was, once Nev's boss, now completely at his mercy, and at the mercy of his lawyer wife. He had to wait for them, and they would advise him as to what to do next. He, himself, could not see his way clear to take any other action than to give up.

And the thoughts rolled in like waves…'If I just hadn't…' and 'If I just had…' The repetition of useless arguments, because the gray reality was that 'he had' when he shouldn't have and he 'hadn't' when he should have.

If one could just push a replay button and start at some point in the past. Fatalists will tell you that it wouldn't work, anyway. And he was enough of a realist to know that he had to look ahead, not back.

He heard the footsteps on the stairwell outside. The strong, determined step of Neville and the daintier step of Celli.

He heard the key in the lock, the turning of the knob and the greeting.

"Hi, John, we are here."

And then the woman's outstretched hand and "Yes, here we are." She couldn't very well say 'How are you?' Because she knew the answer. She looked smart in a dress that was sexy, yet in good taste. She had a good figure, poise and a pleasant voice.

They were so relaxed, so carefree. He almost hated them.

You sometimes start a conversation with something irrelevant.

"Have you found another job, Nev?"

Well, it wasn't irrelevant, but it had nothing to do with why they were there.

"Celli has something lined up for me." He added, "There is some liquor in the cabinet over there. I haven't had time to move that yet. Help yourself, if you'd like."

John took a glass and poured himself a tumbler of Bourbon. "Nev," he said, "I never thought something like this could happen."

At least the conversation was on track.

"Me neither."

"John, how are you taking it all?" Celli asked. She had sat down on the sofa bed. She crossed her legs and then pointed at the bourbon bottle.

"Can I have one?" she asked. Neville grabbed an empty glass on the table and poured her a drink.

"I'll come to the point directly. This is a hypothetical, of course. A man is always better off being free than being in jail when he is accused of something, whatever it is. Our hypothetical person…"

Neville interrupted, "Celli, can't we do without hypothetical persons?"

She looked at him for a moment, and simply said, "No." Then she continued, "Suppose a hypothetical person thinks he is being framed and would need time to clear himself. Such a hypothetical person could leave town making sure that his steps could not be traced. He should do that before the police went looking for him. He wouldn't be a fugitive from justice that way; at least he could claim not to be. He would go somewhere, keeping a low profile, and not communicate with anyone except one person until the coast was clear."

John looked at her, then at Neville. "And how does he do

that - communicate, that is?"

"He would assign a friend to keep track of matters. He would phone his friend from time to time using a public telephone on both ends."

She looked at him. "A hypothetical person would not go by air, preferably he would take a train. He wouldn't use credit cards - at least not his own. He would stay out of the eye of the public. He would find a place to stay for the period he was making himself scarce, so that not too many people would see him come and go. For instance rent an apartment. And, he would lay off the booze."

She rose, finished her drink while standing up and said, "Are you divorced yet, John?"

He shook his head.

"There are men who run away from their wives for a while, just to stay sane."

Again, without waiting for further comment she shook hands with him, went over to Neville, kissed him on the cheek. "See you at home in - how long?"

"A couple of hours," said Nev.

"Lots of luck, John," she said.

Then she left.

"So how do we stay in touch?" asked John.

Nev handed him a piece of paper. "You call me every Friday at exactly noon Wisconsin time, Call this number - it's a pay phone. If there is no answer or it's busy, try again for twenty minutes. When I answer, if there are no news or if the news is bad, I'll simply give you another telephone number. Write it down, so have pen paper ready when you call. The number's for another pay phone, and that's where you call next time. When you call, call from pay phones, preferable fifty miles from where you are staying." He paused as if to collect his thoughts. Then he abruptly changed subject and said, "You did bring your computer, as I suggested?"

John brought out his laptop from his bag and turned it on. Neville went to a chest and took out a disk from it. He handed it to John and John slid it into the laptop. A form appeared on the screen, like a questionnaire.

"This is a program that prints out a birth certificate. You have to enter a name - not any name; I'll come to that - and birth date and places. Select one name from this list..."

'My Lord,' John thought, 'that's the sort of thing Nev was accused of. So he *was* guilty'.

'Jonathan Slowe' was one of the names. He was thinking of Jonathan Swift. Interesting name. He entered the name and the date and place of birth into the form, as well as other particulars.

"Keep the list until we meet again. I don't want to know which name you chose - just in case the police ask me. I have the right kind of paper here. I have paper for social security cards as well. You'll use another program on the disk for that."

"What about driver's license?"

"The best thing is to get settled somewhere and take a driver's test."

"You've thought of everything."

"Hopefully you can throw it all away later."

"I didn't do it, you know. I didn't kill him. I wasn't even there."

"I know," said Neville, "But it looks as if the world is not ready to accept that. So concentrate on what you have to do."

John realized that - more than he had suspected - Neville 'owed him'. He must have been thinking all the time that John had given false testimony on purpose. He just hadn't known; he had made a mistake on the date. He had thought the alibi was true. John caught himself thinking that it was unjust that Nev. had been guilty and gone free and he, John, had to go through all of this. Maybe it would be better to face the music. But he knew better.

"All a DA is interested in is a conviction," said Neville. "They don't care if they have the right guy." Then he added, "Start thinking of yourself as whatever name you chose."

'It's easy,' he thought, it is still John. The H is silent just like the life he would be leading for the while to come. A si-

lent life. That would not be easy. Then he said,
"I feel as if I've lost my dignity,"
"Don't worry, you'll get it back. Think of it this way - you don't have much dignity in jail. Even if you're innocent. I bet you, everyone says they are innocent in jail. How do you tell the innocent guy from the guilty ones?"
"The guilty ones are the others"
"But there are others that are innocent. The thing to do is to treasure the fact that you are free. Stop thinking negatively."
They walked down to the parking lot.
"How are you getting where you are going?"
"By train would probably be best." He added, "All I have will be one suitcase and one attaché case. Could you drive me to the train station in Milwaukee?"
"The Badger bus takes you there, why not take that?"
"Because I want my suitcase with me at all times. They put luggage in the hold on buses."
"How about Columbus? That's just one county over. There's a depot there."
"Fine with me." Nev said. "The reason for the telephone tag we'll be playing is that I don't want to know where you are. But we should know about three months from now how things stand for good. If you aren't in the clear by then you'd either have to face the music, or live under your assumed name for ever."
Three months hence. Yes, by then he should either be cleared or...or what?
"I'll have thought of something for you," Nev said.
He, once again, realized that Nev 'owed him', yet, Nev was a true friend.
They went to Columbus the next day after Neville had checked the train schedules. John, now Jon, headed for New York. He'd go south from there.
He had taken enough cash out of the suitcase to be able to meet expenses on the way. He had it stashed in different pockets. He had packed the small attaché case with a light shirt and

some underwear. He had brought a black garbage bag for clothes he would take off on the way, as he traveled into the warmth. He had his toiletries in he attaché case. In the big suitcase he had all his fifty-dollar bills.

How much? A million dollars easily. He hadn't had a chance to count it yet.

The station in New York was crowded. He heard segments of phrases as people walked by. Inane opinions, said in a meaningful voices, and meaningful opinions said in inane voices.

"This weather has to stop..." and, "Will it ever stop raining..." and, "It is the coldness and the dampness that get you..." And finally,

"I wish I was in Florida..."

Shouldn't it be 'I were'? It was something meaningful said in a meaningful voice. He had been in Florida four years ago with Athena.

He had been so in love with Athena.

"In time we'll love one another," she had said to him, shortly after they had met.

"I love you already," he had said.

"Love is something that comes after having been in love. When you are in love you think of nothing but the object of your affection. When you love it becomes deeper, constant, but with other thoughts creeping in, other obligations. In a way the obligations are there to make the love possible. Like shopping for food. Yet, they don't disturb the devotion."

"But you must love someone to make love to them."

"You are in love with someone you make love to - at all times. You think of nothing but that merging of the two of you while the act is going on. Hasn't it been that way with you?"

And he had had to agree.

He remembered one of the last days of the honeymoon he and Athena had been on in Florida. It was November of 1995 - they had had a flat tire as they were headed up to Ozona on Alternate Nineteen, and they had been lucky enough to be right

by a service station.

As they were waiting, a wrecker came in with a Mercedes with its right front bashed in. It was eerie because the headlights were on - or rather the left headlight, because the right headlight did not function and the pupil of the left one was going on and off in a desperate attempt to join forces with its broken brother.

Two passengers, a man and a woman, stepped out of the wrecker, while the driver went into the office.

The woman was elegant. She wore sunglasses, but one of the lenses was broken. Blood was covering most of her face. Her right knee was bleeding, and her nylons were crisp with coagulated blood. She was crying. "It hurts when I cry," she said. "Why didn't you slow down. I told you to slow down."

"Never mind," he said, "The important thing is to get you to the clinic so someone can tend to your knee and your face."

Later on he thought it funny that the man had said 'the clinic' not 'a clinic' or 'a hospital'.

She was rattled, and kept on repeating, "Why didn't you slow down? What are you going to say to the police?"

"There will be no police involved," he said. "I just swerved into the pole, and there is no damage. Other than to the car. The car is a mess."

"What about my knee? What about my face?"

"Well, yes, that is why I want to get you to the clinic as soon as possible."

"And it's my new car."

She took her sunglasses off, and John noticed how stunning her eyes were, in spite of the blood pouring down the side of one of them. There was a mixture of anger and fear in them. Of great unhappiness. Later, he often thought of the scene. It appeared in his dreams from time to time in one disguise or another.

As they left in the taxi, he heard the man give the address of the clinic.

The mechanic came out and told John their tire was fixed.

Little did he know that four months later he would be in a

similar situation. He remembered Athena's bloody face.

But, unlike the woman in the Mercedes, Athena was dead.

So Florida is where he headed. The trip was strenuous. Two and a half days in all! He tried to stay awake at all times, watching his suitcase, never letting it out of his sight. Somehow - later he couldn't even remember how - he found himself checking into a hotel in Tampa, and having an argument with the clerk.

"We only take credit cards. However, we'll make an exception," said the man, "But you'll have to pay a deposit. People rack up telephone bills, otherwise."

At this point he realized how he would stand out in a crowd by only wanting to pay cash. That was a problem he would have to tackle at a later point. People, if asked, would obviously remember an incident such as the one at the registration desk.

He entered the room, put his suit case as a pillow at the head end of the bed, lay down with all his clothes on, and slept, head on his money, for eight hours. It was nine o'clock at night when he awoke.

He showered and put on one of the sets of clean underwear, and his light shirt.

He called room service and had a sandwich sent up. The water tasted good. The salty taste of the meat and the spices put life back into him.

He lay down again and slept until morning. He realized then how exhausted he had been. And so: what next?

He thought of the area where Athena and he had stayed four years prior. He looked in some brochures he had gotten at the registration desk, and recognized the area they had been in. There were realtors there, and he called one agency.

"Yes," said the lady on the phone, "Renting is possible, but only for an extended period of time. Three months is the minimum. We have a couple of units like that here."

He cheeked out and left by taxi.

"Where to, Mac?"

"Westlake Wetlands, up in Palm Harbor."

They drove the miles up to the Palm Harbor area and through a shopping mall and then through a guarded gate. The taxi stopped at the clubhouse off the golf course. The realtors were in the building next to it - that is what the realtress had said on the phone the night before.

She was a slightly plump lady in her mid-forties, he'd say. She smiled at him. Was it a smile of affection, attraction, or was it the thought of a commission? But her conversation made him think it was the former. She oohed and cooed a bit - something he wasn't used to. Women, usually, were not taken with him until they had a chance to know him better.

"Do you have references?" asked the realtor.

"Well, I came on vacation on short notice. Don't worry. I'll pay in advance. Cash."

Greenbacks have a way of talking. And, of course, she liked him. But he showed no signs of encouragement. Later in his stay, as loneliness crept into his life, he thought back on it many times. It obviously was wise not to get involved. But it would have been nice. Not a one-month-stand. A three-month-stand. It would have made the period more bearable. But it was wise not to have given in to temptation.

The unit was nice. It was in a subdivision of Westlake Wetlands named Lyngwood. 'It's so Florida, you'll love it,' the realtress had said.

And so, there he was, still clutching his hand around the handle of the suitcase. He locked the door after him, drew the blinds, and opened the case. He removed several bundles of fifty-dollar bills and placed them on a table. He looked at the ceiling, and found the trap door to the attic. Judging from the roof the height of the attic was low. He grabbed a chair and climbed up on it, opened the trap door and looked in. The space was too low to maneuver in. It housed the blower for the air conditioning unit. He bent down and took the suitcase and shoved it in next to the blower and then closed the trap door.

He undressed. The day had been warm, and his clothes were damp and stuck to his skin. He felt a sense of tremendous relief as he stepped into the shower. He then dried, shaved.

He found a garbage bag and threw the underwear into it. He didn't dress; he simply lay down, naked, on the couch.

He fell asleep right away. It was next morning when he woke up. He was hungry. He remembered the shopping mall at the entrance to the subdivision - it couldn't be too far. He put on his pants and shirt without underwear. The pants gave him an unpleasant feeling in the crotch as he walked.

He tried to reconstruct the route, and walked down the streets among the golf course and the small ponds. And there it was, the mall. He entered a small diner. It was full of elderly people. It surprised him, but shouldn't have. Florida is a retirement state.

He watched the steam rise from the coffee. He savored it, greedily attacked the food and the juice. He must have looked fairly normal, because people didn't seem to look at him. He didn't hear whispers in the corners about him.

He started contemplating his new life. Neville had said to lay low, and to be as other people as much as he could. What are 'other people' in Florida? Young and poor and old and rich. He watched the older couples, one by one. No talking or, at best, one-sided talking. 'You should have bought that car when it was on sale…' That reminded him, he had to get a car. No way of getting around without a car. Well, he had the money, but how to go about it? As Neville had said: get a driver's license under your new name. He didn't know if they would ask for identification, but he had 'his birth certificate and social security number'. He had better learn the number by heart. Would they look at him in strange ways when he went to get a permit? But how to get there without a car? It was a Catch 22 situation. Again, Neville had said go to a driving school. What would they say on the phone? 'We have an opening at ten o'clock. Well, I guess he could take a taxi there. He could take a taxi anywhere for that matter, but that would not be like 'other people'.

How come Neville was so sage in such matters? Of course, he had been in jail. He had probably been in that situation.

Then his thoughts wondered to the day of doom when all

the problems started. The district manager had come to the store. What would he want? Simple enough. He had opened the envelope and slips were really pink when you got fired. The district manager turned, took out another envelope and handed it to them after having ascertained they had gotten the envelope that had the right name on it. "Severance pay." he had said, "We don't really have to pay it, but the company is generous."

So Neville and he had gone to Frankie's bar down the street and had had a drink. Neville had thanked him. "You've been the best. I'll never have another boss like you." Then he added, "I don't think I'll ever have another boss again, however." John hadn't known how to interpret that at the time. Neville could be an enigma.

It was the bar where he had often rendezvoused with Helen. What had made him so eager to go to bed with her? Well, she was lustfully built, and he was starved at home. Hannah was not one for sex. But did that justify infidelity on his part? Under the law it was adultery, he thought. But it was justified. He could see Hannah's gray face right before she would shut out the light at night before undressing. How often had he seen her naked? Not many times. And she was fairly well built. But breasts can be well formed and not enticing. You didn't feel like kissing them - he hadn't even at first. With other women he had always liked to have his lips touch the nipple, sense the well being it caused in both partners. The expression 'cold as a witch's tit' applied to Hannah. How long since they had had intercourse? How often in their marriage had they actually had sex? No! He was justified in approaching Helen! And she in letting him get to her.

Because, Charlie, Helen's husband, was a jerk too

The morning after the pink slip incident he had called Helen at home - he knew, or at least had reason to believe - that Charlie wouldn't be there - and she had come to the bar. She said, "We can't go to my place, Charlie is likely to come home during the morning. How about yours?" Hannah had gone to a conference out-of-town, so why not. There would be some satisfaction in making love to Helen in Hannah's bed.

But right in the final moments of the passionate engagement, the door had opened, and there was Hannah! "Well," she said. "Well...Well...Well." Then she turned around and slammed the door. It was tense in the house that day. Hannah made some telephone calls, and the next morning a little man showed up. John answered the door and the little man asked who he was. He foolishly (or maybe not so foolishly) answered truthfully. The little man handed him an envelope and said, "This is for you."

Divorce papers.

Would he have to move out? How soon? He asked Hannah and she simply said, "Talk to your lawyer." He called Celli and she recommended a divorce lawyer. They talked at length, the lawyer called Hannah's lawyer, a lot of legal lingo, a lot of apparent insults - were lawyers always like that? But John was permitted to stay in the house for three months.

He was exiled to the basement room. That was OK. He could use the kitchen.

He had called Helen several days in a row, but there had been no answer. So one evening he went to Frankie's bar again. He just needed to sit among people and think things out.

And there were Helen and Tim. Kissing and cooing. He had felt jealousy like never before. To betray him like this.

"What are you doing with my girl!" he had said. Tim loosened his embrace and Helen looked - well 'dumb' is the best way of putting it. Tim was drunk. He pushed John on both shoulders and said, "Why don't you scram!" And he had answered that he would scram when it pleased him and pushed Tim back. Not hard, but a statement in any event. However, it became more than that, because Tim fell backwards and hit a barstool and was out like a light. Helen bent down over him and the bartender passed over some water to splash in his face, and Tim started to come to.

"You shouldn't hit a guy that hard," said the bartender.

So John had left and then he went back to the basement of Hannah's house - his residence for the next three months.

The next morning he met Helen at a diner. She came over to his table.

"Can I sit down?"

He nodded.

"I'm sorry about last night. It doesn't mean anything - I was just desolate - I haven't seen you in a while."

"I would've called, but I never know if Charlie is home."

"Well I have been out a lot. But you know Charlie will be gone next week - hunting, you know. That'll give us the chance to spend the nights together at home, so to speak."

"Hope he doesn't show up like Hannah."

"He won't."

"I'm planning on going hunting as well. I think it is the same group."

"You'd better cancel."

Well, he had a better idea.

The condo he rented in Palm Harbor was convenient. It was the last unit at the edge of the subdivision. On the second floor, so he had only one immediate neighbor, the one in the condo below. The neighbor was a fellow who only came occasionally - there were such people. So Jon had the place to himself. It was ideal.

He called a driving school, and arranged to take driving lessons, then had them take him to the assigned place for driver's tests. He had no problems passing - after all he had been driving for years. He became aware that the inspector who oversaw his driving test seemed suspicious that he should just have learned how to drive. That worried him a bit. But the man got busy with his next assignee.

So he had a driver's license now; he could go to banks and get a checking account.

He hadn't thought there were so many details to take care of - and in the right order - to establish himself in his new identity. He guessed being 'on the lam' was not this complicated if you had someone to hide out with, but that was just what he wouldn't want to do. The fewer people knew about him, the better. He wondered where the expression 'on the lam' came from.

From time to time he took out bills from his money in the suitcase.

'His money', he thought.

Only half of it was really his.

But he would need a checking account.

There was a bank at the shopping mall, so he went there to set up an account. He used his driver's license as identification. He also had his social security number handy. How could he have done all of this without Nev's help, without Nev's computer program?

The bank officer asked him what he did for a living. "I'm an artist," he said.

"What kind of artist?"

"Writer and painter," said Jon. He had thought writer would be good; that is what he had mentioned to the realtress. Why did he deviate from his original intent? Nerves?

"Gee, I'd like to see one of your paintings, sometime," she said.

Problems everywhere, he thought.

"Sure," he said. He could claim he had forgotten. He also thought there were other branches of the bank. He didn't have to come here for banking.

He should never have said 'painter'.

"How do you sell your work?" she asked.

"In fairs. Well, I'm looking for galleries right now. Maybe I'll start my own." Good thought, he thought. But he thought it prematurely.

"Maybe you want to set up a business account," she said.

Man, what a web we weave.

"No, not now," he said.

And that completed the transaction. A week later he had a box of checkbooks in the mail.

He would enter cash into the checking account little by little, and how could he do that without raising suspicion? These bank types were curious by nature, leery of unusual behavior.

At the five and dime store he bought a type money sack, of the kind he had seen merchants use when they deposited cash in banks. He would go into the bank from time to time and deposit money he took out of the money sack.

He was kept busy thinking about things in the beginning of his exile. He had never realized the complications about being 'on the lam'.

CHAPTER 3

> It may seem strange to persons who live in a highly civilized state that he should confide these intimate things to a stranger; it did not seem strange to me.
> Somerset Maugham. The Book Bag

He realized that he would have to establish a daily routine so that he would be noticed as little as possible. Hopefully it was a neighborhood where people kept to themselves. A neighborhood where you could say 'Hello' and leave it at that.

He'd go shopping in the late afternoon. He'd avoid eating out. He found a Laundromat a couple of days later, and would go there in the early morning hours, when there was no one there. But the attendant or owner or whatever he was would see him. Well, that couldn't be helped.

It was almost necessary to get a car, but that was a problem. It would take time to build up enough money in the bank account so he could pay by check, and would it be possible to pay by cash without waking some sort of suspicion?

So, for a while at least, he kept on walking. A lot of people in the compound walked, and so he would not stick out.

He would exchange Hellos with other passers-by, but made sure he would not get into conversation with people. When he went shopping he would see people at the mall.

It was better than nothing but it didn't give him a sense of belonging in the large, sterile expanse, alive only with cars pulling in and out, with angry pushing of carts, and mothers yelling at rebelling children.

Most of the time he was cooped up indoors and watched television. But that made him a slave of what was showing, so he decided to get some books to read. He looked up used bookstores in the telephone directory. He went down to the mall, called a taxi that took him up to a place on Route 19. He bought a bag full of reading, and the cab took him back to the mall. At that time it was dark, and he walked back to the condo by way of the golf course.

And he went back into hibernation. At least he could read something worthwhile. Even so, he realized he needed to get out and mix with people.

The loneliness weighed on him. There is a limit to how much sorrow you can bury in the pages of a book. Man is part of mankind. Isolation, whether voluntary or not, is unnatural.

Yet, he knew he had to be, as Neville had called it, 'on the lam'. He continued to get outdoors very early every morning. He breathed the air and thought that, hard as the isolation was, it must be worse to be in prison. Images of others rolled by on his walks and then, to some extent helped a bit, made him part of a larger whole.

He had to admit to himself that he was lonely. There is a difference between solitude and loneliness. He had often yearned for solitude, when things were too hectic at the store, when Hannah would yak at him on end. But, since his adolescence, he had never been lonely.

He was now.

The sensation kept on coming back to him, almost with anger; he was not a hermit, he needed people. As time went by, whatever little contact he had with the outside world whetted his appetite for belonging. 'No man is a continent unto himself,' he told himself. Maybe having a meal at one of the restaurants would be a breath of fresh air, a type of bonding with the world as a whole. It would be real life, rather than the television and the books that kept him pass the while. But in a restaurant he would be sitting in the light on display for a world that wasn't necessarily without curiosity. Maybe the coffee shop at the mall would be secluded enough?

It was December, as it turned out it was the third Sunday in Advent. He had started his morning walk early, and he had walked - and at times jogged - a long distance.

It was one of those rare Florida mornings when the morning temperature had dipped into the thirties. There was frost on the golf course greensward, and it reminded him of a fine snow in his native Wisconsin. He was gripped with melancholy; he had tears in his eyes. Would he be away from his home all his life?

Then he got to think of the Jews who had been led into foreign lands. His thought went further; actually the soil he was treading - although originally American Indian - had been settled by people far away from their homeland. The pioneers had given up their sense of belonging. They had shaped the homes for their sons and daughters, who now could say, at Christmas time, that 'this is my home; this is where I hail from'.

He had meandered out into the main drag. He was walking on the median in the grass and he started being bothered by the exhaust from the traffic. He was going to turn back.

At that moment the number of cars grew, as if an armada were headed to a goal of sorts, a rendezvous. And he realized they were turning somewhere in the near distance. As he came closer he realized that it was a church. He thought of the Christmas gospel and wondered if a parade of cars could be equal to the shining star that guided the shepherds. He, again, thought of the irony that he was 'on the lam'.

An idea entered his mind. He could go to church. He was originally Lutheran, and it so happened that the place people turned into was a Lutheran church. He hadn't been to church for a long time. Athena and he had never gone to church. At the beginning of their marriage he had attended church with Hannah. As bad as things had been with Hannah he had gone with her on Sundays, until he had found a way to be at work on week-ends, and for the last years he hadn't gone with her. Hers was an Episcopalian church, and he was wondering if the picture he had in his mind of a Lutheran church would not be tainted to some degree with his recollection of the Episcopalian edifice.

He turned where the cars were turning. He saw people get out of their cars, all in their 'Sunday-go-to-meeting' clothes, and he realized that he wasn't really dressed for church, and then he said to himself, 'It shouldn't matter.' The way you are dressed shouldn't matter. Yet, he would stick out in a crowd, and that was exactly what he didn't want to do. And this was the only reason he didn't go in. He looked, almost with a sense of longing, at the lucky people who would go in and stand and sing, would kneel in prayer - no, wait, they knelt in the Episcopalian church; they didn't do that in the Lutheran church, if he remembered right. He envied them because they were part of humanity.

The image of this came back to him several times in the week that followed, and on the following Sunday, again as he was up early, he decided to put on *his* Sunday best. He realized it would be awkward to walk in his best outfit, but both his curiosity and his need to belong was so strong that he decided to go.

He was nervous as he went in. Would they say, 'You're not a member, you can't attend'? Surely not. That is really one very fine thing about Christianity. Everyone is welcome. Yet, he was nervous. He had been away from this kind of service for so long that would he stand up and sit down at the right times?

He was greeted by the entrance, a large anteroom of sorts, by a distinguished-looking older gentleman who welcomed him and gave him a little pamphlet.

He was hampered in his entry into the church by a large group of women and men, all dressed in white, with blue sashes. The choir, he wandered?

The delay allowed him to glance at the bulletin before he reached the door into the church proper - well the anteroom was the church proper as well - into the part of the church where the pews were. It was terrible; he didn't know what the various parts of the church were called. The only nomenclature he was aware of was the words used in crossword puzzles. How heathen!

The bulletin was actually a roadmap to the service, when to stand up, when to sing, where to find the song in the hymnal. He didn't have a hymnal, was one supposed to have one? He found a row where there was an empty seat, and he felt nervous again for having to ask the couple at the end if he could get in. The man on the outside stood up without delay, but the woman tucked her legs close to the wooden seat, looked away from him with an almost insulted mien, and he could hardly get by. Every so often during the service he could feel the cold ambiance she radiated.

He noticed that the first five or six rows were cordoned off, and suddenly a group of children came in. Most of them were girls and they were about eight to ten years old, he reckoned.

The church was impressive, still simplistic. The roof rose high and tall. There were two pulpits, the left one being slightly lower than the one on the right side from his vantage-point. 'Is that stage right?' he thought.

The woodwork was of a lightly stained oak. The wall behind the pulpits was in the same type wood for a certain distance, and centered between the two pulpits was a huge, simple cross, which rose almost to the peak of the roof. The triangle above it was a large, stained glass window with religious motives carried out in a modern style. Parts of the back wall to the left and right were marble.

Next to each pulpit stood a type of tall table-stand with a pot of flowers - large white chrysanthemums and tall roses. Behind each pulpit was a balsam tree decorated with delicate white lights. He seemed to have the same recollection from the Episcopalian church, and he was just hoping that there wouldn't be the swinging of incense pots. He would usually wind up with a headache after service.

But he remembered Father Mann, and what a wonderful person he had been. Some good things came out of his ill-fated marriage to Hannah. It is an ill wind, as they say, that blows no good. He was wondering if Hannah still went to church. If she could go to church in good conscience after what she had done to him. Well, there is this thing about forgiveness, but if there is a way of repairing the wrong you have done, shouldn't you be required to do so before you asked for forgiveness?

There were no kneeling rails in the pews and there was so little room between the pews that it would have been neigh impossible to kneel down anyway so, he guessed, there would be no kneeling. Well, if they had communion like the Episcopalians, then there would have to be some sort of arrangement up by the altars. And indeed, he noticed, now, a low, wooden railing that ran across the width of the church, with an opening in the middle leading up two steps to the altar and the pulpits.

Were there kneeling cushions there? Probably, but it was hard to see, because there were some kind of arrangements, like a music conductor's stand, music holders, which blocked his view and he noticed a rather elaborate arrangement in front of and to the side of the left pulpit, including a piano. Just as he noticed it, some of the white draped women entered the left aisle and took their seats in that particular area and he gathered that that was music that would accompany the choir. But why there? He wondered. Why not up in the balcony; that is where he would expect the music to come from.

He looked around at the congregation. In the row in front of him there were three people who, obviously, belonged together. A youngish woman with long blond hair, and next to her an equally beautiful woman, presumably the mother of the younger woman, and at the end a tall, handsome gray-haired man. They somehow stood out in the crowd. He could observe them because they were in front and at the other end of the pew-row. He only had to turn his head slightly to observe them.

There was a woman in front of him who, apparently, was alone. She was young, slight and there was something very refined about her. It was possibly the clothes. They were expensive clothes, it was easy to see that, but they were also exquisitely tailored. They were black, but not the type of black you would expect from a widow.

Just then his thoughts were interrupted by some of the white-robed women and men he had seen in the anteroom. They were entering the aisle he was at, and the center aisle. They parted at the stairs leading up to the pulpits like water when you walk through it. Half of them went to the left, half to the right, and they took their places on the steps leading up to the pulpit. There were about thirty-five of them. They looked impressive in their white gowns and their blue sashes. He noticed that there was a drape hung on the right pulpit of the same white and blue color as the robes. The word 'Behold' was placed on it, horizontally and vertically. Were the colors of some special significance? Was it because it was the fourth Sunday of Advent, or was it always like that?

The woman all the way at the right end of what was apparently the choir was a woman with very fair skin and dark hair. The rose in the pot on the side table was just of such a length that it looked as if it was in her hairline. He was thinking of Snow-white. One female singer, in the back row, was taller than the rest, and somehow stuck out. She had good features, and she must have been close to forty years of age. Her hair, in particular, was striking - the color of honey. That made him think, why did women bleach their hair?

His train of thought was broken by a woman placing herself in front of the choir, facing the congregation, raising her hands to signal they should stand up and then - suddenly - literally breaking out in song, leading the congregation into emotion-filled song. He knew the hymn but had forgotten the words. Everyone seemed to know the words by heart, so he simply remained standing. The fact that he wasn't singing along didn't make him stand out, he noticed, everyone was so concentrating in joy in their singing.

Through the mass of voices he could hear the voice of the youngish, blond woman. It was a clear voice, a voice of joy, and in his heart he envied people who could experience the joy of faith in that way. He wondered if he could ever find faith.

Or wasn't faith something you 'found'? He had met someone once who said he had had an encounter with Christ. At the time he thought it was a pompous remark, and probably not true. But why not? Maybe that is how faith was born in a man. It wasn't something you could learn; it would have to come all by itself.

If he ever got out of his troubles he would come to this church every Sunday. He suddenly realized that there would be offerings somewhere along in the service, and was wondering if he had brought his wallet. He snug his had to his back pocket and sighed in relief to find that the wallet was there.

Then the pastor ascended invisible steps and appeared at the pulpit. What a man! He was like the old Danes his grandfather had told him about. Like Bishop Absolon who was also a warrior. His grandfather had shown him illustrations of Absolon, with an iron, skull-fitting helmet and body armor. Well, he thought now, that might have been poetic license by the artist, but there must have been something to it. The pastor was a full-chested man with auburn hair and a full beard, and he raised his hands and started speaking. His voice was powerful - it resonated from all the walls. He started reciting something that had happened to him, but it became clear that he was visualizing the shepherds in the fields at the Christ at birth, and taking the role of the son of one of the head shepherds. He told how he had gone with his father about seven miles from Bethlehem, and how the head shepherds had gathered around a warming fire. He - as the narrator - had been lying on the ground and gazing at the sky when he saw the bright star. He pulled at his father's robe, but the father turned around and told him not to interrupt his conversation with the others. He was an obedient boy, and when he pulled again, the father paid attention, and lo and behold, angels came and announced the birth of Christ.

At this point the pastor stopped and the choir rose and sang a hymn. It was a beautiful choir. The male voices supplemented the female voices much like a beautiful painting has a balance of hues and values.

The choir having finished its first hymn stopped and sat down. The pastor then continued saying that 'what next happened I'll cite from Luke' and he read from the Gospels. Then he stopped and suddenly the young girls trooped out of their pew-rows and assembled in front of the grown-up choir.

They sang a hymn, and he was moved by the young voices. Young voices, particularly when in a choir, can't be imitated. Some of them are slightly off key, but the notes are never really sour, and the volume is slighter than that of a grown-up. They also sing in a higher key, and it adds a dimension to a performance - yes, regardless of the religious nature it was a performance - which cannot be equaled by other means. He thought of that, of yore, composition of choir music had sections for castrados. Young boys with good voices were castrated so as to maintain the youthful quality in their voices. He shuddered at the thought.

The pastor came back and continued part of his tale, then stopped and the choir started again. This time there were hand bells from the arrangement to the left of the pews. And the piano was at work most of the time.

Later a girl played a flute and a man a guitar. At another time when the full choir was singing there was trumpet music and it came from the balcony, as far as he could tell.

The pastor's account of what had happened to 'him' was so moving that Jon had tears in his eyes quite often.

At one point the pastor broke his narration, so the ushers could collect money. There were parishioners on either end of each row so that they could receive and pass the collection plates on to the next row. Jon only had a ten-dollar bill in his wallet, but he gladly deposited it. It was a remarkable service.

The pastor now mentioned the fact that the Joseph family was in a small barn adjoining an inn, and described the humble, but warm conditions and that God had chosen such a place to have his son born. Not in the more elegant hotels or inns that might have been available.

Jon started thinking analytically. This splendid performance was like an expensive inn, and was it really appropriate?

Of course, it might not be like this each Sunday - he wouldn't know.

One phrase of the pastor's particularly caused Jon to think. The pastor reminded people that they gave gifts at Christmas time, and he said that the birth of Christ was God's gift to humankind. That we should not only receive it but cherish it and live with it. Jon thought that *yes*, if you got a gift you should open it, and he thought that maybe the religious concepts given him in his youth were a gift he had never unwrapped.

This should really be a period in time when he should seek comfort through God, but the encounter with Christ had not happened. Yet, it was something that would live with him, and through it he might realize the 'mystery of faith'. That was one turn of phrase he remembered from Father Mann's services.

After some announcements the pastor suggested that people applaud the choir and there was a resounding round of applause. He then made a few announcements and told the choir to leave first.

Then people left and passed the pastor in the outer doorway. As Jon left he shook the Pastor's hand. "Wonderful service," he said. "I almost came here last week on an impulse, but I wasn't properly dressed." The pastor looked at him warmly and said, "You could have come in sackcloth and ashes and you'd have been welcome. Please come again."

At the moment Jon walked out he met the lady in the dark clothes. Now that he saw her face and all, he realized how beautiful she was. He had the feeling he had seen her before, but this can happen with look-a-likes.

"Is it always this spectacular?" he asked.

"I don't know," she said. "This is my first time here."

He had to wait for cars that were leaving when he saw the woman again. This time there was a man with her. He had a grip on her arm and was almost pulling her. She looked very upset.

"You know I don't want you to do this. This is not our church. If you want to go to service, you can come to the Assembly. You know that. I've asked you often and..."

The voices faded as they were walking away.

He waited until all - or almost all - the cars had left. Just then a taxi pulled into the lot. The cabby got out of the car and addressed Jon. "Is the thing over?" he asked. "I brought someone over this morning and she asked me to come again after the service. Just - I realized that I didn't know when it was over. Did you see a woman in a black dress?" Then he added, "Good looker."

"If it is the woman I think you're describing, she drove away with who I believe was her husband."

"Oh, shit," he said. "I came over here for nothing."

"I need a ride," Jon said.

"That would be great. Where to?"

"The shopping mall by Westlake Wetlands."

The cabby let him off at the parking lot, and he walked back to the condo.

A remarkable Sunday. He felt good all day, but the next day, worrying came back. And he wondered if he had exposed himself too much to the world by attending church.

Once home, however, he started reflecting. What he had witnessed was a type of 'show'. The pastor, sympathetic as he was, was merely a man. He thought, as he had felt in his youth, that it was all a charade.

At least to him. He had no faith.

One afternoon he decided to go to the coffee shop next to the supermarket. He went into the mall from the compound side and walked slowly across the parking lot, in between bumpers and open trunks and the crackling of the paper bags heaped in them. The coffee shop had tables both outside on the sidewalk and inside.

It was cloudy and cool, and yet there were several people at the tables in front. He opened the door and went in. He got a cup of coffee and sat in the semidarkness of the back of the café. He relished this new nearness of humanity, the bustle of the crowd walking by outside, which he could observe through the windowed wall at the end of the long room.

There were only a few people at the tables inside. An older couple who sat in silence. The man would raise his head from time to time and say something, and his spouse would answer a one-syllable word. No solitude there. Loneliness, maybe. Two people could walk through life together and be together each day of their lives and yet be lonely. They might long for separation maybe, but never have had the courage to go through with it. They wouldn't know the other type of loneliness that would await them should they go their separate ways.

He, Jon, did.

But he must be patient, follow his plan, shun direct contact with people, just sit at the sideline and observe, drink in the presence of others without crossing the line of silence.

Someone asked what time it was and he simply gave it without really looking up. Then he decided to leave.

He went out in the remarkably cool late afternoon. It was getting dark and he walked over the golf course back to his place. 'His place'. Ironic - nothing about it reflected his taste, his convictions in life. The furniture he first had appreciated he didn't care for anymore - it was 'all Florida' as the realtress had said, but it lacked character. It bore the earmarks of assembly line and pale people deciding on bland designs that would not offend people at the time of purchase. Furniture that would disappear from the owner's view, so to speak, blend in with the equally colorless wallpaper and form a vacuous ambience.

Yet, he felt better than in a while. He had been amongst the living. He settled down with a book and fell asleep in the sofa, and when he awoke he didn't feel quite as lonely as he had been.

It was as if the visit to the coffee shop had been an adventure. Interesting how circumstances can alter one's perception of what's exciting. Maybe prisoners felt that way when they got out of jail.

And he thought of prison. He must be careful and patient.

In the semidarkness of the back of the coffee shop he was

relatively unnoticed, yet, he could observe the customers as they came up and ordered their coffee. And he could observe the crowds walking by outside, around the tables, sometimes scolding the customers there for impeding their progress. What right did they have to sit in the middle of the walkway?

One afternoon when he arrived and had seated himself as usual, there was a sudden influx of people. Mostly young persons. It had been cold and no one was sitting outside, so the shop filled up. At this point a red haired girl entered the store. He had seen her before once or twice. She had caught him once looking at her, and rather than looking away and appearing annoyed, she had casually winked at him and then returned to reading a magazine she was perusing.

This time she looked around for a seat after having gotten her latte, and seeing none vacant she headed for where Jon was seated.

"Would you mind if I join you?" she asked, and without awaiting an answer she sat down. What could he have said anyway? Well, he could have said that he was waiting for someone, but the redhead had never seen him with anyone, so he had to deal with the situation. It was the type of thing that he had been avoiding. He had to admit he liked the gal's looks. All these thoughts in a fraction of a second, as it usually goes. When he tried to reconstruct the scene after he had gotten home he could not account for the sequence of thoughts.

"Are you from here?" she asked.

"I live nearby," he said.

"You strike me as being a tourist."

What to answer?

"I took a place for a long rental. I'll be going back up north when it gets too hot."

"A snowbird," she said.

"Is that what they call it?"

"What do you do for a living?" she asked.

She was curious, that one.

"I don't right now. I lost my job, but I got a good exit settlement. A golden handshake."

"And what'll you do when the money runs out?"

"I'll probably pursue good looking women like you until I can find one that can support me."

She laughed.

"You're very secretive, but that has its charm. We should get together some time; I'd really like to know more about you. You're very appealing, you know." Then she added. "Would you care to take in a movie, go eat somewhere, or maybe dance somewhere?"

He had had time to anticipate the question. Usually a question asked by the man, but he had foreseen that this gal was quite aggressive - aggressive in a pleasant way - and that she might ask exactly what she did.

"I have a girlfriend."

She looked at him. "I've never seen you with anyone in here."

"She comes here sometimes. We meet at night, generally."

She took out a business card and wrote something on it. "I'm Shirley Shelly, and this is my home number." She was pointing to the telephone number she had written on the card. "Call me sometime when you have tired of your girlfriend. And when you call, how do I know it is you?" He looked at her. "Yes," she said, "What is your name?"

"Jon," he said. "Without an 'h'."

She stood up. "It's been good talking to you. I think we could find happiness together, so call me sometime - anytime."

How could she know that they 'could find happiness together'? But he was fascinated with her, yet, he was happy he had handled himself the way he had. There had been nothing unnatural about it. He had a girlfriend, he had said, and he had left her with the impression that he was faithful and true.

He went to the coffee shop again. Each time he felt the sense of adventure, the joy of being close to humanity, savoring forbidden fruit in a way, although it still seemed to be hanging on the tree.

One afternoon when he arrived there was a woman sitting at the table closest to the door. She seemed to have seated herself there so she could have a full view of the outside through the room-wide, floor-to-ceiling window. Their glances crossed for a second and then he was out of reach of her eyes. He had seen her before. Where had he seen her?

There was a taxi arriving and the woman arose. He could in that instant take in the entire figure. She was slender and shapely.

Then she bent down to pick up a sack. This tightened her sheer dress around her and her buttocks stood out in the splendor of the mundane surrounding - like the sun in a slum. It was the most evocative backside he had ever seen. Akin to a croup, sending female signals to rutting males, calling for touch, calling for violation.

She had in an instance picked up her package and she used those wonderful protuberances to push open the door. As she was facing the interior did she cast a glance his way? Had she looked at him on purpose? If she had, she showed no sign of recognizing him.

She was beautiful and he suddenly realized that she was the woman he had seen in the church parking lot. As he beheld her he got all excited. His heart beat, hammered. Then he said to himself, 'Be calm. You can't get into anything. You're here to look, not to touch.'

He was in an elevated mood as he went home, and his fantasies took juvenile release. He went to bed, and he dreamed all sorts of happenings with his church lady. 'His' church lady! Had he already cast a die, passing a Rubicon into a dangerous departure from his resolve to be 'on the lam'?

He saw her again at the café, but she didn't see him. She would simply come in without ordering anything and place herself right by the same window. After a while, a taxi would arrive, she would leave, and he realized that she always had a cart with groceries outside by the window. She would sit and guard it until the taxi came.

She was probably in her early to mid thirties. There was seriousness about her, almost a sadness, he thought, as if she was having an internal struggle with problems that she didn't seem able to overcome. She never smiled. Was the man who dragged her at the church her husband? A discontent lover?

He tried to catch her eye a couple of times. She didn't seem to notice his glance, and she also didn't smile.

He had a strange feeling that he had seen her even before the episode at the church parking lot. But that was not possible. He could, if he ever got to talk to her, say, "When I saw you first you reminded me of someone," but he had been told once never to use that introduction, unless you could identify the person she looked like. Or he could say, "Before our encounter at the church parking lot, have we met before?" but that would be equally silly. And who was to say that they would ever get to talk to one another again. If the short episode at the church could be called 'talking to one another'.

He wondered why she was always taking a taxi. She didn't look as if there was anything medically wrong with her, and she also didn't look like someone who had had her driver's license revoked.

Was it that she didn't have a driver's license and that her only mission to the café was to wait for the taxi to come? Probably.

He had told himself never to try to contact people until he knew where he stood on the problems that faced him in Madison. But he became more and more taken with her. And then one day she left without taking her sunglasses with her. He went and picked them up from the table and gave them to the tall gal on duty. "She'll probably pick them up the next time she comes in. If I'm here, I'll remind her."

"This is actually not a lost-and-found department," the gal said with a surly mien. "But, OK." She shoved the glasses in a drawer, and he left.

It was three days before 'his lady' came in again and he had planned on using the glasses as a pretext to talking to her, but when she arrived, before he could do anything about it, she was up by the counter and asked for the glasses.

The gal said, "No, we haven't found any glasses." He broke in, right away. "Miss," he said, "I talked to you about that a couple of days ago. You put the glasses in the drawers."

"Those were sunglasses, not glasses," said the tall gal defensively. She opened the drawer and handed the woman her sunglasses. The woman said 'thank you', placed the sunglasses in her purse, ordered a coffee and as she passed Jon's table she stopped and said "Thank You." There was a gleam of appreciation and life in her eyes, and he noticed how beautiful they were. Then she said, "We have met before, haven't we?"

"Yes," he said, "In the church parking lot."

She smiled - she seemed a bit embarrassed - then she said, "I would join you, except I have to watch my groceries."

"I could move," he said. The right phrase had come to him. Ordinarily, the cat would have gotten his tongue.

She looked hesitant, yet tempted.

"I'd have loved to. Truly, but maybe some other time." Then she added, "Do you come every day?"

"Like clock work," he said. If he hadn't been here like clockwork in the past, he'd see to it that he was here on given times in time to come. "I'm in here the same time every day.

'I'm playing with fire,' he thought.

The next day his fascination got the better of him and he decided to sit at 'her' table right away and see what she did. Was that too brazen? Then in the last minute he thought that, maybe not.   He had come in at about a quarter to three, and as he got his coffee and stepped out in the room there was a great hesitation in him. Then he went to 'her' table and sat down.

She came in, smiled at him, and simply sat down at the table. She was natural about it, as if they did this sort of thing on a daily basis.

"I was sort of hoping you would sit here," she said. "I liked our short conversation yesterday. Unfortunately it will have to be short today as well. I already called for the taxi."

"Maybe it will be late. When I see it I'll run out and let the air out of one of the tires."

She smiled.

"I, too, have a vivid imagination." She sipped her coffee. "I often wonder if there isn't something one could do with a vivid imagination."

"I sometimes write."

"That's funny, so do I. Short stories. I'll show you some of my work - if you can call it that - some day, but I don't think it is any good. What I have experienced in my life I have forgotten."

He thought of that remark later, and thought it bizarre.

"Here's my taxi," she said. "Wish I could stay longer." She had a big smile on her face. The first time she had really smiled. Did he make her happy?

She made him happy.

It was being alive, having someone to talk to. He just wished he could see her longer than the couple of minutes he saw her.

They met approximately every second day.

"You always do your shopping at this hour?" he asked one day. Then he thought it was really dumb what he had said. "That was a dumb question, I know you do."

"Not necessarily," she said. "I could be shopping somewhere else on alternate days."

"Thank you for upholding the honor of my IQ," he said, "Just what I was thinking."

They both laughed.

"It's refreshing," she said, "I don't laugh much in my life."

"Has it always been that way?"

"Whether it has or hasn't, in my adult life, I really don't recall. I laughed a lot when I was a kid."

Again he thought, later on, why didn't she know whether she had laughed much in her adult life?

"It's interesting that you come at a set time every day," he said.

"My husband does his rounds at his clinic about that time of day, so he can't come home then. Otherwise he wants me home at all times."

That sounds like a Mafia Princess, he thought. Is she sort of a prisoner?

"Are you married?" she asked, and then, "Oops, here is the taxi, I'll have to wait for your answer till next time."

The next time she asked, "You seem to come earlier than three?"

"I actually come at two-thirty," he said. "You take a taxi, but I could give you a ride, I'd be most willing to."

He was pleased with having thought of that.

"I'll take you up on that offer a couple of days from now. Could you be here at 2:30 day after tomorrow?"

She all of a sudden seemed worried. Had she made a decision and then changed her mind already? Well, she could always renege.

"I'll be here," he said. And he would drive.

After she had left he wondered. It was all a bit mysterious, but she had gotten to him in a peculiar way. He sat in the café for a little bit, when Shirley Shelly came in. She stopped at his table and said, "Don't forget what I told you. Anytime."

"Why are you so interested in me?" he asked.

"There is something special about you," she said. "But in case you don't know it, I am something special, too."

She laughed kindly, patted him on the back and left.

He felt awkward about it. Shirley Shelly had broken the warm feeling he had had before. But the other woman's words, 'Could you be here at 2:30?' rang in his ears again. There was anticipation in his step as he walked home.

He told himself again that he was on a dangerous path. It was as if his brain wouldn't listen. His heart was beating, and the whole evening, in his sleep and the next morning, he thought of nothing but her. He had fantasies about kissing this woman, about her saying that he was the man she had always wanted.

He took a shower in the morning and let cold water down for a short while. It cooled him off. He had a cup of tea and told himself to forget about the woman. Maybe he shouldn't go to the coffee shop 'day after tomorrow'. It was too dangerous.

Maybe he shouldn't go to the coffee shop at all anymore.

At times luck seemed to smile his way. He had, for weeks, been poring over the classified sections for 'cars for sale'. He had never found anything that suited him, in particular the conditions of transfer. When he called, the seller always wanted to keep the plates, so how would he get the car back to his place? Some people were shy when it meant a cash purchase. Afraid of drug dealers?

But that morning there was an ad for a 1991 Volvo station wagon, which he responded to. When he called, the voice on the other end informed him that the speaker's father had died, and he was anxious to sell the auto. So Jon commandeered a taxi by phone, drove to the seller's place. A cash transaction suited the man fine. He probably doesn't have to declare it now as part of an inheritance, Jon thought, but no matter why - it was what he wanted.

"I have to take the plates off," the man said.

"Well, how am I going to get the car to my place?" Jon asked. "If you can't leave them on I don't want the car."

The guy thought a bit about it, and then he acquiesced. "But you will get the plates back to me." Then he added, "Or destroy them."

"The latter would be the easiest."

And so Jon had a car. He took it to the service station on Alternate Nineteen. It was the place where Athena and he had been years before. It was still the same mechanic.

"I remember you," he said. "Pretty lady, your wife." Should Jon tell him she was dead now?

"She died," he said.

"I'm sorry," the mechanic said. Then, more business-like he added, "Diagnostics will take about an hour. Can you wait for that, so I can assess whether anything is seriously wrong? It'll undoubtedly need an oil change."

So Jon walked over to the strip mall a mile down the road had a cup of coffee at a refreshment stand and walked back. The car was in good condition.

"Rarely you see a 1991 in such good condition," the mechanic said. "It's only got 20,000 miles on it. Where did you get it?"

"Someone died." Jon said. "But couldn't the odometer have turned over? Could it have been 120,000 miles, not 20,000 miles?"

"Not on a Volvo. It doesn't turn over to zero at 100,000 miles."

Jon had wheels! He went to the motor vehicle bureau to get Florida plates. Later, when they arrived, he put them in the storage well in the cargo space of the car.

The 'day after tomorrow' came and he was there. Again he was in a mood somewhere in between anticipation and excitement. Again he found himself between hope and rational arguments with himself. It was a silly state of affairs. No, not 'silly'. Again he realized that the intensity of his emotions came from his isolation. If he hadn't been isolated he might not have given her a second glance. Was that it?

But when she came into the café he felt overwhelmed - an emotion of happiness. He told himself to be cool, not to make any mistakes, not to let his feelings lead him to say things that were outside the rational.

She went by him, touched him on the shoulder as she did so. A pleasant and exciting warmth radiated from the contact. Then she came back with her coffee. She looked at him in a most tender fashion.

"Thank you for being here," she said.

"No, Thank *you*."

She smiled.

"You may wonder about me. You may think I always talk to strangers. Maybe you even think I pick up strangers at random."

"No such thing. You're a classy lady. It is funny you should use the word 'random'. I don't know if you have read a novel by James Hilton called 'Random Harvest'. There is a scene in it where one of the characters observes that if you want to confide in someone you should seek out either someone who knows you very well, or a complete stranger."

"I haven't read the book," she said. "Theroux says the same thing."

They smiled at each other. Then she said, "You know, I have a feeling we have met sometime earlier than the church parking lot. Right now I feel I know you, but it's bizarre that when you see someone you don't know, and pass that person by often enough, you start to say hello, and after a while you *think* you know him. I think I 'know' you, but, of course, I don't. We've already talked a bit, but you don't know all that much about me, and I know nothing about you."

"I think I know you, too. You can't realize how delighted I am to talk to you. I haven't had anyone to talk to for a while."

Mistake, he thought, now she is going to ask why you haven't had anyone to talk to.

"This is actually my big problem, too."

Just then Shirley Shelly came into the café. She went right over to where they were sitting, patted Jon on the shoulder and said, "So this is your girlfriend." She smiled a broad smile and went on her way. As she went to the counter she turned around. Jon was facing her; his companion had her back to the counter. Shirley Shelly waved a small, friendly wave at Jon and threw him a kiss. Then she took her coffee - apparently she had ordered it to go - and left the restaurant.

"What was that all about?"

"She tried to make a move on me recently, and I simply said I was waiting for my girlfriend. Of which I, at the time, had none."

"And your girlfriend is now, not imaginary?"

He said, "Girlfriend. A delightful thought."

She smiled at him.

They were quiet for a minute.

He said, "It's strange. When I was in Wisconsin when I was younger - and later also - there were a lot of women I would have liked to meet and I tried my best - maybe too strongly - but no one seemed to be interested in me. Now, when I have been trying to lay low and not approach anyone, this good-looking redhead approaches me."

"And now I'm throwing myself at you." She laughed. "Everyone wants something they can't get," she added, philosophically. "Coming back to being strangers and not being strangers is interesting. I didn't realize it had been covered so much in literature."

"It wasn't really the problem in 'Random Harvest'," he said. "That was a problem with amnesia."

He had no sooner said that than he noticed a change in her facial expression, as if it froze. He had made a mistake, somehow. What, he didn't know.

"Did I say something wrong?" he asked.

Now she looked sad.

"I was in an auto accident four years ago. Some - in fact a lot - of my memory was lost." She looked as if she was going to cry, then she pulled herself together. "I want to be friends with you, I need a friend. Will you be my friend?"

He had hoped for more, but it was a beginning.

"Of course I will."

"Why do you say 'of course'?"

He thought he might as well come out with it.

"Because since we met I haven't thought of anything but you. It is a difficult to answer why that should be. Your good looks - I hate to admit that - may have something to do with it. But there is a general - what do people call it? - chemistry, affinity, which comes from similar backgrounds, I think, from having something in common."

"Because of my partial amnesia, I have been isolated, and you said you'd been isolated too. Is that what you call 'common background'?"

"It has something to do with that. Is that bad?"

"Not at all. As long as it is not the only reason." She looked at her watch. "I didn't call the taxi, I had better do that now."

"I'll drive you to wherever you are going."

"That's nice, but this time let me take a taxi. I had second thoughts about it. Some day I have to make it so that we can spend more time together. Will you be here day after tomorrow?"

"Absolutely"

"Come by car."

She went to the telephone and called. The taxi came much too soon.

So why did she want to go home by taxi?

"If I gave you a shopping list, could you do the shopping for me? That way I can spend three quarters of an hour with you." She asked him that at their next encounter.

"I'll tell you some of what this is all about." She looked at him. Probingly as if she were saying to herself, 'Should I really trust him?'

"A question you didn't have a chance to answer the other day is, 'are you married?'"

"Difficult to answer," he said, "I'm in the middle of a divorce. I don't know whether it has gone through."

"Why don't you find out?" she asked.

"That's a long story."

"Are you hiding from someone or from something?" She looked at him. "You're never with anybody. It's not natural."

"You aren't either," he said. Then he regretted having said it. He didn't want her to feel bad. He was still saying to himself that what he was doing was completely contrary to what he should do. But he couldn't help himself. He was starved for company, he was starved for affection, and he sensed both of these in the person he was with. He weighed his answer.

"Am I hiding? In a way, Yes, in a way, No."

"You're not married, in a way, you're not hiding, in a way. I don't want to press you, make you uncomfortable, because I like you a lot - in fact I'm already fond of you - but I need to know a thing or two."

"Whether I'm married or not, I'm a free man."

"That's interesting. Could you explain that."

"Can it wait a while? I'll tell you in time. It is a long story, it is painful, and you're probably safer, so to speak, if you don't know."

"Police?"

"Yes."

"What are you accused of? And what are you not guilty of."

He smiled at her. "You trust me, don't you?"

"Yes," she said. "My intuition doesn't have a good track record, but in your case I'm sure it's right. You're a marvelous guy who is in trouble for no fault of his own." She was waiting for an answer. "So what do they want you for?"

This was all wrong. He was putting himself in terrible jeopardy.

"Killing someone," he said. "But I didn't do it."

"I believe you," she said. "You don't have to tell me any more about it right now. But some day...OK?"

"OK."

"I owe you some facts, too. To make it very simple, I want a divorce from my husband, and he doesn't want it."

"Can't you just sue for divorce?"

"He's powerful. I've tried. I need something on him, so I can force him to."

"You mean another woman."

"Not that. Let's leave that alone for the time being, just as you are leaving out details of your own plight."

"OK."

"The important thing is that we trust one another. I don't know why I trusted you from the beginning. I didn't know you. We discussed that, but I don't even know your name."

"I'm Jon. Without an 'H'."

"My name is Leonora, but call me Nora."

"Is that what people call you."

"It is what you call me. I already think of you as someone special."

At that moment he hated Shirley Shelly. She had used the same phrase. But his antipathy evaporated as he looked at Nora.

He felt good again. He felt good about the trust that seemed to have been established.

"Our time is almost up. Where do you have the groceries."

"In my car." (He felt good saying 'my car'). "I can get them for you or I can drive you home if you want to."

"No, I am in the habit of taking a taxi, and I don't want the world - or rather the maid - to see that I have broken a habit."

He had his hands on the table and suddenly she took his left hand and squeezed it. "I don't know how I can be so fond of you. But you're the first person who has trusted me and who I trust - the first person in a long, long time." She squeezed his hand once again and said, "Where is your car?"

"You can see it from here. It is a 91 Volvo. A white station wagon."

"Good," she said. "I'll go get a cart and pick the bags up at your car. Please make it fast. Can we make the same arrangement tomorrow?"

"Sure thing. Just give me the list."

She produced an old envelope with a list of items written in ink. Then they both left within a short interval. She picked up a cart and got the groceries. He saw her go to the phone and then return to the coffee shop. He drove home.

She came in at 2:30 the next day.

"We're in luck," she said. My husband is in the hospital and will be there for a couple of days."

"We can stay together longer than 45 minutes."

"Exactly. I would ordinarily have to figure out what to do with the maid, but she is visiting her sister today."

What did the maid have to do with it, he thought? He had wondered about that two days prior, as well.

"What is the matter with your husband?"

"He started losing his balance. It would appear that his blood pressure dropped too much and that his sodium levels became too low. It will take them a couple of days to correct it. But they are also checking to see if he may have had a mini-stroke."

"Why is it so important that the maid not be home."

"She spies on me for my husband."

He started to wonder if she was a bit paranoid. Should he

bring that up? Maybe she should see a psychiatrist. He would find out later how bizarre that thought was.

"You have the car, right?"

He nodded, and she said, "Let's go to John Chessnut Park."

She directed him, and they parked the car near the boat landing, and walked along the water. They turned in to one of the picnic pads that were hidden in the woods, and they sat on a bench. It was hard and uncomfortable, and it had no backrest.

She put her arm around his back, and he did likewise. She cuddled up to him, He wanted to kiss her, but he lacked the courage. They squeezed one another warmly, then she softened her hold and pulled back.

The window of opportunity had closed. Why was he so shy?

"I told you that I had an automobile accident four years ago. It happened not too far from here, on the day of my honeymoon. Lionel, my husband, and I had been drinking at the reception, I know that much, and I guess I was under the influence. I ran into a lamppost on Route Alternate Nineteen. That's where I suffered memory loss. Some of my memory has come back, most of it hasn't. I can remember my childhood. I can't remember I was a nurse in a hospital. I have forgotten how I met my husband, and there is a period of several years that's completely lost. I'm saying this, because I'm trying to find a means of recovering that memory."

"You don't have to apologize for it," he said. He squeezed her hand. "If there is anything I can do to help, just say the word."

She bent up to him and kissed him on the cheek. "You're wonderful," she said. "I have a confession to make. I didn't forget the sunglasses. I thought we might make contact that way."

His heart jumped again, but all he could say was, "I'm so glad."

"It is not just that I need someone to talk to, you know that. Not anyone would do, it would have to be someone special.

And I don't know - as we talked about yesterday - I don't know why you think someone you really don't know can be special. But you are."

Cat doesn't get her tongue, he thought. She has no problem expressing what she feels.

"We'd better be going," she said. "The maid will be home about this time. I'll show you the way back. I need to get some groceries, so if we could stop at the mall for a couple of things; it won't be but a minute. Then you can let me off a short distance from where I live and I can walk the rest of the way. Can I have your telephone number? I'd like to call you tomorrow. I should be able to arrange something so the maid doesn't get suspicious."

CHAPTER 4

I will always be the virgin-prostitute, the perverse angel, the two-faced sinister and saintly woman.
Anais Nin, Henry and June

She called him at ten ayem. He picked her up at the entrance to the subdivision where she lived - it wasn't too far from Lyngtree where he lived.

They went back to John Chessnut Park again, and went into the same picnic pad. The park was deserted.

"This is our private place," she said. "It belongs to just you and me."

Let's hope so, thought Jon.

They sat on the bench again.

"Should I carve a heart with our initials in it?" he laughed.

She laughed too. "I guess we are like a couple of school kids."

He put his hand around her waist. She bent over towards him, looking up at him and he bent down and kissed her gently.

He kissed her again, and again.

"I'm in love with you," she said.

This was going exactly the way Neville had said that things should not go. But he felt warm all over.

"I think of you all the time," he said. "During meals, before I go to sleep. I can't concentrate on reading, on watching TV. That is 'being in love', isn't it?"

"Exactly," she said.

"My first wife, Athena, used to say that. She said that love actually was spawned by having been in love. 'Love' is much calmer and maybe less passionate and emotional, but it had lasting qualities. You had to be in love before you could love."

He bent down and kissed her again.

Then they sat up, and caught their breath.

She again looked at him with such warmth in her eyes. She seemed hesitant about something, he was wondering what.

He was wondering if he should be more courageous. He touched her breast, and she rejoiced in it, he was fairly sure of that, but should he go further? He let his hand down to the hem of her skirt, but she pulled it away. He knew he had been too forward. She sat herself up straight. Damn it, he thought, he had advanced too fast.

She cleared her throat, and then she said, "When I was a teenager, I wanted to be a virgin when I married. But you can't keep a boy friend without letting him have his way, so I found ways of doing it so that he would be satisfied, yet I would keep my virginity. I don't think we should have intercourse yet, but I can keep you as a boyfriend - so to speak. I hope you don't mind the word."

She loosened herself from him, and opened his zipper. He was quite aroused, and she took out his manhood and gently massaged it. He only wished he could have leaned back. Her hand was velvet, it sheathed his phallus like the inside of a woman, and the ecstasy rose until he finally said, "I'm there." She said, "Spread your legs". She guided his seed to the rocky soil, as it says in the bible. It was the first time he had - in a manner of speaking - been served by a woman, the first time he had had any type of sex since Helen. Several months ago.

She placed his member back in his pants and said, "You zipper it, I'm afraid of getting you caught, but first…"

She rose, bent down and kissed him hard. He could sense his ejection on her hand as she put it on his cheek and it made him feel bonded to her in a peculiar way.

Silence fell for a while, then he said, "We are an item. Whether we wanted to be or not, we are bonded."

"Were you divorced from your first wife?"
"No, she died."
"How long ago was that?"
"We were married in 1995, just about this time of year, and she died four months later. Car accident."
"I'm sorry," she said, "I shouldn't have asked." She kissed him on the cheek. "It's funny, you were married about the same time I was married to my husband." Then she looked at her watch.
"I'd better get home. My husband might phone me from the hospital."
"You can always say you were in the shower."
"He might call umpteen times on end, so we'd better go. Can you drive me home?"
"Of course."
"Later I have to go visit my husband in the hospital and it is around half past noon now. Could you drive down to Countryside Mall? I'll run in to Dillard's and pick out a dress."
"That'll take some time, if I know the female penchant for selection."
"Now, now," she said. "It won't take a bit of time. I'm going to return it tomorrow. I'm going to tell the world that I have been shopping this morning and tomorrow as well."
They turned right on Route Nineteen, and he stopped at Dillard's. "Wait for me here," she said.
She was back in seven minutes. "Can you let me off at Mease Hospital? I'll show you the way. You'll have no problem finding your way home." She added, "I also have to go visit tonight, so we won't see one another until tomorrow. It seems so long."
"Parting is such sweet sorrow," he said.
He had wondered how she was going to manage the maid. Now he knew.
He went home with nothing on his mind but the afternoon's events. He loved this girl, no two ways about it.
Their conversation about Athena brought back memories. He started thinking of his life in the past. He loved Athena,

had loved her. She was dead now, but he guessed he could still love her, because she was a memory of happiness. How had their relationship started? Well, they had known each other for a while and it just happened, sort of naturally. There had been no anxiety on his part, probably none on hers either. It happened because it was a foregone conclusion; it was only a question of when sex would happen. And it happened before they were married.

With his second wife, Hannah, there was no problem. She simply seduced him. There was a void in his life after Athena died, she got him out of a difficult situation, and it was sort of natural that he should say yes when she suggested marriage. But what a mistake.

Then with Helen. They were both drunk. They were both in bad marriages. So they sort of suited each other's needs. But it wasn't love. It was satiating the senses. He had enjoyed sex with Helen and he often thought of it, but it was nothing like this.

He felt as if he was betraying Athena a bit. He hadn't felt that way with Hannah or Helen, because there was no 'love' there. But here there was.

His telephone rang at 9:30 the next morning. He drove up close to her house, and he saw her walk out the door, walk down the street with a shopping bag in her hand. She motioned him to go farther away from the house and he drove outside the iron gate of the subdivision, and she slid into the car when she reached it. They drove the car down the Wetlands Parkway a bit and she said, "Stop here."

He pulled over to the shoulder, and she took his head in her hands and kissed him. "It sounds silly, but I have missed you."

All he could say was a stupid "Me too."

"Let's go out to Crystal Beach. Just turn left at the exit and then go to Tampa Road. Then turn right five miles down when you come to Alternate Nineteen."

"Is that 19A?"

She nodded. As he turned on Alternate Nineteen they

passed by the place where he had had his flat tire during his honeymoon with Athena, the service station that gave the 91 Volvo its physical.

"You know," he said, "During Athena's and my honeymoon I had a flat tire right here. It was lucky that it was right by a service station - the one right here. I remember walking in the rain into the station, and they had just towed in a car…"

My God he thought, that is where I have seen her. It wasn't just that she had reminded him of someone, she was that someone.

"You know," he said. "With your amnesia do you remember anything about your honeymoon?"

"Only what I have been told, actually. Well, what I have been told is compatible with what I think may have happened. I don't remember anything about the ceremony or about what happened afterwards, only that, apparently, I had an accident - actually just around here. My husband had given me a new car for a wedding present. I had had quite a bit to drink at the reception after the ceremony and I drove the car into a telephone pole. I was knocked unconscious, and my husband brought me back to his clinic, and it was about a month before they had got me to assemble some sort of memory again."

"Was your car a gray Mercedes?"

"How did you know that?"

Should he tell her? Well, he had let the cat out of the bag already with his identifying the make of the car. He pulled in to a parking lot at a strip mall, and looked at her. She was wondering why he had stopped.

"When I walked into the service station that day they had just brought in a wrecked Mercedes. The airbag had engaged on the driver's side. The driver and passenger had driven back in the wrecker, and the man stepped out - unharmed - but the woman practically fell out. There was a lot of blood covering the right side of her face. The man called for a taxi and said - and these were his words - 'I'll take you to the clinic, you need attention'. She was saying, 'You shouldn't have been driving so fast. After all, it is my car. You gave it to me.'

And the part that bothers me is that in your story, you, not he, were driving."

She sat in stone silence. "Then what happened?" she asked. She was addressing herself as much as she was addressing him.

"Is that why you don't drive?"

"He had to report it to the police, they came and took a blood test, and my license was revoked for six months. But he had the car repaired and sold it. He told me never to drive again. It would be too traumatic for me."

"Did they restore your license?"

She nodded. She was like in a trance.

"You want to drive this one right now?"

"I don't have my license with me."

"Next time bring it," he said. "If the horse has thrown you, you get right in the saddle again. Except in this case the horse hasn't really thrown you."

Suddenly she turned towards him; she had fire in her eyes. "I'm so glad I met you. So glad. Not only because I love you, because I think you can give me back my life."

Then she smiled quietly.

"If we told this story to someone, no one would believe us." She gave him a kiss on the forehead.

She came into the coffee shop at nine o'clock sharp. "I have so much to say to you," she said, "but right now the time I can ... afford, shall we say is limited. Lionel may come home this afternoon. Right now I need to toss a coin. Except I'd like to put a more human touch on it."

He looked puzzled. "How can you put a human touch on tossing a coin?"

"You'll be my coin. Simply say to me, Yes or say to me No."

"Yes," he said. Then he added, "I should probably have thought this over before I answered."

"Exactly what you shouldn't have done. Now you have answered, let me ask you to do me a favor."

This time he took his time answering.

"It isn't illegal, is it?"

"No," she said,"Not this time."

"There's going to be a next?"

"Depends, but from what I can sense, Yes."

What was he getting himself into? Again he had a fleeting thought of Neville and Celli. This was the type thing he definitely did NOT want to do, yet he couldn't help himself.

"What is the favor you want me to do right now?" he asked

"I'll give you more detail later. My husband has a safe, and in it, I believe, there is some very sensitive information. I have wanted to get my hands on it for a long time, but I haven't known quite how. It is mainly because I don't know too much about safes."

"You don't want me to blast open a safe!" He could see himself with sticks of dynamite looking like David Niven with a brimmed hat and a cigarette in his mouth, nonchalantly imploding a safe door.

"I asked Lionel for a divorce once. He simply refused. 'LOLAs don't divorce' he said. Did I tell you that Lionel is a LOLA member? A member of considerable standing."

"Whatever LOLA means, you'll have to explain that to me some time."

"Officially it is 'Love of Life Assembly'. But as long as I have been associated with it, I'm still not quite sure. In any event, it's like your, for instance saying you're a Catholic. Yet, there is more to it than that."

"I'm a Lutheran."

"Well, you know what I mean. In any event, I had reasons to want to divorce him. Reasons I'll tell you about in a moment. But it's even more imperative that I lay my hands on something I can hold over his head. I think the safe contains information about my life after I met Lionel. Right now my memory starts with my leaving the clinic a month after we were married. Except you have filled in one gap."

"OK, so what do you want me - or rather us - to do?"

"Lionel puts stuff in his safe every night. He used to take out a small book and write in it, Now he takes out a laptop computer, composes on it, and then puts it back. I know he has a book in there, which I believe is a diary. Those are the things I'm interested in getting a hold of right now."

"But he'll soon know they are missing."

"If they are what I think they are, then he'll grant me a divorce in return for my giving them back to him. You know, Lionel is an extraordinarily good and renounced psychiatrist. But he can't remember numbers. If he looks up a number in a telephone book, he can't retain the seven - or ten - numbers; he has to look at least twice during the dialing. It's the same way with his safe - he can't remember the combination. I saw him one evening, on the sly, open it, and what he did first was to take out a little crumbled sheet of paper and read it off as he opened the safe door. So one evening when he had left in a hurry and had not taken his coat, I copied the number. Except I don't know how to use it. I tried it one night, and I couldn't make head or tail of it."

She handed Jon a piece of paper. "This is simple enough. I can explain it to you," he said.

"No," she said. "I'll get the maid out of the house. I'd like you to sneak in, open up the safe and take out the book and the computer. There isn't much time. We'd have to do it before Lionel comes home."

With the way her husband had treated her in the church parking lot, he could see it was not a happy union. He could also understand her wanting any kind of information, which would help her get ammunition in her quest for a separation.

"So when do we start?"

"Right now," she said. "I'll give you a pair of thin gloves. First you'll drop me at the rent-a-car agency on 19."

"You're going to rent a car? You'll drive?"

"Yes. As you said yesterday, get back on the horse. I know I can."

"But do you need a car? Don't you have your husband's, now he is in the hospital."

"He has the keys. He won't give them up. The maid asked him."

"But you're not the maid."

"He doesn't know my license was reinstated and he doesn't want me to drive. He wants me to stay put. Anyway, you'll follow me and park away from the house. I know I can drive. The problem is, I'll probably have to pick up Lionel, so I'll be coming back with him. At that time I'll be in a taxi.

"I'll tell the maid I'll need her help with getting Lionel into the car. You'll see me leave with her and get in a taxi and drive away. I'll keep her occupied for about one hour. Get the stuff, then leave. I'll phone you to make further arrangements. It is, of course, possible that they'll keep Lionel for another day, but in any event I'll have the maid out of the house."

She had been saying this in a very concise and rational way. Then she looked at him. "I'm sorry to be so business-like, but this is really important. Follow me out right now. I'll cross my fingers. I'll call you at your place when I'm back at the house, sweetheart."

She had never called him 'sweetheart' before. They left the café and sat in the car for a spell. She kissed him passionately, and touched his crotch.

"We'll pick up where we left off later. I wish I could make love to you right here."

What did she mean by 'making love'? Real making love or the velvet hand? In any way, it was a pleasant prospect.

"Let's go to the rent-a-car place now," she said. He still was not quite sure why she needed a car, but an extra set of wheels could come in handy.

As they were about to pull out she grabbed his sleeve.

"Please wait a minute. Do you see that man there?" She indicated a tall man, somewhat stooped, who was walking in the row between the parked cars. There was a woman by his side. "Look outside and see where he's going."

Jon went outside. The fellow went into the supermarket. The blonde he was with must once have been beautiful. She was still pretty, but in a cheap sort of way.

He turned and told Nora where the couple had gone. "Who

was the guy?"

"He is LOLA. He is one of Lionel's best friends. His name is Harry."

"Who is the gal he was with?"

"Oh, that's his bimbo. She was at the house once, but she behaved pretty badly."

"Not invited again."

"Right."

He dropped her at the rent-a-car agency.

CHAPTER 5

Faint Hear Ne'er Wan A Lady Fair
Robert Burns

He felt uneasy about it. Uneasy, at first, a bit scared later on. As a young man he had always wanted to play the role of the knight in shining armor. And here was his chance. And he was afraid. As he got closer and closer to 'her' house, the more his fright. He had never done this type of thing before - walked into a house that was unknown to him. He realized that basically he was a coward.

He brought his computer bag and drove up and parked down the street a small distance from Nora's house. He waited about five minutes and he saw Nora and the maid leave the house. The maid was a woman, he'd say, in her late thirties. Not too bad looking, but she - even at the distance he was at - didn't look too swift.

He let the taxi drive away and then he walked up to the house. He knocked on the door, as if he had rung the doorbell, and then opened the door. It was open, as Nora had said.

He entered the house. It was an eerie feeling being in a place you had never seen before. He felt a bit faint - a sinking feeling in the stomach. He couldn't wait to be out of there again.

He followed her directions to the safe. He felt as if his footsteps could be heard a mile a way. He saw a neighbor working in the adjacent back yard. Could he see Jon?

He found the safe without trouble, but his hands were shaking. It failed to open for him the first time and his hands started shaking even more, but the second time it clicked. He saw the diary. He also saw the computer, and noted it was the same make as his own. There were also some newspaper clippings, a journal type book, and a pocket book. He didn't know what the significance of the pocket book and the clipping was, but they didn't take up much room, so he removed them, put all of it in his computer case and shut the safe.

He felt like running out of the house, but he disciplined himself, put one foot forward of the other. But suddenly he heard voices. He got terribly nervous. He went to the back of the house by the swimming pool and hid at the wall facing the neighbor's place. The only way out was either to climb the wall or go back through the house.

He listened at the door and heard a man's voice say,"Harry, I think Lionel is wrong. There hasn't been anyone here."

"Let's check the safe,"

"Do you have the combination to the safe?"

"No, but there may be tell-tale signs."

He heard them go into the computer room. From where he stood he could watch the door that led into it, and as he saw it open. He went into the hallway. The floor creaked a bit - he hadn't noticed that before, but he simply proceeded to the front door quietly.

Once outside he turned around and bowed towards the door, as if he was talking to someone, then closed the door and - again disciplining himself - walked towards the gate. He was breathing heavily - his heart was pounding. Why was it pounding now? He was out of there, so why was it pounding now?

He went quietly and deliberately to his car.

He stopped at a Mail Place and copied the diary, then went home and waited. Ten minutes later the telephone rang.

"Did you get it all?" asked Nora.

"Yes. And I made a couple of copies of the diary and a newspaper article. There was a book there, as well. I took it too. I hope it's worth the while. I'll start reading it in the meantime, if you don't mind. But I have things to tell you. Harry and a buddy of his were there."

There was silence at the other end, then, "Oh, my God. Perhaps I shouldn't go back to the house at all."

"You can come here if you want to."

"Till it blows over?"

"I don't think it will. They were obviously sent by Lionel."

" Let me go visit Lionel. Maybe I can get a feel for it by then. I'll call you again in an hour's time," she said.

"Do you think that's wise?"

"You said that they were there, but they also said they thought that Lionel was wrong, that there hadn't been anyone there. So they don't really suspect you've been there. And they couldn't get into the safe."

He thought a bit. "OK," he said," But the minute you suspect anything, come home. I mean home to me. Maybe rather 'Home to us'.

He could almost hear her smile.

"I'll be careful. Anyway, they are going to keep Lionel one more day in the hospital."

The newspaper articles were about the case. He perused them. The name of Dr. Ondmand was no place mentioned. Just in case she thought he had been involved.

He started reading the diary and it contained a lot of the information Nora had wanted, he was sure. He read parts of it; he could read the whole thing at a later time.

He read the diary at night in bed. It was an account of someone's, a psychiatrist's or psychologist's, life. To a great extent it was filled with records of patients. The patients all seemed to be poor, often not able to pay their bills. It was fairly obvious that the office was located in a poorer section of Tampa.

It was also clear from the reading that Nora was working for the fellow. He referred to her often, and when mentioning her it was obvious that he was quite taken with her. He earmarked some points of interest.

January 15, 1995

When I approached her at the hospital and suggested she come work for me, I didn't know what a treasure I had acquired.

She is intelligent, so intelligent. I love discussing things with her. She is an ardent environmentalist. A point we have in common. Furthermore, she has the most exciting behind of any woman I have ever known. That, however, is not her strongest point. Come on, Lionel, who are you kidding. You know you are physically attracted to her. Now, how to go about it...

January 22, 1995

I loaded her down with work so she had to stay late. I suggested dinner at Fredo's and she accepted. We had a nice evening. I drove her home and asked if she would invite me in. She said I was moving too fast. Disappointing, although encouraging, too. She seemed to accept the fact that 'I was moving'.

January 27, 1995

We went out again, and this time she let me in to her apartment. We had a glass of wine, and I put my arm around her shoulder. She didn't pull back, so I bent over and kissed her. She kissed me back, but not passionately. When I put my hand on her breast she gently moved it away.

"You need a ticket for that," she said.

"How do I get a ticket?"

"In this case by moving on me more slowly. Mind you, it is not that you have to stand in line, there is no line, but let's progress a bit more slowly."

February 1, 1995

I was at her apartment again. As we entered we kissed, and this time she let me touch her breasts. They are nice, not too large, not too small, well-formed nipples. I let my left hand down her back and as I neared the dividing line between those wonderful globes she pulled back.

As we sat down I felt her breasts again, and I was so excited that I ejaculated in my pants.

She noticed both the erection and the wetness that suddenly appeared.

"It is too late for me to do something about that now," she said. "But next time."

February 2, 1995.
We were in the office late, and I kissed her. We sat down on the sofa, and suddenly she unzipped me. I was aroused, and she fallated me. I wanted to stop her before I climaxed but she held steadfast, and my little men disappeared in her mouth. And she kept on tonguing me, and it tickled so that I almost went out of my mind.

February 3, 1995
We went out, and went to her apartment. Again she repeated what she had done at the office. I tried to let my hand down her front. But she wouldn't let me. I let my hand down towards her buttocks but again she wouldn't let me.

February 4, 1995
We went out again. I asked her why she didn't want to have real intercourse. She said, "I'm keeping that for my wedding night." If that is her game, then she is mistaken. I don't take ultimatums.

February 10, 1995.
We haven't spoken much of late. I thought silence would get her interest up. There was a patient who came in - her name was Dolores and she was quite a looker. We stayed in the office a long time, and Leonora must have heard the moaning. This gal was a bit of a screamer.

Maybe Leonora will show a bit of jealousy.

February 11, 1995.
She's an enigma. When I came in this morning she said, very calmly, "I hope you enjoyed yourself last night." Is she not human?

February 16, 1995.
There was a girl I had met in the luncheonette down the street before I came to work. Her name was Susie. She was well built, but her face was not the best. I talked her into a free session, when she had mentioned some problems she had.
She came in close to closing time, I took her into the office, and the same events unfolded as they had with Dolores. I was anxious to see Leonora's face when we left. But Leonora had left.

March 15, 1995.
I talked to Leonora about an article I'm planning on writing, and it peeked her interest. It is all well and good that we advocate control of environmentally hostile practices. But the fact of the matter is that each person on the earth contributes to environmental exhaustion in some form or another. Even if automobiles were made very fuel-efficient and with minimum pollution, it stands to reason that the more persons drive, the more the pollution will be. It is a matter of overpopulation. In fact, it is possible to extrapolate and calculate how many people there is oxygen for with a given plant population. We could eventually all be affixiated because of lack of oxygen.
She encouraged me to write it.

March 16, 1995
I wrote a draft and showed it to her. I asked her to read it during the day, if she could, and could we discuss it in the evening over supper? She agreed.
At night over dinner I had a long conversation with her, and she seemed to warm up a bit. She liked what I had written, and made a couple of suggestions. I'll see if I can get her to go out with me again. She drives me out of my mind with

that derriere.

However, the article is not part of the scheme to seduce her. I meant everything I said in the article, and she meant her enthusiasm and suggestions equally unrestrictedly.

May 5, 1995

I had to take my time, but Leonora finally invited me up to her apartment. We have been having really good ecological and population discussions of late. During dinner she asked, "Why have you been going out with all those women? None of them are worthy of you."

So I may have gotten through to her, anyway. But I can see it is going to be a long haul.

May 9, 1995

When I came in during the morning, she was excited and waved a newspaper at me. "The article has appeared. They didn't change anything." She was truly excited.

May 10, 1995

Three men in blue shirts and tan slacks came in to see me. They were from an organization called LOLA, which I have heard about before. Except it is not just an organization, it is a type of religion. They asked me to treat our discussion confidential. They are advocates of limiting population growth, in fact of reversing the trend. They need psychiatrists in their organization or church, whatever you may call it. They had a tempting proposal. They'll acquire a new clinic for me with full power to practice as I see fit. But I need to join LOLA.

Leonora was curious after they had left. So I took her out to dinner, and told her about the clinic.

"It's a no-brainer, unless there are conditions," she said.

"Well, there are," I said. "I would have to join LOLA."

"Oh, LOLA, that's what it is about. I don't know too much about it, but I think they have a following of people who have joined to achieve happiness."

"That's my impression, too. I'll meet with them at their 'church' tomorrow, and they'll describe what it is all about."

July 10, 1995

I finally reached an agreement with LOLA. It's exciting. I went to see their governing council. They indoctrinated me and told me I would be a beta member of the church. This refers to professional people who are privy to information not for public consumption.

They were very interested in my success with hypnosis, as well.

Leonora and I went out for dinner, and I didn't tell her about confidential matters such as the beta membership. Just that I had joined, and that we would probably be moving in October,

She said that one thing she regretted was that I would no longer be working with poor people. But she was generally enthusiastic.

July 17, 1995

I thought I would make a move on her tonight. It was like deja vu. She let me kiss her, but no more.

August 8, 1995

She let me hold her breasts for a long time. I thought I heard her moan a bit in pleasure. But the events earlier this year seem to be playing out again. It's driving me out of my mind.

September 15, 1995

I gave in. I proposed to her. I gave her a nice ring. She accepted.

We were passionate on the sofa, in fact I almost undressed her, but she would only fallate me.

"But we are engaged," I said.

"We are ONLY engaged." She looked at me and then said, "You don't cut the wedding cake until the ceremony is over."

September 30, 1995

We set the wedding date for December. I asked her for a list of people she wanted at the wedding reception. She said, "Only you."

She's remarkable.

She added: "You can invite whomever you want. Do you want a big wedding?"

"Sort of."

"The thing that any little girl dreams of."

"Of course I do."

November 10, 1995

We finally moved into the new facility. I have a couple of other LOLA psychiatrist on board, but I call the shots. They are all lesser beta members.

November 13, 1995.

Leonora is getting prepared for the wedding. I see excitement in her eyes. It is something she had been waiting for for many years, and we are obviously a good match.

I want her to join LOLA and she is thinking it over. We should simply be married at the LOLA headquarters. The ceremony would be performed by one of the superior beta members.

Leonora is a bit put off because it is not a Lutheran ceremony. She'd rather be married in church, but the council told me that would not be acceptable.

So it will be a LOLA ceremony.

November 23, 1995.

She has agreed to be married by a superior beta council member.

"As long as it is legal."

I checked with City Hall, and it is legal. Those guys are authorized to perform weddings. The certificate, of course, will be issued by City Hall.

December 10, 1995
I simply can't wait. We'll have the wedding, then we'll be going to my apartment to change clothes. Actually to consummate the marriage.
I just can't wait.

That was the last diary entry. The last half of the book had only empty pages. Did he simply stop writing a diary after they got married? You would think that with all the sexual stuff he had written, he would have elaborated on that.

Nora called within the hour, and they decided to meet at the coffee shop again. It was shopping time, anyway, so she'd probably use that as an excuse.

At the table he handed her one of the copies. "I have sent the other one to a friend in Madison whom I trust."

"I don't want to read anything - and I mean anything - until later," she said. "I'm fairly sure this is of importance, otherwise why would he keep it in the safe?"

"I think you should read this, though," Jon said, "It might have some bearing on whatever you decide."

"That's why I don't want to read anything. I have already decided," she said. "That was the significance of my Yes/No question to you the other day."

But she did look at the newspaper articles. She said, as to herself, "That's what I thought."

"But they don't mention Dr. Ondmand by name."

She looked at him. "There is so much I didn't have a chance to tell you." She looked sad all of a sudden.

"I might as well tell you now," she said. "My memory loss can't be simply amnesia. Something can happen one day and a month afterwards I'll have forgotten it. So I, at one point in time, took to writing down things I thought and observed. One day, it was shortly after I had had a LOLA session, Lionel talked in his sleep. He did this several nights, in fact he still does. It started about the time and continued for a while after the time of the death of Jessica Kreutz. He talked about things that would imply that he was the one who engineered her death. Words like 'I didn't really want her to die'. I wrote it down, and a month afterwards I had forgotten it all. But I had it written down and that's when I got scared of him and wanted a divorce. And when he reacted the way he did when I brought it up, I just gave it up. I got depressed and he sent me to a session, and I felt OK after that. I also wrote that down.

"It was just about that time when he went up in the LOLA organization. He is now on the council of the supreme betas. He is an important and powerful man. He hired Dolores Juanita, the maid, and he has me under surveillance all the time."

Things are falling in place was what Jon thought.

"If you are looking for material of significance, I think the computer will tell you a lot. The evidence here he could just shrug off," he said. Then he added, "I'm glad you asked me to take everything in the safe. If you want to use it as a weapon, tell him you'll give it back to him when he grants you a divorce hearing."

"Of course," she said. "Can you open the computer? Do you need a password?"

"I won't know until I try to open it."

"Will that be difficult?"

"I have to guess at it. You say he can't retain figures very well. He may have troubles with his password too. Let's gamble on it. I somehow have a feeling that the answer is in the book I took from the safe."

"What book is it?"

"Heart of Darkness. Conrad, you know."

"I all of a sudden get scared. Is it dangerous to stay around?"

"Yes, I think so. There would be no harm in us - shall we say taking a vacation."

"Not only do I love you. You're such a gem." She seemed relaxed again. He realized it had been a difficult decision. Once the decision was made she didn't want any post consideration muddying the waters.

She was quite a gal.

She said on the telephone, "He's staying in the hospital at

least one more day. They are running a lot of tests. But he is not in critical conditions or anything. They just want to make sure it wasn't a ministroke. It's late now and I'll call you in the morning." Then she said, "Very early. We have a lot to do. I love you so. I miss you. Pretty soon we may be able to stay together all the time."

"I tried to open the computer, but I *do* need a password. Do you have any suggestions about passwords? Words he might use." "Alpha, beta, gamma, epsilon, Helligman. But," she said, "Don't work on it now. Wait with that until later. It is good to be focused. Let's get the work at hand done." She then added, "We should relax a little after all of this is taken care of."

"I'll work on it, anyway," he said. "I think it is important."

She sounded a bit irritated. "Let's stick to the task at hand." Then she added, "I'm sorry, I didn't want to snap at you."

She was tense, indeed.

He was tired and went to bed. But he couldn't sleep. There were so many events that were interwoven that his thoughts jumped from one thing to another. He finally fell into a light sleep.

He was awakened when the phone rang at seven o'clock. Nora must have noticed how out of it he was. "Is anything the matter?" she asked.

She met him at the shop at noon sharp.

"We're still on track with our plans?" she asked

He nodded.

"What I'd like to do is to go to a lawyer today and file for divorce. I'm sure, with enough money, he can serve papers by tomorrow or the day after, when Lionel is back."

"Are you just going to wait at your - at his house until he comes back. I was hoping…"

"What you were hoping is right. I'll pack the most important things I have, stuff them in the rent-a-car, and I'll see you at your - at our place. So now you know what I wanted the rent-a-car for."

He thought - with delight - she was thinking of this already when she got the rent-a-car. She added, "I have never been by your place, but I know the area fairly well."

"I'll pull my car out of the garage and place it in the visitor's lot and you can drive right into the garage. I'll give you the garage door opener out at the car."

He shook his head to himself. He was laying himself open, doing things that he definitely should not be doing. He should be at home in the shadow of the television, or reading to pass the time, until things in Madison were settled. Or? But, once again, he was mesmerized by her because she did something that warmed him all over. She got up from the table, went over to him, took his head in her hands and kissed him. She took him by surprise, but then he kissed her back, and in the kiss, short as it was, lingered the promise of the future.

His heart was jumping as he drove home. He had forgotten the computer for a while. They were going to live together. He had no more qualms about how it came about.

He picked up a flower in front of the house and took it in and sat in the sofa and picked the petals and said, "She loves me, she loves me, she loves me..."

After a while he went to the supermarket and bought some sandwich meat, some Italian bread and some wine.

He had taken his time. By now it was dark and he went home, wondering whether she would be there already or not. Or whether she would really come. And if she didn't would it be because she had changed her mind or had she met with some of the LOLA people at her house, and were they keeping her from leaving?

His feeling of elation got mixed with fears of what might happen. He shouldn't have let her go back to her place again. She probably was *not* paranoid.

Again he wondered what type of power these people had over others.

CHAPTER 6

> A…nymph with moist and parted mouth, and now bending down over my bare belly, crooning her glorious obscenities, prepared to take between those lips…the bone-rigid stalk of my passion.
> William Styron. Sophie's Choice

The garage door was closed and there was no car in the driveway, and he was hoping she'd be there. He parked his car in the visitor's lot.

She was standing right by the door as he opened. She embraced him and kissed him.

"Were you standing right by the door all the time?" he asked.

"It wasn't too long, but I was waiting impatiently," she said.

They walked up the stairs into the front room. She had placed a tablecloth on the dining table, and she had put silverware and glasses out.

"I thought it should be quite festive," she said.

"But where did you get it all?"

"It was in the outermost closet."

He had never looked there.

She went over to him, held her hands around his face, pulled it down and kissed him. As in the coffee shop it was more than a warm and tender embrace - there were intentions hidden in it, deep emotions, strong passion.

She loosened her arms from him and let them down to his belt. She undid the buckle, all while kissing him, then undid the top of the zipper and opened it without looking, all the while with her lips kissing his. He felt his pants starting to fall, and at that moment she let go of her grip on him, bent down on her knees and liberated his phallus from its confine. He was already aroused, and she placed it in her mouth. There was in him a surge of at one time serenity and enormous thrust. He felt his essence rising and wanted to be inside her other lips, but she kept her lips and teeth around him and he couldn't hold back the essence that issued forth in her mouth.

She lingered until his arousement started to leave him. Then she stood up and kissed him as if to let him partake in the essence that he had left in her.

After a pause she said, "I knew I was in love with you the minute I saw you in the coffee shop. That doesn't sound rational, but it was that way."

"It is rational enough. We have talked about the difference between 'being in love' and 'loving.'"

"But then we didn't know each other - really."

"Didn't we? Sometimes body language is more eloquent than words. I saw you looking at me, and you gave me shivers of delight. I bet you didn't know I was looking at you, though."

"No, and I didn't know that you thought I was looking at you."

She laughed and caressed his cheek.

"I love it. You are so naïve." She went over to the refrigerator and took out a bottle of the white wine. "I'm serving you wine in our house." She made a joyful dance as she said it.

"Oh, you found the wine I had bought."

"No," she said. "I happened to have a bottle in the car." Then she laughingly said, "I keep one at all time for occasions that happen but once in a lifetime."

He took her hands, and they stood for a while gazing at one another.

They drank a glass of wine, and sat, saying nothing, then she said, "I have to tell you the thing that didn't go right."

"Again, I repeat, I don't' think we are safe around here."

"Less so than you think," she said.

"Maybe we should leave right away. It would actually fit in with my plans."

"Which you haven't told me about. Should we leave tomorrow?"

"Sure," he said, "Regarding my plans, I have all the time in the world. I have to make telephone calls from time to time, but traveling will actually make that better for me."

"Good," she said. "Do you need money?"

"Not at all."

"I took my holdings with me, but it isn't all that much, maybe twenty K. But I need to get the rent-a-car back. And - as I said - I'd also like to get some more stuff from the house. I should say, I left a note for Lionel that 'I' had the contents of the safe and that I would return it to him when he granted me a divorce."

"That might not have been too wise."

"Well, Lionel will not be back until tomorrow and won't see it until then, so it should be OK."

"But Harry and his cohort?"

"I think they'll report back an OK to Lionel."

"What about the maid, what's her name, Dolores Juanita?"

"I think she already reported to Lionel and that Harry and Company was a result of her talking with Lionel."

"We have to stay, at least until tomorrow. I'll have to see a divorce lawyer before we leave," She was uncomfortable as she said that.

"I don't think you should go back to the house again. Don't you have enough of your stuff in the car already? I think going back would be too risky. And - again - Dolores Juanita will see the note. She'll tell Lionel."

"I was thinking of what you were saying about it not have been too wise to leave the note just yet. You're right. She may see it and call him, and either he or someone from LOLA may spot me if I go back. But I have to get the business with the lawyer settled before we leave. Can you help me find a lawyer?"

"Sure, but how'll you know he won't be a LOLA member?"

"Good point. Suppose we find someone who isn't all that successful."

So they went through the telephone book, and tried out a couple of locations. They found a Mr. Skifter in Tampa who had his office in a run-down building and she decided to try him.

"Do you want me to come with you? I'd actually rather not." He thought, again, how much he was deviating from his resolve to stay out of sight.

"Just wait for me in the car."

She knocked on the door and tried the knob, but it was locked. Rather than a receptionist or secretary opening, a man in his mid-fifties opened the door for her and bade her come in.

She sat down in the old wooden chair in front of the desk in a barren room and stated her business.

"So why do you want a divorce?" he asked.

"My husband sodomizes me all the time, and I tell him I don't want it."

"Legally, that is actually rape, but the point is to prove it so we can use it to get you a good divorce settlement. Could you have intercourse - if you'd call it that - with him, and go to a hospital afterwards? Better even, could you tape it?"

"You mean video-tape?" she said with some horror in her voice.

"Well, that would be nice, but an audiotape may suffice. Do you have a small tape recorder?"

She nodded.

"But I can't really wear it as a - what do they call it - a wire. After all I won't be wearing all my clothes."

"Do you always have intercourse at the same time and location?"

"We have intercourse when he comes home. Any time of the day."

"Place a tape recorder in a bag or something. Start it and let the microphone out a bit. Then come back and see me. In the meantime I will prepare papers. There is a retainer of one thousand dollars I would need."

"When?"

"Well, before I start. I charge three hundred dollars an hour."

"Let me think it over," she said, "On second thought, OK. I'll be back in a minute with the money."

Down at the car she asked John if he had a thousand dollars on him. He had 800 and she had 200 plus, so she went up and gave the man the money. He didn't give her a receipt, but she didn't think of that until later.

"I need your husband's name and address," he said.

When she mentioned it was Lionel Ondmand he was startled. But he didn't say anything.

She left the murky little office, and drove back with Jon.

"What reason for divorce did you give him?"

"That my husband was a pervert. But you don't need a reason. No-fault divorce."

"I was wondering, as I sat down here, if it might not be better to go for the divorce somewhere else," he said. "In my divorce my lawyer said it would have been to my advantage if I had established residence elsewhere and if I, not she, had filed for divorce."

"We are leaving anyway," she said. "We could do it in another state even. We'll talk about it on the way when we drive. Where are we going?"

"All over, sort of," he said. "It is certainly likely that someone will try to follow us. I'm sure Lionel - or LOLA, rather - will want the computer and the diary back. So we'll drive around at random. Best way of not being followed."

"I wish I had more clothes with me," she said, "But what I have will do OK. I won't be all that elegant."

"Beauty is in the eye of the beholder, but in any event, it's not what clothes you wear, but how you wear them and what you have to put in them. So don't worry, you'll do fine."

"You're nice," she said. "But maybe we should make one more trip to my place." Then she added, "I've got to get out of the habit of saying 'my place'. In a divorce I'd surely lose custody of the house. Then again, I still don't know if he'd agree to a divorce."

In the evening they went to get more of her clothes. They drove out on Eastlake Road and turned off at the road that led to her complex. He was driving the rent-a-car and he drove slowly

"It is probably good you are taking precautions," she said.

He shut off the headlights as he passed the gate to the subdivision and parked a short distance away from her house.

"I'll wait for you here, and keep the passenger door ajar. If something happens run back and I'll open it all the way; then jump in as I take off."

He saw her walk down in the dark. Her shape would reappear as she passed under a streetlight, and then disappear and become a shadow. It was enticing to see the move of her sensuous gait in the semidarkness.

As she came close to the house, she suddenly turned, and first walked, and then ran towards the car. He then saw two men emerging from the house and pursuing her. They were gaining on her, but he opened the door, didn't wait for her to close it, and made a fast U-turn. The front runner still was a good fifty feet away as he sped off.

"Some of Lionel's friends. I saw their shapes through the side window - there is only a sheer curtain there. I recognized the shape of one of them. It is very characteristic. He is at the clinic."

He drove some side roads first, just in case the men had spotted her car, and brought it back and drove it into the garage again.

"We'd better get the car back to the rent-a-car agency," she said. "Will that be dangerous?"

"Who knows," he said. "The sooner the better. I'll get in the Volvo and I will follow you. I'll check the car in for you at the rent-a-car place, just to be on the safe side."

Driving into the rent-a-car place he parked his car in the street in such a fashion that it was pointed away from the gate.

Then he went over to her car and she got out and kissed him and she went over and sat in the driver's seat in the Volvo.

"If anything happens I might be running like you did before, and you just do as I did."

"I don't know whether I can do it as well as you."

"Well, you don't have to make a U-ey," he said, "Just go straight ahead. But everything will probably be OK."

The rent-a-car office was a cubicle that was lit and formed a strange beacon in the night. There were two men inside, talking to the attendant.

Then suddenly there was a voice behind him, and it startled him so much that he jumped. He turned around, and there was an attendant right there.

"I'm not off duty yet," he said. "I can check you in, if that is what you are looking for. I saw the car pull in. You should actually leave the lights on so we can see you,"

"I will in the future, and thank you," Jon said. Then he added, "I hate these lit-up offices in the middle of the night."

"I hate them all day," the attendant said grinning. "But it is a job."

He took care of the checking-in on a hand-held computer. He had just finished when Jon saw one of the men come out of the cubicle and come towards them in a brisk walk.

He simply took off, ran towards the Volvo, jumped in and Nora took off without a hitch. She was shaking, though. They got out on Nineteen. He said, "You'd better put the headlights on now." Then he added, "Do you want me to drive?"

"No, it's OK. Shall I go straight back to your place? - Our place."

He had looked in the side view mirror, and didn't notice anything. "I think we're OK. Just go into the compound by the main gate. When you go in, make an immediate right turn, then I'll direct you. We'll be able to see if we are followed."

But they were not.

She parked the car in the garage and they went upstairs into the condo. He poured himself a glass of bourbon and her one, too.

"I haven't really seen you drink strong alcoholic beverages," she said.

"It was a tricky evening and I need something."

"Right," she said.

"We'd better hit the road as soon as possible. Would tomorrow before dawn be OK?"

"I can obviously drive all right, but I don't know if I'm up to highway driving." She looked sad, all of a sudden. "You're doing everything. I'm not much use," Tears were coming down her cheeks.

"Don't worry about that. Necessity is the mother of invention. If I need you to drive on the highway you may have to, but I plan on doing most of it myself. You're doing just fine."

"What are you going to do about the condo?"

"It's paid for up to March the first," he said.

He packed several suitcases. He brought his and Lionel's laptop computer and his printer.

"You're taking the printer too?" she said.

"Well, you never know if you want to print something, do you now?"

He took their luggage down to the car in the garage.

They had a couple of sandwiches.

"Should I pack some of the stuff from the refrigerator for the road?" she asked.

And it came time to go to bed.

"Can I sleep with you?" she asked.

"I'd love it. I had sort of taken it for granted. I guess I shouldn't have."

"Yes, you should."

In the bedroom she went into the bathroom. She opened the door and came out. She had a cotton nightgown on. It hid all her wonderful shapes. He was wondering why.

She cuddled up to him in bed, but before he could say or do anything she was asleep. He felt like touching her, then he thought better of it.

In the morning they drove off and headed out Eastlake Road and took the byroads over through Land O'Lakes to Interstate 75. Once on the highway she started to relax.

"I think we are out of their reach now," she said.

If it hadn't been for enough evidence that *he* had seen himself, he would think she was paranoid. But there was something very real about it all.

It certainly was a chain of events that didn't fit with his original scheme of 'laying low'. He was wondering if 'laying low' was something he had to do for the rest of his life. Did he really have a right to take Nora with him on some sort of Odyssey through the Southern states?

Then she looked at him and said, "We're on our way."

Somehow, that relaxed him again. Yet, on her behalf, he worried. Indeed, their fates were tied together.

They overnighted in a cheap motel in Ocala.

In the morning she said, "The motel couldn't be better. It is sort of ours."

Again the magic word 'ours'.

CHAPTER 7

> O, speak again, bright angel! For thou art
> As glorious to this night, being o'er my head
> As is a winged messenger of heaven
> Shakespeare, Romeo and Juliet, II,2

She had been right. It was the thing to do, not to read the diary, not to look at what was on the computer. He also shouldn't think of whether or not he could unlock it at all.

They drove and they were happy. Around nine, he took an exit and stopped at a gas station.

"I've been here before," she said. "They have a counter with tapes. I guess the truckers use tapes a lot to stay awake."

"Good idea," he said. "What kind of music do you like?" he asked.

"Any kind you like."

"Mind Ellington and Shaw and Goodman and stuff like that?"

"That's fine, but mix a little Mozart and Beethoven in as well."

He ran through the racks and picked ten tapes. He thought the cashier would wonder about the mixture, but she just stood and chewed gum. He wanted to get out fast and get on with the trip, but the paper in her cash machine ran out, so she had to put in a new roll. She fumbled with it, but finally got it to work.

She said, "Have a nice day," as she was bending down to pick up a strip of paper from the old paper roll. She was fairly slender, but she had a big behind. Too many lollypops. Behinds mean a lot.

He got in the car. "Everything clear?" he asked.

"Nothing suspicious," she said. "What did you get?"

He handed her the bag with the tapes.

"Let's start with Shaw." She stuck the tape in the player, and it started playing 'It had to be you.'

"It *did* have to be you," she said. And she leaned over on his shoulder.

"We are driving into our life," she said.

"How do you feel?" he asked later. He was wondering if she had ever driven a lot as a passenger in a car, taken road trips and such.

"I feel much safer now," she said. Then she held his hand and squeezed it. "I haven't even said thank you for all you've done."

"Thank you is what you say to strangers, where you couldn't expect help."

"That's right. We aren't strangers anymore, are we now." Without looking he could discern a smile on her face.

"What a strange way we met. Meeting people is difficult." She looked in the mirror on the visor. "Is my hair OK?"

"It looks fine. The wind has tossed it a bit. Do you want me to close the window?"

"No, I like the fresh air." She sat for a while, looked at the dark sky.

"I felt the attraction for you right away. The first time I saw you," he said.

"So you wanted to seduce me?"

He smiled. "To tell the truth...maybe," Then he grinned, "Is that bad? I am just trying to think of how it really played out. You forget very fast."

She thought she hadn't forgotten, and he really did remember. You remember good things. You remember really horrible things. But in between you don't.

"Something protects you from remembering mundane things. Also irritating things that aren't important."

She was sitting there with the most adorable smile on her face. She was enjoying.

"It is good to remember."

"Yes," he said, "But it also good to be aware of Right Now."

The wind had started up, and there were a few raindrops on the window shield.

"But I like to think of the good moments."

"Don't get me wrong. No sense in having good moments if you can't think of them."

"Do you think that most people do?"

"I don't know. I think most people don't have too many good moments to think of."

"Do you think that they change their memories in their minds?"

His mother had been notorious for changing stories she told about his childhood.

"Sure. I remember my mother did. She told about the same event many times, and it always changed a bit."

"But real good moments you don't talk about. You share them with the one you had them with. Like you and me."

"Like you and me."

Her smile was like a lasting mood in a woods where birds sing and the breeze whispers.

"I'm more than just in love with you," she said. "I love you. I know I keep on repeating myself, but it is so true. It's such an indescribable feeling." It was like a declaration out of nowhere, one, which they both knew existed, but which bore repeating. Like the prayers and the benedictions and the declarations of faith in church. You have read them, yet they are repeated each Sunday

"Do you love me? Say that you love me."

John the Baptist.

"I love you. We'll say that every day of our lives."

"Promise?"

She had fallen asleep in the seat. It was a nice, calm sleep. Apparently the strain of the flight had left her, she felt safe, maybe for the first time in days.

He was wondering how he should proceed. He had called Nev the night prior and the news were the same as the last time. He had gotten the new number and jotted it down. He would call again a week hence.

But the question was, would she become bored or tired after so much driving around? Or should he simply find a motel somewhere in nice surroundings and should they stay there for a while?

He was thinking of how he should sign in, when they registered at motels. In Ocala he had signed in as Al Smith. Best to make it under a name different from Slowe. Someone might have made the connection with the white Volvo. And to protect her further - and himself as well - he would sign in as a single. What name to use?

His thoughts wandered off, and he started thinking of the bliss he seemed to have with her, the bond. And he wished that he could just stay in one place with her, and he decided to drive up to Tennessee and find a place there where they could stay for a while. In any event, check in, and then they could make up their minds.

She woke up all of a sudden and said, "Where are we now?"

Southern Georgia.

"Where are we going? Not that I need to know, I was just curious."

"Eventually, I figured we'd go to Tennessee - we'd be there tomorrow - and check in some place nice, and make our plans then. But I'm taking my time. You'll not have noticed, but I get off the highway every so often, so that we don't just travel in one line."

"Tennessee and see," she said and laughed to herself. "I'm not quite awake yet. Did I sleep long?"

"About half an hour."

"I dreamt of you. You were out fishing. Do you ever fish?"

"Well, Yes and No. There is a bit of a story to that. I can tell it out of sequence, but it belongs to the Hannah phase of my life."

Hannah had been angry with him because of his insistence on working in the sporting goods store. He knew why. If he worked in the bank, she could keep tabs on him all the time. She didn't love him - he was sure of that - but she wanted to possess him. He realized that he had to get out of this grip. The sporting goods store had been a god-sent. He had gone to his father-in-law's office and turned down the offer.

"I simply don't understand young people," said the old man, "in particular you. You have a great future here, yet, you turn it down. And for what? To go and sell Green Bay Packer T-shirts to nimcompoots. Why don't you talk it over with Hannah? She has a good head on her shoulders. She is making money. She is successful. You could be too, so why don't you follow her example."

But he had stood his ground. It still came up from time to time. The fishing worked out well for him. Nev got hired into the store and when he announced to Hannah that he had to work weekends, Nev was always there to cover for him.

It was Nev's idea to go fishing. Well, Nev liked fishing, and by this means Jon could escape from home. Whenever.

"Why this sudden interest in fishing?" Hannah asked.

"A lot of customers come in for fishing gear, and I need to know something about it."

"But when you have learned you can stop, can't you?"

"You get hooked." Then he added, "That's a joke." He shouldn't joke with her. She had no sense of humor.

"Just like the poor fishes," she said.

"That was deceitful," Nora said. "But the end justifies the means - sometimes."

"The beginning as well," he laughed, "like the alpha and the omega."

"Greek letters bring back a past I'm longing to forget."

"I'm sorry. I wasn't thinking."

"I know. I have to learn to deal with it. So you went fishing?"

"It made my life bearable."

"But you have said things from time to time that indicated that you weren't faithful to Hannah. I can understand that - you didn't love her and she didn't love you. Tell me more about it..." and then she added, "Yes, sometime. It doesn't have to be now."

She looked a little sad.

"I'm a bit jealous," she said. "But I guess I have reason to be. Like your red-headed girlfriend, Sherry what was her name?"

"Shirley Shelley." He was going to say that Shirley was not his girlfriend, but before he could go any further she was talking again.

"I guess you knew her in a biblical sense too?"

"She was not my girlfriend. I hardly knew her."

"Come on, now," she said. "No need to hide it. It was before we met."

"But she still wasn't my girlfriend."

He was a bit irritated.

"I'm actually not jealous of her," she continued. "But in the case of Hannah, it is more like anger. I'd like to have smacked the bitch. She must have been awful. I'll never be awful to you."

Then he said, "I'll never be unfaithful to you."

"Did you ever say that to Hannah?"

"Never."

"Say you'll love me forever. I just never want this to go away, I don't want anyone or anything to come in its way."

"I'll love you forever."

She squeezed his hand. Then she fell asleep again.

He thought back to the conversation about Shirley Shelly. It was frustrating that Nora didn't want to believe him. Then he thought about what Celli had said that it wasn't the truth that mattered but it was what people perceived the truth to be.

He parsed the question she had addressed, namely, "What was the name of your girlfriend, Sherry...? He had answered Shirley's name spontaneously, In so doing, however, he had acknowledged - at least in her perception - that Shirley had been his girlfriend. If Nora, with a simple question, could cause him to say something that conveyed what he didn't mean, how easy, then, wouldn't it be for a sharp lawyer to twist his words around!

Celli was right.

But Nora would never be able to understand that. She hadn't experienced the situation.

He stopped at Byron, Georgia, for gas.

They got some coffee and some packaged snacks and used the facilities. "They're clean," she said, "I hadn't expected it."

"It must be owned by a lady. The men's room was filthy."

They drank the coffee and ate the snacks.

"Do you feel fairly safe now. Away enough from danger?" he asked.

"Sort of," she said. "I forgot for a while. Every time I was holding your hand. Maybe you shouldn't have asked?"

"I'll hold your hand again."

She smiled and, indeed, squeezed his hand.

"I got stiff," she said.

"Sorry about it, but it is the best I can do in the line of chariots."

She smiled again. "I know," she said, "And it's actually a marvelous car. But we've stopped for gas quite a few times. Is it a gas guzzler?"

"Small gas tank."

"That is like a girl being small-breasted, isn't it?" she laughed.

"At baby-feeding time, I suppose," he said.

She thought a while, and then said, "Do you want babies?"

"With you, yes,"

"I like that answer," she said, "It is so contrary to Lionel's philosophies. But we can't wait too long. The clock is ticking."

He kissed her. "I love you," he said, "I can't just say it enough." Then he added, "Maybe we should stop soon and find a place for the night."

They turned off at the next exit and stopped at a small motel. The type where there is only one long building and twenty rooms with a space to park in front of each room. They were the only ones there.

"You stay in the car," he said. "I think it would be best if I check in as one person, just in case someone is trying to track you."

She looked worried again. "So you *do* think we are not out of danger."

"No, I think we are fine, but you can still be cautious."

She smiled. "I guess so." When he came back she asked, "What name did you give?"

"Bob Browning. A single room. I thought that would be best."

"How did the man react - the owner or manager, I mean?"

"It was an old gal. Nothing unusual. She seemed to like the idea of being paid cash. But that's a weakness. People remember stuff like that." He added, "Chances are she'll just pocket the money."

"Robert Browning," she mused. "You can wax poetic, if you want to."

He smiled. "The best I can do is, 'Roses are Red, Grass is Green, You're in my heart, not in my spleen."

"That's terrible," she said,"Where did you pick that up?"

"There was a girl in high school who wanted her friends to write poetry in her so-called 'verse book'. It was awful dribble, so I cooked that one up. It has a good ring to it doesn't it."

"You're awful at times. And I think you knew a lot of girls."

"I've told you already, Not So."

She shrugged in delight. Then she kissed him.

They got into the room. It was spartanic, but clean. "It'll do," he said.

"Any place with you'll do," she said.

That's nice, he thought. The right thing to say. She seemed to be calm again. He kissed her. They sat down on the bed, and she took off his jeans, and he felt the same divine ecstasy once again. Well, can it be divine and yet of the flesh?

"I love to do this to you," she said. "It makes me feel that you are in me, and that you are physically part of me."

"Strange," he said, "I feel the same sort of thing, as if we are together in a different dimension. Like Siamese twins."

"But the feeling at the end is so great too. I hate to let go."

"And I hate to," he said. He held her tight. Then he ran his hand over her breasts, and she seemed to like it, but when he moved his hand further down, she took it away.

"Not now," she said. "Later."

Why, he wondered, why not now? They were this far in their relationship already.

"Can I use the car for about half an hour?" she asked.

She went somewhere and got some cheese and crackers and a bottle of wine. She came back with a big smile on her face and said, "The housewife is back, time for dinner."

They ate, quietly, then he said, "Tomorrow we'll have a good dinner somewhere, OK?"

"Isn't this good?"

"It's superb," he said. "And that's not what I meant. We're both tired - at least I suppose you are tired -". She nodded, "and it would probably be good to get an early start. I don't quite know where we'll overnight then, but somewhere less out in the sticks."

She went out in the bathroom and again she came back out in her cotton nightgown, which didn't reveal much of her figure. He was wondering what she looked like in the altogether. He'd know, eventually, he was sure of that.

They both fell asleep rapidly, but he woke up in the middle of the night. He got up and drew the curtain a bit and looked out at the parking lot. Theirs was the only car.

Thoughts crept in about what might be on the computer and about what news, if any, Nev might have next time. And the bliss disappeared. What did he face? If nothing had cleared up, how should he proceed? How could he offer her a decent life?

He knew he loved her, but he was suddenly gripped, again, by this terror about the future. He could, himself, go somewhere and continue his life as Jonathan Slowe, but what sort of life could he offer her as Mrs. Slowe?

He went back to bed and fell into an unquiet sleep. Then deep sleep suddenly came. He awoke by her standing by the side of the bed and bending down and kissing him. She had brought in two cups of coffee.

"Sleepyhead," she said, "I love you."

"There was a song like that, once," he said.

She smiled. "I know. I like it better when simply recited."

"Me too."

They drove off and stopped at a restaurant a couple of exits up the road.

"Can you tell me about Hannah now?" Why not he thought.

CHAPTER 8

> He said he loved me that going into me
> He said he was going into the world and the sky
> He said all the buckles were very firm...
> He said Just don't cry
> Muriel Rukeyser. Waiting for Icarus

He was aware that he had to talk about his past. They had sat down at a table near a window. The curtains could stand washing, and he thought of the expression, 'to air ones dirty linen in public'. Well, this was in private, and he would have to talk about his past at one point or another.

"For instance," she said, "How did you meet?"

He looked thoughtful - collecting thoughts, arranging words and events in a logical fashion.

"I told you that Athena died in a car accident. I was practically unscathed. A little cut over the eye, and a sore elbow and some muscular pains, for instance in the stomach. I guess from the seat belt.

"Aside from my grief, I had to think of funeral arrangements. Nobody can fathom this double insult, the loss of your wife and the almost commercial arrangements you have to make.

"I had no one to turn to, so I called a funeral director in the neighborhood, and he was a big help. He asked me for the wording of an obituary and placed it in the paper. He had a picture of Athena included. It was a nice picture.

"I called her parents to ask them how they wanted to be included in the wording of the obit, and this was where the third insult came in. They were absolutely hostile - not grieving, but hostile. You killed our daughter, how dare you have the audacity to call us."

"They were looking for money," Nora said.

"Exactly, I'll come to that."

"They placed their own obituary, and it was sort of all out there for the world to see. Two obituaries, one following the other.

"At the viewing in the funeral home it was even more awkward. They stood in the opposite end of the room, glaring at me.

"I was to some degree distracted from it, because a large group of friends of Athena's showed up. She had many more friends than I had known of.

"A woman came in. She went over to Athena's parents first; then she came over to where I stood. 'I'm a good friend of Athena's - 'I was', I guess is the proper tense. I was awfully sorry to hear about her death. We roomed together the first year at the university, but we have lost touch of late. Did she ever mention my name? I'm Hannah.'

"I said, 'She may have', and thought that was going to be the end of the conversation.

"She looked at me and said, 'Is there any way I can help'?

"I muttered 'That is very kind of you, but all the arrangements have been made. We are having a small wake at our - my apartment after this, and you're welcome to come.'

"'I certainly will,' she said, 'but that is not what I meant by help. I sense there is some very bad feelings between you and Athena's parents.'

"I admitted as much and she said, 'They are looking for money. They'll probably take you to court for wrongful death damages.'

"I said something like 'You're kidding' and she said something like 'This is no place for joking. Do you want me to help you?'

"She went over to the parents and they palavered for a

while, then she came back. She was followed closely by the man and the woman, and they said to me 'We are sorry for our telephone conversation. We were overtaken by grief. Please forgive us.'

"But I didn't invite them to the wake. I asked Hannah, 'What exactly did you do?'

"She answered, 'I told them that you were not where the money was, the money was with the trucking company. The truck that hit your car.

"And Hannah came to the wake, and that is how it all started. I'm ashamed to admit it, but after everyone had left she and I had sex. In retrospect it was rather incongruous. She appeared passionate, almost wild. She dug her fingernails into my back and for weeks I had bruises as if I had been whipped.

Later - not too soon afterwards - the passion disappeared."

His thoughts went back to the introduction to her family.

"My father is the somewhat heavy-set man over by the window," Hannah said. She had an air of being very proper. She was not tall, but stood erect.

They walked over towards the heavy man. He had a drink in his hand, and as he turned some of it spilled. He wiped the drops off his pants and said, "Darn it."

Then he looked up and saw them and he smiled, extended his hand and said, "You must be Hannah's – what shall I call you?"

"We are going to be married, dad," said Hannah. "His name is John."

The father looked over in another corner of a room and waved at someone and said, "How are you, you old son-of-a-gun?" Then he turned to them again.

"So it would be more appropriate to say that you are Hannah's fiancé. Why didn't you tell me, Hannah?"

"I did, dad," she said, "Two days ago."

"You couldn't have said it very enthusiastically," he said. "Well, I can see why."

I was taken aback by this - impoliteness - to say the least.

The man was inebriated, but had an air of distinction, anyway. Like a Southern colonel, in the days of the civil war.

"I am not going to ask you if you if you can support my daughter financially," he said. It was as if he was at the point of concluding a financial transaction. "You know she is financially independent."

"No," said John. "I didn't know that."

"My sister, Dorothy, died a couple of years ago. The old wench kept her nest egg in a coffee tin. She would have had more if she had put it in the bank. Anyhow, she willed it to Hannah, and Hannah is working wonders with it"

"Father is the director of the bank here," Hannah explained.

"Oh," said John.

"Come work for me," said the father. "You are a college man, right?"

He thought the expression 'college man' a relic from the thirties. Or was it meant to be derogatory?

"We'll talk about that later," said Hannah. Her lips were pursed. She'd have liked the conversation to take a different direction.

"We'll go mingle with the other guests," she said.

And so they mingled.

When he graduated he hadn't been able to find a job in his field. What was his field anyway? Political science. Diffuse. He entered the employment agency, and the woman sitting at the desk said, "Still no luck?"

He shook his head. He looked at the girl. She was ugly, but she had a job. She took out a Kleenex and blew her nose.

"Hay fever," she said. She smiled. She had bad teeth. "If you are willing to bend a bit, there is a position available in a sporting goods store. Would you be interested? You could take it for a time, you know."

He thought the expressions 'bend a bit' and 'position' were, perhaps suggestive. Did she pick up romances on the side? Possibly. She had a vulnerable audience.

Mr. Thompson was the assistant CEO of the sporting goods

chain. He was in town.

"It is a responsible job," he said.

John got the job and he liked it. He'd meet fishermen and hunters - that bothered him a bit in the beginning, because he had never done either before.

"You should work for father," is what Hannah said. On several occasions, at that. John actually went to the bank one day, and after her father had introduced him to people and explained the functions, he asked if he could interview with the Personnel Department. Hannah wanted to be there, but he persuaded her to go have a cup of coffee.

It didn't take him long to figure out that, first of all, he had a lot to learn about the business, that he didn't care for the business, and most of all the he would be looked upon as the director's son-in-law.

So he turned down the job.

"You remind me of the character in the film 'Good-bye Columbus.' You've seen it, haven't you?"

"I read the book."

"There you go again, being so snooty and cultured and educated. Too good for a real-life job."

But he stuck to his guns.

"You're just like Neil Klugman in Good-Bye Columbus," Hannah said

"I don't think I'm undecided in life," he said. "I liked what I did, and that was that. If she was as rich as she implied and as her father implied why would she want more?"

"Rich people always do. Anyway, I would say that Neil Klugman wasn't undecided. He just knew he didn't want anything to do with the establishment. Did Hannah see herself as Brenda Patimkin - was that what her name was in the book?"

"I think so. I don't even know if she would have recognized the name. She just saw the movie and she thought that Neil Klugman was a jerk."

"You were running a sporting goods store," she said, "Your father-in-law should have looked at you as a business man, and as such respected you."

"Not so. I didn't own the store, I just ran it."

"I see your point. But was Hannah really rich? You must have known from your income taxes."

"That is another strange point. As April neared, I said to her we should start filing our taxes. And she answered, 'I already filed mine.'"

"You filed separately? As a couple you must have wasted quite a bit of money that way."

"She not necessarily, and I'll come to that."

"She was cheating on her taxes, is that it?"

Nora, he thought, you're very perceptive.

"Right on! But there is much more to that, and that is an installment to come."

"Yes, you've talked enough for one session."

She bent over and kissed him.

"That's for being such a naughty boy and marrying twice without me in the picture."

He laughed. "I guess I should have torn you out of Lionel's arms that evening in the garage."

She smiled again. "What a wonderful thought that is. But what would you have done with Athena?" She smiled, impishly. "Try and answer that."

Then, saving him from having to answer, the waitress came over with the check.

After he had paid she said, "Maybe I should tell you a bit more about Lionel. Sort of a tit for a tat. But first continue with Hannah. And also, I don't know much about this friend of yours, Nev."

He really wanted to find a spot where they could settle down for a little while, but he was wondering if they dared stay at one spot for more than one day. He was, forever, looking at the cars whenever they overnighted somewhere. In the morning back on the Interstate he saw a green sedan with the license plate '2MANY' and it bothered him. The morning was slightly foggy. It was still early and the traffic was not heavy.

She squeezed his hand again. She had taken to doing that,

and he liked it.

"You have to tell me things at your own pace," she said. "But you've said yourself that you're running away - No, rather, hiding sort of - from the police. But you can't do that forever."

"Well," he said, "I could take on another identity."

The thought came to him that had not been telling the whole truth, so he added, "In fact, I have. My name is not Jonathan Slowe. I shouldn't tell you my real name, just in case things go wrong, and you should be interrogated some day."

"That sounds ominous," she said. Her relaxed mood seemed to disappear for a moment. "If you do that, then I have to run away for the rest of my life, too."

He thought 'Maybe you have to, because you may have problems getting a divorce.' Then he thought 'No that was dumb. She would get the divorce eventually. Just a matter of time.'

"Have you ever thought about your friends, if you keep on running away?" she said. "If we just run away and become someone else we'll never see our friends again." She added, "You don't have to worry about me, I don't have any anymore."

At one point he got behind the green car with the license '2MANY' again. The plate bothered him. It could refer to overpopulation. Then he thought that, well, there were other people than LOLA who were concerned about that problem. And maybe it stood for something else. He decided not to say anything to Nora about it.

"You know," he said, "I've had second thoughts about going to Tennessee right away. Maybe we should stop some place on the way."

"If you're getting tired I can drive for a bit," she said. Then she added, "What made you change your mind?" Was there a bit of anxiety in her voice?

"Nev used to say it was not just a woman's prerogative. Men could change their minds as well."

She smiled and said, "I thought that Tennessee was - is - just fine with me."

It made him wonder. Had she seen the green car and the license plate?

"Does Nev stand for Nevada?"

"No, Nev stands for Neville."

"Like Neville Shute?"

"Yes. Well, I call him Nev. Nev worked for me in the store."

"Tell me about him. And tell me more about Hannah," she said. "I want to know all about you, as if we had known each other for all times past."

The thoughts came back to him in a jumbled way. It was not free from being painful. He sensed again the anger and anxiety he lived with before he knew Nora. It was as if a spell had been broken when they met. He thought that, maybe, she should have asked the question some other time. Let it come with time, as they - hopefully - lived a whole lifetime and they could share memories bits by bits, as they came back to mind.

Hannah came into the breakfast nook. The sun was shining through the East window and she put the newspaper on the table. She had had a bad night. There were rings under her eyes.

"You're so silly, not working for dad," she said. "After all, you have a degree and you are squandering it away.'

"You sound like your father," he said.

"Anything wrong with that?"

"He's a drunk," he said.

"So are you."

He thought he ought to spend as little time as possible at home. She was getting intolerable.

He was late getting to the store. Nev had opened up.

"Thanks," he said. He went over to the telephone and called a customer. "Your rod just came in."

Nev looked at him. "Why don't we go fishing?" he said. "We could go over on the causeway and fish between Monona

Bay and the Lake."

He thought of Hannah and said, "Can't we go further away."

"Sure," said Nev. "Shall I pick you up at your house?"

That would be good. Hannah would see them.

A customer came in. He was a young man with long hair. "I'll be going hunting this fall. Do you have hunting clothes? I see you have guns next door, so I assume you sell guns."

He selected a red mackinaw and some thermal underwear. "I like to go deer hunting. I haven't hunted in Wisconsin before. Where is the hunting best?"

Nev answered, and John left them alone. The man paid and took his bags with the clothes and left.

"That's a guy who wants to get away from his wife. She's probably a chatterbox who won't leave him a quiet minute."

John thought a bit then said. "Just like me and my wife."

Nev smiled. "Trouble at home again?"

"You know, she feels it's below her dignity to be married to a store manager."

"So what does she think of me?"

"She isn't married to you."

A second customer came in. He roamed around in the store, looking at this and at that. Buying a present, maybe, thought John. Nev went over to him after a while.

"No thanks," he said, "just looking"

But after a while he came over with a couple of hand weights.

"That's a lot of money for a pair of measly weights. They couldn't have cost one tenth of that to produce."

Nev looked at him and said, "What you sees is what you gets."

The man leaned on the counter and looked at the bill. It was lying on top of the package with the weights.

"My wife isn't going to like it." he said, "She had said that it shouldn't cost more than one half of what you are asking. I don't mind, but she does."

"I can sell you each weight separately, and you can tell her you thought she meant that she wouldn't pay more per weight. She'll be proud of you."

The man paid and picked up the package. On the way out he was still looking around.

"I should take up fishing," he said. "That way I could get away from her from time to time." He didn't give them the time to answer. He left with his weights.

Hannah continued to make John's life difficult. In small ways - she was, never agreeing, always being 'hurt', always remarking that her family didn't really accept him. That he was simply jerking off being at the store, not at her dad's bank.

"I'm going fishing tomorrow after work. Nev is picking me up."

She didn't answer. She just kept on washing the good silverware. No meal without first class service. Her food was good. But her company wasn't.

"Do you want a bourbon?" she asked.

She had taken out the bottle and two glasses. She put one down at the table and the other in front of her own chair. "We have to talk."

"What makes now so different. We usually don't talk much, it's you who talks..."

"That's why we have to talk. You are absenting yourself from me. What I really want is a husband I can be proud of. It's bad enough you work in a store, it is even worse that you want to take up low class habits like fishing. We have enough money to buy food. Let the blacks and the homeless do their fishing over at the causeway. They need the protein."

He thought it was going to be another soliloquy, but Nev saved the day. He was honking the horn outside, and John said, "Got to be going."

They went to a lake up by Wisconsin Dells. Nev caught several fish, but John didn't catch any.

"That's not why you're here," said Nev. "Just sit down and relax."

John sort of had a bad conscience, but he started enjoying

sitting looking at his fishing pole and catching nothing.

"Take this one home with you and ask her to fix it," Nev said.

"She won't."

"That's just the point."

And he did take it home, and she said she didn't want those stinking creatures in her house. And so he kept on going fishing

"I'm turning the sewing room into a room of my own," she said one day. "I don't want to be awakened by you every night when you come home. From fishing, or whatever."

"OK with me," he said. They didn't have sex anymore, anyway.

He drove off the highway and drove well 'inland' so to speak.

"Where are we going?" Nora asked.

"I just thought we'd reconnoiter a bit."

"We should stay at one place for a couple of days, don't you think. It should be safe now."

"Maybe," he said.

He was still thinking of the green car with the '2Many' license plate. He decided not to tell her. She was nicely relaxed. She had made a decision, she felt herself out of danger, better to leave it like that.

He continued his maneuvers with the same excuse. He was finally sure he wasn't followed. Maybe he hadn't been, in the first place.

'Nerves,' he thought.

He found a place well off from the highway. The sign said 'The Dogwood.'

"This place OK?" he asked.

She smiled, "Fine. How far to the next town?"

"I'll ask the manager. Why?"

"I need to get to a laundry."

He checked in as Ben Disraeli.

"Oh," the manager said, "You can walk there, if you want

to. Right at the next corner."

She had bundled some clothes into a plastic bag. "Do you need anything laundered?"

He pulled some dirty underwear and a shirt out of his luggage and gave it to her.

"Do you want me to come along?" he asked. She said No and took off.

They were going to spend a week at the Dogwood. The setting was nice and the first day they went for a walk. The weather was spring-like, in spite of it being January. There were birds out, chirping away, and at one point they saw five deer.

"They're so graceful," said Jon

"They're also too plentiful," she said.

"Does Lionel's philosophy about overpopulation apply for deer as well as for the human race?" he asked.

"No," she said, "I didn't mean that. I'm an environmentalist and I think we have done away with natural predators."

They went back home, and she made love to him. That's what falacio is - a woman making love to a man. Maybe at climax it is a shared thing.

He had to broach the subject. "Are we ever going to have real intercourse?" he asked.

"But we are having intercourse."

"You know what I mean. It is really driving me out of my mind. I want to be IN you, that's what my love for you craves. Don't you feel that need too?"

"But you are IN me. I feel you in me, I feel the unison, I feel the love." Then she hesitated a bit and said something odd. "Let me see what I can do."

CHAPTER 9

> Love and Marriage
> Go together like a horse and carriage
> Dad was told my Mother
> You can't have one without the other
> Rogersa and Hammerstein. "Oklahoma."

They slept late the next morning and they were slow getting up. They went to a local diner in the little town. The manager had been right. It was actually within walking distance.

She smiled at him. "I'm having a hard time waking up this morning. I awoke in the middle of the night and started thinking of things." She hesitated a bit, then said,

"Were you, and are you still in love with Athena?"

"Were you in love with Lionel, at one time or another?" He was saying this as a defense against the last question she had asked. Then he said, "We can't tell each other lies. I wish I could say No, but I was in love with her. Whether it had gotten to the stage where it was 'love' rather than 'being in love' I don't know."

"I'm not jealous of Athena." she said. Then after a short pause, "Well, yes I am."

"Were you in love with Lionel at one point? I guess you must have been, since you married him."

"Well, you married Hannah, and you weren't in love with her." He didn't like the direction the conversation was taking.

"Attraction, infatuation, comfort. Time to get over Athena.

It looked like a comfortable life. It was a way to get started again. And she was clever."

"Or you were dumb."

"Blunt, but correct. We've got to be frank with one another. But tell me about Lionel. Tell me about yourself. You told me about your amnesia, but you said you remembered your high school years, about your boyfriends and how you managed to remain a virgin through those years until Lionel married you." In an unkind way of thinking it was the ultimate price for seduction.

"I conjecture, and I know from our present - no just past - life that he was terribly attracted to me, physically."

Jon realized that she had a hard time talking about her sex life with Lionel. He had gotten some insight into this from the diary.

"He also was intellectually attracted to me. I gather from things he has said that I was a nurse at a hospital when we met. Most of the nurses he had dealt with before were simply that - nurses."

"Well, weren't you just that? I know you are intelligent, but there are probably other intelligent nurses around."

"Well, I am also an English major, and was actually going for my Master's Degree in English Literature, when I switched to Nursing. That is one thing I remember."

He thought, again, that the conversation was dangerous. They had purposely - or at least tacitly - agreed not to worry about those aspects in the first days they were together.

"I know you are going to ask why, but the answer is quite simple. I like to help people. I was immensely popular in college because I actually was more interested in helping others with their assignments and often skimped on my own.

"And the males I dated were always happy for a while. But like in high school, after a while my brand of sex - the 'heading' so to speak - was not enough for them. They wanted the whole nine yards.

"In fact..." she laughed a bit, "I am getting to think a bit like you. Most of them didn't even have nine inches to offer."

They laughed.

"That is probably the way it was with Lionel but it is blocked out of my memory. I must have been in love with him, I must have wanted to marry him, but I'm fairly sure I must have been sticking to my principles. I can't even remember how he greeted me in the beginning. Did he say, for instance, 'Good morning, Ms. Kristina.'"

"That's your maiden name? What is it? German?"

"Danish."

They sat still for a while, then he said, "You have quite a bit of education. That explains your knowledge of literature."

"Actually, I got most of that reading on my own, but you are right. The education helps tie things together. Bit I don't ever think anybody told me about the similarities between Joyce and Thomas Wolfe, for instance. The same pedestrian type of structure, the same way of writing."

Then she snuggled up to him. "I don't want to let education come between us, but you have a college degree as well. We talked about what draws people together, and similarities, of course, do. Education is another similarity between us. You have a college degree, but you went to work in retail. I think we both found our educations to be wanting, because what can you do with those degrees? How can you actually contribute to society - no to humanity - with amorphous majors like English, for instance?"

"The answer usually given is that you are more 'well rounded'"

"Should you then diet?"

"You are getting to be a punster supreme," he said. "It's true, isn't it, that those in trades are different. A plumber, after apprenticeship, knows how to plumb, a carpenter knows how to carpent."

"And a dentist knows how to dent." She chuckled. Then she added, "But you see, this aspect of two people having reacted the same to similar situations is a basis for attraction." Then she added, "Oh, we are getting too serious. I just want to think of you, and not to think of anything but you, and I don't want anything to come in the way of that."

"It's an intellectual fig leaf," he said.

"What do you mean by that?"

"It is, once again, the concept that the tree of knowledge was more than knowledge of sex and the pleasures of the flesh. It was also that the ability to think distanced man from God."

"So you are a believer?"

She kissed him.

"Will you always love me?"

"I can't see how I couldn't."

"You know there are people who say that love is just an illusion, that you fall in love with an illusion. John Erskine has written about that. And when the illusion is gone, then one of two things may happen. Either a deep friendship evolves, or great unhappiness results."

"If that be true," he said, "then let's always be happy after the illusion is gone. But I somehow don't think it is an illusion. I think it is very real."

"Let's not talk about it anymore. Let's be in love, not analyze it."

"D'accord, as they say in France."

"You know French?"

"You just heard the extent of my knowledge of French."

He was still thinking of the green car. Maybe they should drive in a different direction for a while.

"I think we'll drive south again, if you don't mind," he said. "I still have time to burn up, and being with you is not a function of where we are."

"You're right," she said. "The weather, further north, might not be pleasant. But first let's have something to eat."

It was Friday. He went to the payphone at the restaurant and called Madison. Nev's voice came on and delivered a phone number, first slowly, and then he repeated it for good measure.

"Who do you call?" she asked.

"I call Madison to see whether there is good news?"

"And?"

He just shook his head.

"It is funny how you pass one particular car, and then you pass it again some time later," she said.

So she had noticed

"Well, you stop for a while for gas or at a rest stop and the other guy doesn't and he gets ahead of you."

"And you're going the same route. Like the car hauling the boat saying 'Leaking Lena'."

"You noticed that too," he said.

"Yes, I noticed. Hard not to," she said. She added, "Like the green car we just passed."

This time he hadn't noticed. He looked in the rear view mirror. The car behind him was a green Saturn.

"It is a green Saturn."

"I wouldn't know. It is a green car."

"How many times have we played tag?' he asked.

"Oh, only twice."

Jon was going 72 and it was a 70 mph zone.

"He probably likes the speed we are driving. He has cruise control, no doubt. He just likes the speed."

"It is a good speed," she said. "It is not too nerve-wrecking."

"Well, I go faster when I pass trucks."

"I thought so," she said. "I guess you want to get past them fast."

Quite right, he thought.

He pulled into a rest stop and the green car went on. He had thought for a minute that maybe they were being followed, but in that case the car would have pulled into the rest stop as well.

"At least the guy isn't following us. That could be the case, you know," he said.

"Yes, I was worried about it. But he didn't pull in to the rest stop."

He suddenly felt uncomfortable. Suppose the green car was - really - following them. In that case he'd play cat and mouse and be sure to be behind at an exit and he could simply pull off at the exit and wait. Silly, he thought, his imagination was running wild on him. But he wouldn't say anything. They were in such a nice mood. He didn't want her to worry.

"He could be stopping at the next exit and simply wait for us," she said.

"Oh," he said, "That's silly. That is sort of like a detective flic."

"I guess so, but so are our lives right now. Aren't they?" she said.

She was right, he thought.

"If they are detective flics, then I'd like the female lead."

She laughed. It was good to hear her laugh. She was relaxed again.

"We talked about it earlier - in a light vein, but how do you feel about children? Do *you* want to have children?" she asked.

"Not while I am driving," he said.

She laughed again. Things were back to normal. Normal can be so abnormal and so wonderful, he thought. Then he thought of the normal error curve that he had learned about at the university.

He looked back as they were driving along. No green car in sight. About fifty miles down the road there was another rest stop.

"Let's stop again. I have to go to the bathroom," she said.

"Me too."

That would give him more of a chance to check on the green car, he thought. He was apprehensive - he realized it. He wished she had never mentioned the car. But he would keep from mentioning it, and treat it lightly if it came up. It was probably coincidence, in any event.

The rest stop was full to overflowing. He wondered what was going on in the area, because it was not vacation time. He had to wait his turn to get to a urinal, and then went out in the hall. She wasn't out yet. The small anteroom was full of people. There was a young couple looking at a map, and he observed them. The man had his hand half way into her buttocks, and she didn't seem to mind.

Then Nora came out and said to him, "Watching naughty movies at the big map?" He laughed.

"You won't do that to me, ever, will you?" and then she added, "In public, I mean."

He laughed again and patted her on the backside. She wiggled coyly.

"I feel like doing it right now," he said.

"Now, now, don't pick up habits from the epsilons." She added, "There are more acceptable venues. Like: right now let's get in the car so I can sit on your hand."

He thought, had he finally changed her thinking about real intercourse?'

He laughed again. "Well, that wouldn't be in public, I suppose."

They drove off, and some miles down the road he saw the green car behind him. He started accelerating going 10 mph over the limit, and the car disappeared from view.

"You're going too fast, dear," she said.

"I guess so. Thank you." And he slowed down again.

"I don't want to be a back seat driver, but..."

"No that's fine. I just forget myself once in a while. The last thing we need is to be stopped by a cop." The green car was still out of sight.

They stopped at a motel in Southern Tennessee. He could have gone further, but the weather was starting to act up. The clouds were dark and ominous.

"I am leery of going further today," he said. "And we don't really have to. Why don't we settle in for the night?" He had bought a bottle of Jack Daniels, and said, "We won't go out to eat. We'll stop and get some sandwiches and have them in the room. We can have a drink and make a night of it right there."

The motel was the 'I DO INN'. "Why the name?" Jon asked the man at the desk.

"I'm the owner," he said. "I was married here." He looked a bit old for that. Well, the motel was old. "My third marriage," he said. "We pooled our resources and bought the place we were at when we were married."

"What a nice thought," Jon said.

The room was nice.

"It will be a nice night," Nora said. Then she went over and kissed him. "You just don't know how much I love you," she said.

"You'd be surprised, but I do know. There are certain things you know."

"And you know."

They sat down in silence, and munched on their hero sandwiches. They sipped Bourbon.

"Have you always liked Bourbon?"

"No," he said, "but Hannah got me into the habit. She had one every night when she came home. Sort of celebrating the financial gains of the day."

"You mean you celebrated with *her*."

"No. But in the beginning I kept her company. Later on I just drank the Bourbon by myself."

"I am not really jealous of Hannah because you didn't love her. But she had you all those years."

"If it hadn't been for Hannah and her lousy lies about me, we would never have met."

Nora smiled. "What lies? You've got to tell me about that, but for now, OK," she lifted her glass, "Here is to Hannah."

"Here is to Nora. I'll keep on calling you Nora, is that OK?"

"Certainly, Nathan."

"No, call me Jon."

After dinner they undressed and sat on the bed. She bent over him and fondled him, then placed her mouth around him and started to consume him. But when his hands wondered over her back towards her loins and past the point of the small door, she sat up and said "All in good time", then she bent down and he felt the ecstasy he had felt in the apartment.

But, once again, he wondered why she wouldn't let him go further. Then she said, "I told you yesterday that I have a solution for all that. A temporary one."

What did she mean? At times she was an enigma.

The next morning early he went down the outside stairs and entered the lobby to get coffee for the day's trip. He noticed the green car parked further down in the parking lot.

There was a man in the lobby talking to the desk clerk and getting coffee. When Jon entered, the man turned away with his coffee cup, and went out in the hallway to the first floor rooms. Did he know him? Maybe he was imagining, but it did look like what he remembered Harry to look like in parking lot at the coffee shop.

He didn't tell Nora. She was all packed, and they walked down to the car. He drove the long way around the motel, so she wouldn't see the green car.

"You could have gone the other way," she said.

"I guess you're right," he said. "It is early; this time of day I am not all that alert."

And off they drove.

They got further into Tennessee. It was starting to snow, and the roads were getting slick. The snow came down finely, as a mist, and at the onset lay on the ground for a moment and melted. Then it didn't melt fast, and you could see the tire tracks as dark, angry streaks in the white innocence. And then it started getting coarser. The flakes came down like pieces of cotton, caressing the world they met.

"I don't like the weather. We'd better pull into a motel again, and weather the storm..."

He stopped the car at the 'Happy Bells Motel'. Where did they get those names?

He signed in. Asked for a single again. The man was friendly and not inquisitive.

"If you need anything - as long as the 'Vacant' sign is on - just ring the bell."

They got settled and she said, "Can I have the car for about half an hour?"

He was wondering if it was wise. First of all the snow - she wasn't all that accustomed to driving. How much snow driving do they do in Florida? But secondly, the thought of the green car still was on his mind. "Sure," he said.

She came back to the motel two hours later with Italian bread and cold cuts. She had also bought some red wine and two glasses. The glasses were quite elegant.

"Where did you pick all of that up?"

"You drive around a bit, and you find places. There is a deli about a mile from here, and the glasses I got in a gift shop that sold all sorts of stuff. The wine came from the liquor store."

"All that in two hours," he laughed.

"I know," she grinned, "it was a bit long, but I did a lot of things. I bought some other stuff, too."

"You are being coy."

"Yes."

She had also bought a tablecloth, red and white squares.

"You should like that," she said. "You said once that your grandfather was Danish." She smiled at him. "See, I know my flags"

"What is the banner of Lichtenstein?"

She laughed. "OK, not all of them." Then she on a sudden became a little more serious. She placed two candles in candleholders on the table, and it was all set, and they sat down.

"Do you want me to light the candles?"

She nodded and went over and switched off the room light.

"We used to say grace when I lived at home, and I would sort of like to do that again."

There was a bit of silence.

"I guess you don't like that idea?"

"Well," he said, "the problem is that I'm always turned off when I go into someone's house and the host says grace. It's his privilege; he says grace daily, and he has a right to say it when he has company as well, but I don't much care for that custom. It is like someone is pushing their religion on you."

"But aren't you a Christian?"

"That depends on your definition. I believe in God."

"But not in Jesus."

"Well, I believe he existed, I live fairly much by the rules he set forth. But one of them is 'go in your closet and pray', and this he said in conjunction with chiding those who got the good seats in the synagogue and prayed the loudest."

"But you don't believe he is the Son of God?"

"I'm undecided. You can make me come around to that and you probably will and that's OK. But you would have to do it subtly, not by saying grace. Could we maybe hold hands and say grace to ourselves?"

"I like that," she said.

"But not in public, for instance in a diner. I really dislike it when people do that."

She smiled. "Me too."

He held his hands across the table and held hers, and said,"I love you." Then she bent her head and closed her eyes, and he did likewise. After a short while she squeezed his hand and he gathered that she was through with her prayer, and they both looked up and gazed at one another.

He had simply said the Lord's prayer to himself, and their release came simultaneously. Maybe they were saying the same prayer without knowing it.

There was quiet happiness glowing in her face.

"Let's always start a meal like this. You know the pre-LOLA Lionel did a lot of family counseling. One thing he told me was effective was for people to hold hands and say, out loud, at least once a day, that they loved one another. He had a lot of good ideas. Also a lot of bad ones."

"People might say that we both have a lot to pray about, because we are both in some sort of trouble," he said, "but that is not what prayer is really about, is it? You can't pray to win the lottery."

"You pray for others, not for yourself."

"Well put," he said. "One advantage of unions like ours. You can pray for me and I can pray for you."

She poured the wine from the small bottle. The glasses were nice. They clinked them. They savored the food and the wine, and she had made coffee. She had bought mugs too.

"Are those the 'other things' you were talking about - the mugs and the plates."

"I hope you like the pattern. It is five-and-dime premium ware."

He laughed. "But that's not all you wanted to tell me."

"No," she said. She got serious - he could see it in her face. "You do love me, don't you?"

"I told you." He looked deeply into her eyes. "I love you."

"Will you love me for all your days?"

"I will."

"Will you marry me?"

As carefully as she had planned the question, it still came to him as a surprise.

"Give me your intuitive answer."

"Yes. But"

It was he, now, who was struggling with the words. "First of all neither of us are divorced yet - at least I don't know - so it would have to be a while."

"Disregard that for a minute and what else?"

"The question usually comes from the guy."

"Don't hold back."

He felt it an exceedingly important moment. He knew he wanted to marry her. Marry in haste, they say, and repent at leisure, but he had no doubts.

"Will you marry me, Nora?"

She went over to the other side of the table, took his head in her hands and kissed him.

"Yes." A simple Yes but said with all the happiness in the world. "We have our problems but they are completely forgotten, aren't they?"

"Yes."

She went over to her bag and removed something. "I don't want you to think I'm completely nuts, but my intention is for us to marry right here and now. Marriage is between man and woman, and ordained only by God. Society has gotten to mingle into it, but they really have no right to be part of it."

She took the two candles from the table and placed them on a tall chest of drawers in the room. Behind it was a large mirror.

She lit them with a lighter she also removed from the bag. Their light flickered and cast an uncertain, dim light in the room, giving it a feel of a church, a monastery. The drabness of the interior vanished, and was transformed into a lascivious, beckoning divineness.

They placed themselves in front of the candles and she said,

"Let's take off our clothes."

The disrobement somehow went with deliberation, like a priest donning a cape. There was something solemn and holy about it.

Then, "Stand here with me," she said. "Now face me."

He did.

"Do you, Jonathan Slowe, take this woman to be your wife until death do you part?"

"Yes" he answered. "I do."

Then she had him repeat the same ceremony.

"You have to say, 'Do You Leonora Kristina…"

When she said, "I do," she added, "With this ring I thee wed," and she placed a small, cheap ring on his finger and one on her own.

He was half in a daze, as if he didn't know, really what had happened.

"You may now enjoy the bride."

Was this entire procedure a manner of justifying her not having sex before she was married? She had talked about how important that had been in her teen years.

She looked magnificent, with the random shadows accenting her breasts, her Venus mound, and the slight roundness of her stomach. He bent down and kissed her nipples, and she shuddered a bit as if cold. Her skin was aglow; there must be a fire in her loins. He bent further down and kissed the mound, but she took his head and lifted it up, and she embraced him. He divined the valley between the two magnificent mounds and felt the time had come, the time he secretly had been waiting for, longing for since the first time he saw her in the coffee shop, nay, maybe even when he saw her in the church parking lot. Then he felt her hand feel his manhood, she caressed it a bit, feeling the sensitive spots with the expertise of a strumpet.

He guided her backwards to the bed and was about to help her lay down all while gliding his hand towards her center. He wanted to lie down on her, but she turned around and lay on her knees. As he put his knees on the bed to mount her she took hold of his phallus and guided it. What he thought was going to be a simple deed became a difficult and different from what he had thought.

The pole in his flesh was mysteriously and unexpectedly strayed from its expected trajectory, like a guided missile finding the wrong target. And he entered into a sultry night of dark gods rather than into the mossy paradise of the center of the universe. He was going to pull back and start again, but it was obviously not what she wanted. As he started pulling back, she moved her buttocks with him. He realized that he was at the Gates of Gomorrah and he knew better than to turn away. He remembered the fate of Lot's wife.

But much as being at the Gates of Gomorrah was a surprise, what ensued was even more astounding. She moved her buttocks in cadence with his thrust and suddenly started to moan, then more wildly and finally she uttered words he would never have expected from her. "Fuck me...fuck me hard...Yes, yes, come in me...oh, yes."

It sounded like a pornographic movie. Both the sex itself and the utterances made *him* speechless. Just at the time when he was about at climax he felt a convulsion in her body, then another, then another. Then it was as if she woke up and looked back at him.

She moved her legs back so she lay prostrate and squeezed her legs together, tightened her buttock hold on him and kept him in a scissors hold, and she shuddered a few times. "See," she said, "you are my prisoner." The convulsions continued, but at longer and longer intervals.

Finally, when he got too insignificant, she said, "I'll let you go now." She rolled over on her back and he lay down next to her. She bent over and kissed him.

She said, "I loved it, sweetheart. I'm sorry, we should have done it earlier. But this is one case where I needed to know you better. I didn't know how you would take it. What was your reaction when I had you...approach in a manner different from what you had expected?"

"You know," he said. "It was strange. I got just for a moment - before...you know - a series of thought just flashed through my mind. One was that of Joe Buck's encounter with the rich lady."

She smiled. "I know the sequence. Not from English Lit 101."

"Have you always talked out your feelings when you have sex? I mean with Lionel?"

"He taught me. I wouldn't have known that unless I had written notes to myself because somehow my memory took a dive every session I went to. The sessions calm me, make me sort of happy. What I wrote is actually a diary. I'll let you see it. It explains a lot. That's one of the aspects of the sessions we have each month..."

She is still talking about it in the present tense. Will she ever completely divorce herself from her ties with this sex fiend?

"They call it vocalization. Unhappiness in people comes from taboos."

"On that I agree," said John.

"You are simply describing a beautiful act. Why should a verb be so offensive to society?"

"Because some people use four letter words in every sentence."

"You are right. That's denigrating something of great special importance. But it shouldn't lead us not to use the proper terms. There is poetry in the Anglo-Saxon words. There is sentiment in the word 'fuck', one of the most important sentiments in the world." Then she said, "You aren't disturbed by what happened. I hope not."

"No," he said, "I felt the unison, just that it came in a different form than I had expected. But I think I would feel more in unison with you if I could see you while we make love."

"Now there you don't have to say 'fuck'. In that context I like your words better."

They had a glass of wine.

It was a red-letter evening.

"Where did you learn the thing about closing your legs?"

"A classmate told me. She was right. The togetherness feeling last much longer, so does the ecstasy, it is as if it has time to wear down."

"Like a diver not coming up too fast from the deep," he said.

"Sort of," she said. "Remember today's date. It is our wedding day. Agree?"

"Of course."

"Would you like to marry officially? Like before a justice of the peace?"

"It would possibly make me a bigamist," he said.

"Me too, but does it matter?"

"To me it doesn't."

"Where should we get married?" she asked.

"We'd have to wait until your divorce comes through. If everything goes right in Wisconsin, I'll get mine in about a month's time, but then by law I can't marry for another six months."

"What does the law mean, really? It is an imposition on people. Neither you nor I are really married to our so-called spouses, are we? Do you share your bed with Hannah? No, you don't, really. And I wouldn't have remembered anything about my wedding to Lionel at all, had it not been for you being in the service station at the time. You haven't had a marriage and neither have I, so in God's eyes we can marry."

"Yes, but we both in each our cases are still contracted, legally,"

"It is what God thinks that is important. Why don't we simply go somewhere, for instance out to Las Vegas? I think it is easy to get married out there."

"It's OK with me," he said. Then he reflected a bit. The

thought was fascinating. He felt a feeling of purpose in life, a feeling of worth, a feeling of ecstatic warmth.

She said, with some concern, "We'd have to show some identification. I have my birth certificate with me. I'd marry you, so I'd be Leonora Slowe. But what about you?"

"I have a birth certificate for Jonathan Slowe. But I'm afraid that Lionel and LOLA would hunt us down."

"They're looking for Leonora Ondmand, not Kristina."I'd use my maiden name, and I don't think they'll track us down in the aisle, so to speak. They think I have other things on my mind."

"I'm glad. So you think you could marry under your real name," he said. "I guess if we married in Georgia or Tennessee it would be fairly safe for us. Let me think about it a bit."

"You're still afraid because of what happened in Wisconsin. Something you haven't told me about, yet. We are man and wife, and you owe me that bit of your life's story," she said. "You haven't told me yet why you are - what did you call it - on the lam?"

"I will," he said. "And it is nothing dishonorable."

"I know you well enough - I told you that in the coffee shop - so that you don't have to say that.

In her inimitable way she took his head in her hands and kissed him. With the same three warming words about love.

She smiled one of those Mona Lisa smiles and kissed him.

"Better go to sleep. I love you."

"Sweet dreams."

And surely they both had sweet dreams.

In the night he woke up. Dreams were sweet to start with, but then troubled. Was the green car for real, or was it just his imagination?

She slept deeply, and he got out of bed quietly and tiptoed over to the window. He looked out. Then he fumbled around for his pants and his shoes and found the key to the door.

She heard him vaguely as he left and then she awoke. She felt to her left. Where was he? She started getting up when she heard the key in the door. She was frightened. Suppose it wasn't he.

But he entered with a "Sorry, I didn't want to wake you."

"Where were you?"

"Just catching a bit of fresh air."

He went back to bed, and she cuddled up to him. "Can we do it again?"

They did. "Even nicer," she said, "You were in me for a longer time."

She went back to sleep. There had been no green car in the parking lot. It was as if she sensed his unquietness, for she woke up again.

"Something is bothering you," she said. "Whatever it is, stop worrying and get some sleep." Then she added, "I would really like to get married legally."

"You'd be Mrs. Slowe, and Slowe is not my real name."

"OK," she said. "If you get things squared away in Wisconsin, then we'll simply get married one more time. You'll have been married four times - Athena, Hannah and then myself twice, and I'll have been married four times, once to Lionel, once in the room, once legally and in the case things work out for you, once to you under your real name."

"You have an interesting sense of logic," he said, but it's OK with me."

In the morning, early, he went to the office and rang the bell. The manager came out. He was sleepy.

"I'm sorry for the imposition," Jon said, "but do you know where I can get information about how you go about getting married here and in the neighboring states?"

The manager smiled. He reached down under the desk and brought up three sets of papers, two pages each. "Georgia, Tennessee, Kentucky. That's all I have." He smiled proudly. "I get that question quite often. They'll be a dollar a piece."

"That's fine."

"Are you going to bring your fiancée here?"

Jon hadn't thought of that question. He had signed in as a single.

"Yes," he said.

The manager smiled knowingly. He knows, thought Jon.

He went back to the room. She was still sleeping. She woke up slowly from the noise he was making.

"Morning," she said. He liked that she looked as good in the morning when she woke up as she did at night. Her hair was disheveled but it looked great.

"And how is Mrs. Slowe?"

She smiled. "It has a good ring to it. I'm glad I cleared out my checking accounts. Now I don't have to go through the bother of having my checks changed."

He told her about the manager and showed her the marriage procedures in the three states.

"You're such a dear," she said. "Let's go to Macon. I'm so happy. My only concern is that I can't find my slippers."

He laughed. "My father once told me that a Norwegian or Danish author, back in the eighteenth century wrote a satirical play called "Love Without Stockings." It was in the period of the French Tragedy, and the plot was that these two people couldn't get married because he didn't have any stockings."

"So now it is Love In Spite of No Slippers."

"It's not a catching title, but it is a wonderful concept."

They left shortly after breakfast.

"I'll count this as our honeymoon. We *are* married, *just* married, and it is a nice honeymoon," she said. "A nice way of spending it. No expensive motels. Togetherness. Do you think anyone else has ever thought of just driving around on their honeymoon and staying at motels as they came up?"

"I doubt it," he said, "but it is not completely an unplanned trip. After all, there is a goal - a place we have to be at a certain time, because at one time or another I have to meet up with Nev. But I guess this is like honeymoons usually are. They are terminated by the fact that one or both have to go back to work."

"What is the deadline, actually? Other than the fact that we are heading for Macon?"

"Nev said at the onset he would like to see me - wherever I was - after three months, if things weren't settled. Some place like Paducah."

She looked pensive. "This waiting out time until your friend will be in Paducah is a bit like 'Waiting for Godot.'" She said.

"Or 'The Iceman Commeth.'"

But of the sudden the thoughtful expression vanished from her face and she gave the impression of happiness. It was strange how she alternated between great worry and an almost blissful state.

"Life is an imitation of literature," she said.

"Is that original with you?" he asked.

"In the sense that I haven't read it or heard it, but I am sure someone must have said that at some point or other. It seems like something obvious to come up with."

"Not to everybody."

CHAPTER 10

"Then it is thyself who will forgive thee the killing.
Ernest Hemingway, For Whom the Bell Tolls

They went back onto the Interstate, and headed south - towards Georgia, towards Macon. Then he saw the green car again. Once more he decided not to say anything to her. It was a great moment in their lives, and she was relaxed and relishing it. Best simply to lose the car. If there were really someone tailing them, then it would be a mistake to stay on the same route.

He was getting back into the southern part of Tennessee. He turned off at the first exit, and started driving on byroads.

It started raining. Small drops at first, distinct, like transparent pearls on the glass, then they started to flatten out, then they started to build up on the wiper blades. The heat was on in the car, and he directed it towards the window, but it still kept on glazing over.

He didn't have a scraper, so he stepped outside from time to time and used the backside of his comb. Then he finally came to a small gas station. He bought a scraper.

"We'll sell a lot of those today," said the fat woman behind the counter. "Happens every year."

He left the store. The woman was looking at him. He scraped the window down thoroughly. She was still looking as he got into the car.

The car had gotten cold during the time the motor hadn't been running. Nora sat with her arms crossed in front of her, shivering a bit. "You'll be all right after a while. It is heating up fine."

They drove for a while. The roads were getting slippery. Nora was getting warm again. She was putting her hand on his from time to time, and squeezing it. It was a different kind of 'warm' he thought, different from the warmth of the heater. It was warmth that went all through him, and he enjoyed it, but it left him as two persons. One who was at one with the woman at his side and one who was concentrating on the road as it wound into the countryside.

The heater, once it got going, made the interior very hot and he couldn't seem to control it.

"It's nice," said Nora. "Like sitting by a fire." She looked over at him and smiled. "Wouldn't it be fun by a fire. The old image, on a bear skin rug. I get all excited thinking about it."

Nice thought, he thought.

There was a motel sign up the road. It was barely visible through the falling snow, but as he approached it was like a beacon, and he was going to suggest that they stop when she said, "Stop here," she said. "I want to make love to you. I want it so bad."

He felt a delight go through him. He stopped the car. The motel had seen better days.

He got out of the car, but leaned in. "Be just a minute," he said. "Keep that thought."

He paid the man in cash. It was a nice old man who wanted to talk. You could see it, deliberate, slow movements giving him time to start a conversation.

"It's cold," he said, "colder than usual. We have the heat on in the rooms."

Was heat sometimes not available, thought Jon. Well, maybe so - the place was old. But he cut the man off. He felt sorry about it and said,

"We'll talk in the morning. But you know...the little woman...we were just married."

The man smiled.

"See you in the morning. We have continental breakfast, you know."

How many times have that scene been played out in love stories he thought. He looked at the man as he walked out. He was bent like a question mark, and his slow movements were like out of the past. The celerity of society had left him behind. And the only car in the lot was theirs. It was early in the day, though.

"Hurry," she said.

He watched her undress. He marveled at her breasts; the nipples sprung out at him like explanation marks. Her behind was jutting out, almost beckoning, and as she bent down when she took off her panties, the valley between the globes showed in splendor. You divined the secret place of entry and he felt the rise in his loins as she came towards him.

She simply straddled him, without any preparation, and he glided into her forbidden door like a key into a well-oiled lock. And the door opened to vistas of the unknown, and they lived in this never-never land for how long? It was a departure from sex, as he had heretofore known it.

She had been sitting up straight, and he had been holding her about the breasts, sometimes on the breasts, but once the fire was over she bent forwards and laid her head in the cup of his shoulders.

"Only love can make it this way," she said. "Only love." She sighed. "I'm so happy. You're happy, too. I don't even have to ask."

"Why don't you anyway?"

"Are you happy?"

"I'm happy."

"Like never before."

"Like I didn't know I could be."

The green car had been forgotten. If, indeed, it was tailing them.

"Let's eat in," she said.

She was smiling as she put on her clothes, at times doing

dance steps, humming 'April in Paris'. This place was as far removed from April in Paris as imaginable, but it was a moment in his life, a special moment, part of a milestone. Something they would reminisce about at breakfast time in years to come. 'Remember that motel in Tennessee.' They might forget the name of the state in time, but they would never forget the motel, the room, the event. Maybe they would make love instead of eating breakfast. Life would be wonderful together.

"Yes, we'll remember," she said. "Always. And we'll be together always." She sat down on the side of the bed for a spell. "I have forgotten all about our troubles."

"Me, too," he said. "But we have to come back to earth. Let's go downtown and get some cheese and some wine."

"Where is downtown?"

"I'll ask the guy at the desk."

"Is he nice?"

"If you don't mind listening to the story of his life."

"Then will we ever get downtown?"

"I promised him a conversation session tomorrow morning. I told him we were on our honeymoon."

"We are," she said.

They bought cheese and wine at a general store in the little village. He didn't know that such places existed anymore. The downtown was charmless, but the little store had class.

"You need something to cut the cheese with?" said the clerk. He was a thin teenager with bad posture and pimples. He looked dumb, but he wasn't. 'Don't judge a book by its cover' thought Jon.

He brought a knife.

"It is a pretty big knife," said Nora.

"It'll work," said Pimples. "It's the only one we have in stock. People hunt and fish around here."

My kind of people, thought Jon.

He bought three bottles of wine, and they returned to the motel. They ate, and fell asleep, he with his arms around her, and her with her head on his chest. Her hair tickled him and he gently moved it over. She awoke.

"Tired of me already?" she said. "Seduced and abandoned," she laughed.
"Your hair tickled me."
"I could tickle you some more."
And she did.
The day was rainy and cold as they woke up. They started out and stopped at a restaurant before they got on the Interstate.
"You still want to get married - legally?"
"Yes. But do you?"
"Yes,
It had cleared up as they headed south. The road was still slippery. The traffic was fairly light, but everyone was going five miles over the speed limit. 75 mph, mostly. That in spite of the road conditions

He drove at the speed of other cars, and he savored the presence of Nora. She was still worry-free, relaxed, happy. She'd look at the landscape and make comments and then, from time to time, put her hand on his thigh and squeeze it gently. He would smile and take her hand and he would feel the pressure of her fingers around it and he would feel that the concept of two shall become one was further-reaching than he had thought at first.

It was at such a moment that he, again, noticed the green car in the rear view mirror. The traffic was still fairly light at that point, and he was in the middle lane. There were slower moving cars in the right lane, but no cars right behind him, and there was only the green car in the immediate distance in the fast lane. As it came parallel to him, it started moving closer to him.

"What's the matter with the guy," he exclaimed. He became, in a fraction of a second aware, that he was going to be side-swiped, and started moving to the right, then he applied his brakes, and just then the green car moved to the right at great speed. Its right back fender caught his left front fender ever so lightly, and his car started spinning on the wet pavement.

He turned the wheel counter to the spin, and overcompensated, turned it back, forth, back, and finally had the car righted in the fast lane. There were no cars there, and just then did he notice that Nora was unconscious. She looked as if she had hit her head, maybe on the front window.

In a fraction of the second when he saw the green car move towards them, the face of the passenger had imprinted itself on his memory. It was the pale blonde he had seen with Lionel's friend Harry. After that, as he turned the wheel, it was as if his mind was blank. He was just reacting to a danger situation in the manner he had been taught and in the manner his reflexes dictated.

"Look back and see what you can see," he said.

Silly of him - she was still unconscious. But as he started to get concerned about that as well, she came to, all of a sudden. She looked around, at first with an astonished look on her face and then with a look of recognition.

"What happened? Don't say, I know, I remember what happened." She looked bewildered. "And I remember. I remember things."

"That's great, but could you look back and tell me what you can see.

She looked back. It seemed that the road was void of vehicles, that there was a pile-up of cars well behind them and she confirmed it.

"There is a big pile-up. I think the green car is on fire."

Her voice was trembling. "What an idiot," she said.

He was no idiot, Jon thought. The guy was trying to drive us off the road. He was angry.

"Maybe we should go back," she said. "We are actually leaving a scene of an accident."

"I think not."

She was quiet. He was thinking, 'Should he tell her?' He decided not to. She was upset enough, and it would ruin the tranquility they had experienced so far. Then after a pause, he said, almost to himself, "We better get off the highway. I'm a bit shaken."

He turned off at the next exit. There were a few gas stations, and he passed them all. He came to a small town with a few stores. One of them was a hardware store. He stopped and parked the car and got out and assessed the damage. The left part of the front fender had been ripped loose but wasn't quite touching the ground. He tried to lift it, and he could lift it almost in place.

He said to her, "Wait here," and went into the store. He bought a pair of fine-nosed pliers, some coated electrical wire and a wire cutter.

"Trouble with the wiring at home?" the man behind the counter asked.

"Sort of," he said.

"If it is more than you can handle, my brother is an electrician."

"That's kind of you, but 'no', I can handle it."

"Just trying to help."

He went back to the car, and got in.

"I'll drive on. We've got to find a place where we can park and be undisturbed."

Outside town the road became two-lane with a wide shoulder and it was deserted. He drove about five miles and stopped the car.

"Come out and help me," he said.

She got out, and said, "What do you want me to do?"

"Just hold the fender right here, can you do that?"

She tried, but it kept on slipping back on her.

He let it fall back, and took the wire and passed it trough the support bar behind the fender, and up and to the outside.

"OK," he said, "Let me hold it, then when I tell you to, slip the wire around the fender about five times. Then cut it with the wire cutter."

She did it.

"Now take the fine-nosed pliers and turn the two ends of the wire."

She did that. She was holding the tool awkwardly, but managed to carry out the task and the fender stayed in place. The fender being fairly secure, he took the remaining wire and repeated the operation. He turned the wire hard. He cut the excesses of wire off with the wire cutter.

"I guess I didn't do it well enough," she apologized,

"You did fine," he said. He went over to her and kissed her. She kissed him back.

"I am afraid," she said. "But I think we should tell the police."

He shook his head.

"Let's find a motel, and clear our heads."

Several miles out they found another old motel. All these motels on the byways that the I-system has passed by. He was wondering when they had last had customers. It reminded him of the Bates motel in the film 'Psycho'. She waited for him in the car, while he checked in.

"Queen size or two beds?" the man behind the counter asked.

"Queen size," he said. "Pretty empty. Is it the weather?"

"It is not always this empty. There is a pea-shooting festival here in March, then the place is full. This time of year we don't get hardly nobody."

They settled in. He had brought in the bottle of bourbon he had in the tire well. He poured himself a drink.

"Want one?" he asked.

She got a plastic glass and held it out.

"Yes, I need one too."

They sat on the bed, side by side, and he held his arm around her. She snuggled up to him, and then suddenly started crying.

"We should talk to the police. They may need witnesses."

He was getting upset.

"Don't you realize I can't do that. If you insist on talking to them, I'll take you tomorrow," he said. "Not now. But I'll just drop you at the station. You will have to say that you were hitchhiking or something. You can take the little carry-on. I'll give you money for traveling. You obviously can't take all your luggage."

She was crying. "You have never been angry with me before."

"I'm not angry with you. I'm just trying to make you assess the situation. The situation from my point of view. There must have been scads of witnesses, anyway. They won't need us."

She was still sobbing. "And you know, I don't think they'll believe me. Could we just meet some place afterwards? I mean after I talk to the police."

"No," he said. "My cover would be blown. I would need a couple of days to get away. You could stall them for a day or so. I'll be out of sight by then. You've got to do that for me."

Her sobs got louder and more uncontrolled.

"We were going to do everything together," she said. "I'll never see you again."

"If I went with you to the cops, you'd never see me again, either. Unless you'd spend the next eighteen years visiting me in prison."

"I will. I'll wait for you. I love you so." Then she added,"Eighteen years! Did you really kill someone?"

She had been so sure of him before. Once again it was a bit like John the Baptist.

His lips were pursed.

"I'll tell you all about it in the morning."

He went over and put on the television set. "The local news must have something about the accident." He turned to the program channel. The local news was not on until half an hour later.

They lay down on the bed. He bent over and kissed her. He put his hand on her breast.

"Not now," she said. "I'm too upset."

"I understand."

He got up and poured himself another drink, When he held out the bottle in her direction, she just shook her head. She was still crying.

"Let me wipe away your tears," he said.

She smiled through the tears. She looked beautiful and vulnerable.

"That's so nice," she said. "I guess I'm silly. I can see your point. I'm just egotistical. Since it's your involvement that is at stake not mine I'm starting to get moral qualms about something where I can't help anyway."

"I can help you see that even clearer," he said.

"How so?"

"The gal in the green car was Harry's girlfriend. He was probably the driver. You know, with that license plate."

Then the news came on. The first item was about the eight-car pile-up on the Interstate.

"The driver was from Tampa and he and his passenger were killed. The police are urging witnesses to come forward, since the reason for the accident is not clear, but apparently the Florida car careened across two lanes of traffic and was rear-ended by a car in the right lane. The cars spun around and were hit by traffic behind them..."

He turned down the volume.

"Your talking to the police will not bring them back. What difference does it make what the actual cause of their death was. They're dead."

She sat still for a little while. "And to the living we owe respect," she said. "Never mind, You're right. She looked worried and preoccupied.

"You think they're after us? Me, rather."

"The computer and the book, rather," Jon said. "What a tangled web we weave..."

"Shakespeare," she smiled.

"No, Sir Walter Scott."

"You're kidding," she said. She had a smile on her face. "Except we had to weave webs. We had no choice."

They needed to relax, somehow.

"Shall we go somewhere to eat? Or I could go and get something in one of the three shops around here. I think there is a food counter at the gas station. We need gas anyway."

He came back with some prepackaged tuna salad sandwiches.

"Not the Ritz," he said.

She smiled sadly.

They undressed and went to bed. He had another shot of bourbon. He thought he might sleep better, but they both slept unquietly.

They got up at eight.

When they got in the car he said, "It's time, I think, that *you* take a look at the diary. I have already read it; I hope you don't mind."

"Of course not. But I'm glad I haven't read it so far. I have really enjoyed our honeymoon. I guess it is over."

"It will never be over."

"You're sweet."

"I'll take a look at the computer tonight. You can read diary on the way. When you became conscious again in the car you said that you remembered everything. Did I understand that correctly?"

"Exactly," she said, "The wedding, the sessions, the parties.

"You must tell me about the things you remember."

She smiled.

"After all, something very good came of it. Thank you, Harry."

"Worth a busted fender."

CHAPTER 11

> He had an immediate… knowledge of the weaknesses of men and women… like a priest…
> F. Scott Fitzgerald, The Rich Boy.

They had stopped at an out of the way motel in the afternoon.

"I might want to stay here for a while," said Jon as he registered.

"Well, how many days?"

"Let's say three to start with. I can always extend it, right?"

"Sure."

There was only one other car in the parking lot. They got settled and decided to go out for dinner. She took her time, dressed up. As she emerged, like a finished work of art, she said, "Do I look all right?"

She always looked all right. She looked all right when elegant, all right when she was casual. She had a way of being able to wear clothes that complimented her.

"I don't know if I'm a good judge. You seem to think that I'd look at you as the average public would."

"You have a point," she said. "If you were average public, we'd never have found one another." Then she added, "But do I look all right?"

She was using him as a mirror. And in times to come he would become accustomed to that, because she'd say it almost any time she went out in public. She had started it now, and it would become a ritual. He didn't mind, but he was wondering, at this moment, how she would react if he said No.

"You look exquisite," he said.

They went to a rather classy place for the little town they were in. It wasn't too crowded

"Business slow?" he asked the maitre d'.

"Crowds come later," said the man. "People know they're in for a treat when they come here. It's the sort of thing the owner, who is also the chef, has dreamed about all her life. But she is working on a slim profit margin. It's much too good a place for out here in Nowhere. The restaurant should be in New York. She'd have success there. She is a marvelous cook. You're in for a treat."

At the table, Nora said, "This place calls for elegant clothes. I'm glad I dressed up. I just felt like it. Clothes have an impact on how you feel."

"Lack of clothes does as well," said Jon.

She laughed.

"Why did you think she started a restaurant here in the boonies?"

"Isn't there something you always wanted to do, but never did?"

She looked pensive. "You know, it's strange, with my memory coming back, it's as if it comes back in bits and pieces - as a response to things that trigger the recollection. When I was a nurse, I wanted to go to a war zone and be like Florence Nightingale. I had forgotten that."

"I can't arrange for a war," he said. "I hope not, there is enough conflict in the world. But do you really think many people see their dreams fulfilled?"

"It's probably nice that she can live her dream for just a while. She must have gotten some money, somehow, and decided to use it this way. Thinking also that, maybe, it could be a living for her. The food is certainly excellent." Then she said, "I'm living my dream right now, being with the man I love."

What do you say to something like that? He felt warmth all over.

Back at the motel they lingered a bit and undressed. She fallated him gently and said, "You want me to lie on my back?"

His heart leaped. She was ready.

She turned out the light and moved her legs up over her shoulders. She guided him, once again, but it was still into the Site of Sodom. It progressed in a fury and he felt good to be able to sense her face, to savor looking at her as she started vocalizing again. She must like it, he thought, but he was unsure. Was she doing it just to please him, had she done it in the past just to please Lionel? Yet, it was a call to the dark gods, he thought, a wailing in a night that was full of fire.

She let go slowly, as before, holding him in as long as she could. He bent down and kissed her, and her kiss was moist and warm and full of satiated desire. Then he said, "Did you enjoy?"

"Yes. I felt one with you again, more so even," she said. "It can't be wrong, can it?"

"Do you have doubts?"

"Sometimes," she said. "Now that I remember more of my past I have figured out that one of the occurring situations that made Lionel have me go to the sessions was exactly the fear that I might falter in my belief in the sodomic union, as he called it."

"Was it part of the LOLA's teaching?" Jon thought that maybe the campaign against overpopulation had led to this type of sex. No kids that way.

"I'm not sure whether or not LOLA had anything to do with it." Then she added, "You know, I have been unquiet after the accident. This is the first time I've missed the sessions. They cleared me of anxiety, actually emptied my mind."

"Maybe the two were connected. If your mind has been cleared, what anxiety can it contain?"

She thought a bit. Then she said, "Could we afford an analyst sometime? I would like to have some help with some problems I still have."

"OK with me," he said. "But right now we should go to sleep."

They dozed off, not really sleeping.

His enjoyment of the experience warmed him. Not quite what he wanted, but certainly close enough, and he felt it an expression of love - more so than the first time she had let him into her. Would she do it this way all her living days? Hopefully she would get around to other ways.

Presently she stretched and she started waking up. He kissed her as she was coming out of her sleep.

"That was nice," she said.

"Shall we do it again?"

She kissed him hard. And they did what they had done before. They separated and she lay, relaxed and stretched out on the bed.

"You can put on the light," she said.

He looked at this - what the artists call a declining nude. She was beautiful.

"What were you doing in the bathroom for so long before? And the other night, too?" he asked.

"Too personal to answer," she said.

He later deduced that she had taken an enema and had lubricated herself.

She fell asleep in her naked state. She murmured a bit, and he covered her up.

He felt like having a shot of bourbon but he had no more in the car. He wrote on a piece of paper: 'I've gone to the bar down the street,' and he noted the time. 'Come down if you wake up, but I should be back in about an hour.'

There was only one person in the bar, a man who looked like he had lost his best friend. He was bent over a glass of whiskey. Jon positioned himself at the other end of the bar.

He ordered a shot of sour mash.

"Do you know the guy down there?" the bartender asked.

"No," Jon said.

"He is really down in the dumps. He keeps on talking

about the damn Lulu or Lula."

"LOLA?"

"That's it. I guess it is some dame."

"Whatever Lola Wants - do you remember the song?"

He did. Jon was wondering if he should talk to the guy. He decided yes. He took his glass and sat down at the stool next to the fellow.

"So what's up?" he said.

"The world sucks," the man said. "And God damn LOLA."

"I thought LOLA was strictly Florida," Jon said.

"LOLA is over the entire Yoonated States." He had another sip of his drink.

The bartender came up. "You'd better pay up. You've had quite a few."

The man started looking in his pockets. "Damn it," he said, "I can't find my money."

The bartender was about to get angry, but Jon said, "How much is his tab?" The bartender stated a figure and Jon paid.

"We're mighty generous tonight," the bartender said.

"Why don't we sit at a table?" Jon suggested. He asked the bartender for one more drink for both of them. They went over to a far table, and the barkeep brought the drinks.

"Are you LOLA?" the man asked.

"No," Jon said, "but I've had some trouble with them."

"Trouble," the man said, "you ain't seen what I've seen. They ruined my practice, they caused my wife to divorce me, I'm broke and I don't know what to do." He looked down in his glass. It was already empty.

"How about a cup of coffee?" Jon asked.

"How's that going to help me?"

"I can talk to you better. And I can help you."

"Those are my lines," the man said. "Did you get them from LOLA?"

"No, and how about a cup of coffee?"

The man just looked out in space. Jon waved his hand at the barkeep and ordered two cups of coffee. He made the man drink one, then gave him his own. The man drank that, too.

"Now, how about a bit of fresh air?"

He coaxed the man outside, and held him by the arm while they walked or stumbled up and down the street.

"Do you have a car?" Jon asked.

"Down at the motel," he said. He pointed down the street in the direction of the motel where Jon and Nora were staying.

"Good, let's go there."

They got there and when they were at Jon and Nora's unit Jon said, "Stop here for a moment." He opened the door and looked in. Nora was still in a deep sleep. They proceeded to the man's unit, which was four doors further down.

There was coffee and a coffee pot in the room, so Jon brewed a bit more coffee while the man was sitting in an arm chair, obviously coming to a bit and now battling with staying awake.

"Tell me what happened. It's important to me."

"Nothing's important anymore," the man said. "I'm finished. Tomorrow you may find me pumping gas somewhere."

"What do you do for a living?" Jon asked.

"What did I do, not what do I do. I was a psychiatrist. I worked over at the State Hospital. You know for psychiatric patients."

"What's your beef with LOLA?"

"You mean LOLA's beef with me. A patient belonged to LOLA. I started treating her, and she was making progress. Her husband, apparently was LOLA, and I told him some of her problems stemmed from that. Then suddenly she didn't come to see me anymore. I learned that her husband reported my comments to LOLA. What happened next was that she called me late one night and said, 'I need you, I need you.' There is always a possibility of suicide in such cases, so I rushed to her place. Her husband opened the door and said, 'She is in the next room.' It was the bedroom. The bed had been slept in. Suddenly she came out of the bathroom, naked to the skin, threw her arms around me and said, 'I'm so glad we made love, I'm so glad you love me' and words to that effect. I tore myself loose from her, and left, telling the husband off on the way out. They had video recorded it all. I was charged with having had sex with a patient. I can't practice anymore. They sent a copy of the videotape to my wife. She's divorcing me and getting me for all I've got. That's not much by now. They got to my CPA and found something I didn't know anything about and Internal Revenue sent me a letter that I owe them a huge sum of money, including a fine for misreporting. So you can see why I needed a drink or two." He looked at Jon, and his eyes started closing on him.

"What's your name?"

"Ron"

"Rhymes with mine. It's Jon. Do you think you can remember all of this tomorrow morning?" he asked the shrink. "Because I think I can help you. And you can help me."

The psychiatrist didn't even answer. He just stumbled over to the bed and went to sleep the minute he was prone. Jon saw the key on the table. He took it. He would come in and wake up the guy in the morning.

"I did something I would usually have consulted you about, but the situation was such that I couldn't."

"What happened?" she asked.

"I went to the bar down the street last night."

"I didn't hear you leave," she said, "But I somehow felt you weren't here for a while. You should always wake me up."

"I left a note."

"Oh, that's good. That works, too. I prefer you wake me up."

He told her what had happened.

"Do you think he could help me with my anxiety? Also maybe help me fill in things I may still not remember? Then again, I don't know. You really don't know the man. Do you think he's any good?"

"One way of finding out is to try him. Would you mind if we have breakfast with him?"

"OK."

They went to his unit and Jon used the key to open the door and went in. Surprise, Ron was already up. He was shaving. Ron was startled as Jon entered the room.

"How did you get in?"

Jon simply lifted up the key. "Stole it last night when I brought you home. Thought you might need a bit of assist this morning, too."

"I'm fine," said Ron. "I gave up hangovers a long time ago." He laughed.

"Do you remember the deal I proposed last night?"

"Vaguely. You can help me. I need it."

"Let's go have breakfast. I'm bringing my wife."

"OK, but I have to check out at noon. I'm out of money."

"Don't worry about it, OK!"

It was a nice diner they were at. There was a fair amount room, and they sat in a corner away from the counter so they had some privacy.

"My wife has suffered from amnesia," Jon said. "She still has many spots of missing memory and I was wondering if you could help. For instance would hypnosis help?"

"What makes you think I know how to hypnotize? In fact I do. But for hypnosis to work there must be a trusting relation between hypnotist and subject and that usually doesn't come just like that. I hardly know your wife..." He smiled at her, "She seems awfully nice. But what makes you think that she would...what shall we say...trust me?" He turned to her and said, "Would you be willing?"

"If you could bring back memories I'm still not clear on. You make a very good impression."

"I must warn you," he said, "Hypnosis is not what most people think it is. First of all the trust must be there, secondly, this stuff about altered states that you see in movies is not correct. At least it is believed to be incorrect. One never knows, you know. It is more of a state of great relaxation where the practitioner can suggest things to the subject. But you can never, for instance, make a person do what he or she doesn't want to do. In the case of amnesia there is also the problem with confabulation. I might suggest things to you that you would really like to be true although they are not. The courts don't allow witnesses to have their memories intensified by hypnosis. Lastly, I can't be of any positive help in just one session. In most cases it would take years. But it depends on how deep the trauma was that caused the amnesia."

Nora looked at the man and said. "I would be willing to let you hypnotize me. You seem to be quite honest. Of course, that is probably a silly statement, but my intuitive feeling about people is often right." Then she said suddenly, "No, that is quite untrue. I have made terrible misjudgments in my life. But tell me this; could someone have hypnotized me so that part of my memory was blocked out?"

"I would say No," said Ron. "It would have to be more like a hit on the head or some trauma to the head, like a fall."

"When do we start?"

"Well," Ron said, "Let's finish our breakfast. Also your husband and I have some business to attend to after breakfast. So why don't you meet me in my room in about an hour." Turning to Jon he said, "Can you pay for my motel room for a couple of more days. I think it will take at least that long if I stand a chance of any success."

"I'll take care of it."

They finished breakfast, and went back to the motel. Nora went back to the room, and Jon and Ron went over to his. As Jon was leaving Nora in the doorway to their room she kissed him and said, "This is the first time I have voluntarily let you leave me."

"Newlyweds?" Ron asked from the outside.

"Yes," Nora answered.

In Ron's room Jon said, "The deal I'm proposing is the following. I have a friend in Wisconsin. He can fix you with a new identity, passports, birth certificates, high school and university degrees. Everything you'd need. I'll give you enough money to get to Wisconsin. Gas and the like. I'll write a note to my friend. I'll give you a bit of seed money."

"You don't look that rich," Ron said. Then he hastily

added, "I'm sorry, I didn't mean to be impolite."

"Natural comment."

"It's a deal," Ron said. "I would never have believed that I would enter into such a pact. But both you and your wife look on the up and up." After a moment he said, "You know, I'm not allowed to practice anymore, but that may have its advantages."

"Such as?"

"I can talk to you freely about what she has said, what she thinks. I have a feeling that is, to some extent, what you want. But first, can you give me an inkling of what it's about with your wife."

Jon looked at him. "It would probably help that I told you what I think. It's conjecture from some documents that I've read. Her husband was a psychiatrist who belonged - in fact was in a high position - in LOLA."

"I take it you don't like LOLA."

"You take it right. It is my feeling - No, it was my feeling that he was hypnotizing her into submission. I also think that he hypnotized her so that she would like his brand of sex."

"Which is?"

"Sodomy."

"Well," Ron said, "I don't think he could hypnotize her into liking it if she didn't really like it. I'm sorry to have to say it. Don't forget that there are large sections of the populations - male homosexuals - to whom that is the preferred sex style."

"Well, they presumably can't do it any other way."

"One of them, maybe, not the other."

"I see your point."

"Have you, yourself, been involved in anal intercourse?"

"Not until very recently."

"With her?"

"Yes."

"Did you like it?"

He hesitated a bit, then he said, "Yes."

"So that is not really a problem I have to address, is it?"

"You're right."

"But I'll try to tackle the amnesia and anxiety. From what you have said so far, she has some of her memory back."

"It was strange," Jon said. "We were in an accident - not a bad one - but she hit her head and was unconscious for a short while. When she came to, she said 'I remember everything.' But is it really everything?"

Ron worked on her, two sessions a day, for three days. It became clear that the hit she had taken on the head in the accident on her wedding day was the prime suspect as a cause for the amnesia. But Lionel could not have planned that. Even if he had planned the accident, he couldn't have foreseen the amnesia. Unless those fellows knew something that the scientific community didn't know of.

"Always a possibility," Ron said. "It's not an exact science, and there is more between heaven and earth…"

He told Jon, in private, that the first sodomic experience could have been a shock to Nora, but that she basically either had nothing against it, or maybe actually liked it or got to like it. He agreed - because he knew that already from his own practice - that the so-called sessions were probably hypnosis, but he reiterated that one could not make someone do something that was against his or her convictions.

"The Manchurian Candidate is based on this, and it is fiction. Unless, as I say, there are some types of hypnosis and hypnotists that we are not aware of.

"I asked her if she liked it - because I did, something you don't usually do. You suggest ideas to the patients who will make them say what you wanted them to say. When I asked her, she answered 'I love it with Jon."

"That makes me feel good. But did she like it with Lionel?

"I asked that, but never got an answer." Ron said. "She loves you. Note I didn't say she loves you very much. For her - as it should always be - love is love. No such thing as more or less." He then added, "It is such a pleasure being able to talk to someone about sessions. That's something lacking in the ethics of the field. Incidentally, have you made arrangements for me with your friend in Madison?"

"Yes," said Jon. "I talked to him on the phone yesterday. I talk to him on Fridays." He handed Ron a piece of paper. "Call this number and ask for Celli, give your name. She'll do the rest."

From his conversation and the arrangement he had suggested he had concluded that Celli somehow was involved with the set-up where they could produce fake papers. He wondered what her role was. He knew she was unhappy with the firm where she was working and that to be a successful lawyer was not easy.

He shook hands with Ron and they parted.

"I mustn't forget to call Nev on Friday," he said to her. "Our happiness seems so much more important than the troubles I left behind."

"Maybe you'll be cleared," she said.

"Man, that would be nice," he said.

"Maybe your divorce will have come through."

"That would be nice, too."

"But not essential," she said.

CHAPTER 12

Some vices were then so unnatural that they didn't exist...
John Fowles, The French Lieutenant's Woman.

The next morning she said, "I'm so glad we're staying here for a while. It will be safe, won't it? Actually it should be safer not to move around a lot?"

"You can look at it both ways, but it can be safer to be a moving target than to be stationary. If someone identifies us here and gets back to LOLA, then we're sitting ducks. But we need a little time in one place. We have some reading to do."

She started reading Lionel's written diary. She went back and forth over several passages several times, and finally laid it down. Then she said, "It is such a strange coincidence that you should have seen me right after the wedding."

They were lying on the bed and she bent over and held his hand. "It is painful to talk about but I remember it clearly now. The real surprise of my entire relationship with Lionel was at our wedding night. I wasn't suspicious of this until you told me about my not being the driver of the car.

"I had - for years - guarded my virginity for this occasion. And when the moment arrived he simply said to me, 'take off your panties'. I had expected something like, 'let's go to bed, but he said, simply, 'take off your panties." I did so. Then he moved over to the back of the freestanding hide-a-sofa and I was wondering what he was going to do next. He simply said,

'Bend over it.' I was surprised, but I did. He lifted my beautiful wedding dress over my head and I was in total darkness and he had exposed my behind. He caressed it, placed his finger where it shouldn't have been, and then I felt myself penetrated in a place not meant for penetration. It hurt, and he simply said, 'You'll learn to appreciate it.'

"I asked him once if he didn't want to do it the natural way, and he simply said, 'The Venus mound can come later.' Why should he want to rush into the … little door…?"

"But I felt, on my wedding night, my head enrobed in my dress, completely out of contact with the outside world, only feeling the pain, and then the awful, humiliating sensation of an invasion I didn't want. I felt it was unnatural at the time, I felt degraded by it.

"All through our married life it was like that. I hate to admit it - don't get disgusted with me - but I got to appreciate his brand of sex. I think Ron was right, that I must have had some predisposition to it. And I came to appreciate it because it was his way of showing affection. He would hold my breasts as he came in me, and there was some tenderness there, at least I imagined there was, I wanted to believe there was.

"Right at the beginning he told me to give him head after the act but I revolted. 'I won't do that,' I said. And I steadfastly refused. That is simply filthy. I would at times give him head before. And, of course, during our dating period I had done it that way. But he no longer really wanted it before the act, and after the act I refused.

"Do you think I was wrong, Jonathan?" she asked. There was a special effect in what she said because she called him 'Jonathan' not 'Jon'. "He had other desires that were unnatural - I can't even talk about them - but maybe if I had caved, would that have saved the marriage?"

"Only if you believe that a woman should be a slave to a man."

She looked at him appreciatively. "Thank you," she said. "I was beginning to wonder."

Jon looked at her. He wasn't going to ask what those other

practices were.

"I'm thinking of the Manchurian Candidate again, the film," he said. "Every thirty days you were given 'instruction' and that was probably comparable to their brainwashing sessions. It indoctrinated you to acceptance, to submission. I know that Ron said that was not possible unless you deep down wanted to, but I think it *was* possible.

"Lionel often said that this was a natural way of reducing the world's population over the long haul. That sodomy should be taught in schools as the 'natural' way of intercourse. No unexpected pregnancies.

"I really have been a piece of meat." She looked as if she was going to cry, then she pulled herself together and said, "I think all he wanted from me was the sex. He would come home late afternoon, have his brand of sex, have dinner, then go back to work. But, as I said, I appreciated his fondling of my breasts. But I know he wrote on his papers every evening and locked them up."

"Well, we have the papers now. I'll open the computer and we'll read them tonight"

"We fought a lot for getting them, and we don't even know what they are, the ones in the computer," she said. "That's my fault - I wanted to be with you for a while without having to think of anything but us."

"And we have been busy with ourselves. No, we have been relaxed with ourselves."

"I won't mind if that continues."

"Forever."

"But we'd better be acquainted with what we've got.

"I guess I was fascinated with Lionel from the start. I had admired him at the hospital. He was good-looking, he had poise and, as they said about the officer from Capernaum, he would say Come and they would come and he would say Go and they would go.

"We talked earlier about whether there is such a thing as affinity between people, but with me at the time it was more than mere fascination. Maybe I had fallen in love with him when I worked in the office and didn't really want to admit it to myself.

"When he offered for me to work in the office at his practice I didn't even think it over. I jumped at the opportunity. I worked at a lower wage than at the hospital, but there were compensating factors. Anyway, I wasn't wanting; I had enough to get along on. And he was an interesting man.

"It turned out that I got to see how he developed, how he eventually shaped a magma of opinions and ideas into a philosophy, and how this affected both his and my life.

"He had a habit of having me come to work one half hour before his first appointment. I couldn't understand at first, but later I thought it might be one of two reasons. One, he wanted to talk to me because he wanted a sounding board. Apparently he felt me sufficiently intelligent to comment on what he said. Second, he too, was probably infatuated with me from the onset and wanted to - eventually - seduce me.

"He was an ardent environmentalist. One day he told me about his concerns about the Earth.

"'You know,' he said, 'Some Danish geologists bored down through the floor of a lake in Denmark and could, from the layers, gather information about the climate at the time of their formation. And in each case - I think there were seven - there was global warming prior to an ice age. But they were natural warmings. We help create the global warming.

"'When I drive down Route 19 for instance, I can visualize an oil field spewing out oil right into the air. I can see the emission of the field; I can see the exhaust gasses floating into the atmosphere. I can see the interaction with the ozone in the higher layers.'

"I asked him if he wasn't, perhaps, exaggerating a bit.

"'I'm not,' he said. 'I don't know how the ice age theory works, but for one thing the melting of the ice caps will change the currents of the oceans and if, for instance, the golf stream changes direction, then Northern Europe will get to have a climate like Siberia.'

"And some mornings he would talk about the rain forest,

and of the felling of the redwood trees on the West Coast.

"I argued that if you took environmentalism to the extreme there would be a lot of people out of work.

"'If someone is working towards the destruction of the world, then he should quit and get another job.'

"I thought that a bit rash. But the more I thought of it, the more I agreed with him.

"'We need a complete restructuring of society. We need to rethink our way of life. There should be a more rational organization of jobs, of how and where people live. It is silly that someone has to drive 80 miles to and from work. It would be more rational for him to live near-by.'

"I argued that this would be a sort of centralized economics approach and we were now talking socialism.

"He thought about that. In fact he didn't talk to me for about a week, and then one morning when he came in he simply said to me - not even saying Good Morning - 'You're right.'

"I didn't know what he was talking about. By then a week had gone by, but little by little it dawned on me.

"As you see I got insight into his mode of thinking and it was important because it showed me how it changed - or rather how it developed - as time went by.

"He told me one morning about an old patient whom he had seen for a while and that all of a sudden this patient had opened up. He had never before told Lionel that he had been a prisoner in German concentration camps.

"Why hadn't he talked about it? I asked him and he simply said he never did. So I asked him - to goad him - if he felt ashamed of it, and he answered that No it was a sort of red badge of courage that he was proud of, but that you actually could not be proud of suffering - ever. It was an interesting comment, I thought. And it is possible that the people who talk about such things all the time haven't really suffered and those who don't, have. Or maybe haven't suffered at all.'

"I remember saying that to some people certain events in their lives were the only thing that mattered. For instance the old soldiers at Veterans of Foreign Wars. These fellows have something to be proud of but it becomes such a center in their lives that they spend the rest of their lives thinking and talking about nothing else.

"'Exactly,' said Lionel, 'We live in the present not in the past. The past has formed us, and if we have problems with certain things in the past we have to come to terms with them. That is one reason for my profession.'

"I admired him. He wasn't really interested in money or position at that point in time, only in helping people. And, I think, in seducing me. Why me, I thought? Because he was much sought after by, shall we say, the modern aggressive female. And they were all good lookers, and it wasn't until much later I realized the common trait in the ones he liked. He would have me work late and then have them come to the office. I knew they weren't patients, but he had them in his office and I know he locked the door and I was - audibly - aware of them having sex. And the 'ladies' would have their garments well reconstituted when they came out, but there was always some sign that a skirt had been lifted and that panties had been shed and then put back on. At one time I noted from the place where a gal had a run in a stocking that it was on inside out at the time they left.

"I knew they went to expensive restaurants, and one time I happened to see him with a lady friend in such a place and it was the lady who paid. But I guess that happens often now a days. I never would do that. I was brought up differently.

"He had started out being a champion for the little man then, but it changed. It happened after the morning he came to work and simply said 'You're right.'" We had a long discussion before and after work that day. He was saying that democracy was really illogical - and furthermore it was incompatible with the environment. But to the first point first. Politicians would cater to the desires of 'the little man' without really caring what happens to him. Give them a lollypop but one which is not wise for society, get elected and then we're all stuck with the bad decision. 'We'll get bad teeth from the lollypop,' he'd say.

"'For instance,' he said, 'By now I think that the minimum wage is much too high. American products will not be able to compete in the world, and when the Free Trade notions really take hold, we'll find ourselves losing all kinds of industries until we finally don't make anything at all in this country. Then our debtors will come in and buy all of us and we'll be a nation of serfs. Can't they see that? No they can't. The catastrophe will have to happen before we become aware of it.'

"He later added, 'We do need a centralized government of sorts. But not for the US alone but for the world. Because the more important problems can only be solved by a global council.'

"That was the first time he uttered the words 'global' and 'council.'

"'Have you ever read Huxley?' he asked me.

"'Gioconda smile,' I said. 'I started Point Counterpoint and I'm still asleep.'

"I had meant it to be humorous, but he didn't laugh. 'No,' he said, 'I mean Brave New World.'

"'I remember vaguely - Alphas, Betas, Soma and people created in test tubes. Something like that. All a bit far fetched. A bit frightening, too.'"

"'Test tube babies may not be far fetched,' he said. 'Cloning, you know.'

"'You don't really believe in human cloning?' I said.

"'When I was a kid,' he said, 'My father told me that in the fifties people didn't believe that beer could be put in cans and that a twist-off beer cap was possible.'

"I laughed and said. 'I don't drink beer.'

"But he didn't laugh. Not that he didn't have a sense of humor, but I saw, suddenly, the emergence of a way of thinking that had to be taken seriously.

"Like a religion.

"Things like this happened little by little and he changed from being a liberal champion of the people to one who believed in intellectual control of the nation. Of the world.

"But these were, at the onset, isolated instances. In general our conversations were in a way lighter. That is to say not of such a revolutionary nature.

"Often political, though. For instance on the subject of suffering he was just as adamant about reparations for suffering. As a doctor he was furious about the terribly high cost of malpractice insurance and said it was due to a few bad doctors and a lot of scheister lawyers. And it was becoming the order of the day. There was a day and age where, if a doctor made an unfortunate decision, the patient might consider it bad luck and would get on with his or her life. Now the first reaction is Sue for Malpractice or for Deep Pockets.

Everyone wants money, and no one seems to realize that in a society there is but a limited sum of money. Well it can be expanded by government at will. These sue-happy people want an unfair share of it. Of course, there are exceptions, but the feeling of Sue, Sue, Sue seemed to pervade society.

"Again, where years before he would have been a bleeding heart liberal man who had lost a toe or something, he'd now say, 'So learn to walk on it.

"I recalled my father telling about Dizzie Dean who couldn't pitch after he lost a toe.

"'You'd have to prove it to me,' he said, 'and a lawyer today probably could. But what did Dizzie Dean do? He became a successful sports announcer. That is the right attitude. If you have a lemon make lemonade.'

"I remember laughing and admitting he was right. But again, it wasn't funny to him.

"He became more and more conservative - in a way - in his thinking. In his thought that the masses were too stupid to see what was happening, and that it took deep thinkers and intellectuals to run the Nation so that the Nation could remain strong. And eventually to run the World, so the World could be saved.

"However, he wasn't becoming a Republican. And I think that is where his opinions started to crystallize. He started to think, so to speak, on a higher plane. The reason he wasn't a

Republican was that he was an environmentalist, and Republicans are lackeys of big industry and their lobbyists.

"And apparently, one day, he had managed to fuse his opinions into a philosophy, for that morning, when he had his one half hour brain session with me he said, 'No laws are going to succeed in keeping us from ruining the planet. Suppose North America did all that was really necessary to do its bit to maintain the Eco, other nations wouldn't and they would seize the opportunity to exploit the weakness that would ensue. Because there is one thing that really is not considered in all of this and that is the population explosion.'

"That was a turning point. At this point he stopped taking 'ladies' to the office and he started approaching me. Well he had on several occasions but it had all fallen down because I didn't want 'to go all the way' as he said. And apparently he hadn't been willing earlier to marry me. And suddenly he seemed to respect me, to date me without the final sexual event.

"Then he wrote his article about overpopulation. The day after it appeared the men in the blue shirts and tan slacks came and visited and it became clear to me, later on, that they were LOLA.

"He moved his office out to the outskirts, he built the clinic, and you know what happened from that point on. At least up to the point we were at when he and I were married.

"The wedding ceremony was fine. I was brought up Protestant, like you, and so it was a bit odd. The LOLA have alphas and betas and gammas and epsilons, and we were married by a 'high beta'. Only alphas and high betas were present. With their wives. He was sincere, but it bothered me that the spiel he gave contained the phrase for me 'to honor and obey.' I almost didn't answer, but we were so far into the proceedings that I didn't dare cut out at that point.

"We had a reception - all LOLA people. There were five people in blue shirts; the rest of the men were wearing their various varieties of Sunday suits. I asked Lionel afterwards what that was all about and he said that the blue shirts were alphas. The men shook my hand lightly and Lionel was given strong handshakes. The women gathered about me. They all seemed so subdued and it bothered me a bit. Then again, I was standing there in a bridal gown, experiencing what every red blooded American girl ultimately wants.

"We left the party, and people threw rice and I threw the bridal bouquet. All conventional. Then we went to his apartment - our first stop on our planned honeymoon. From there we were going to go on to a resort hotel somewhere. Lionel had given me a car as a wedding gift - you heard that in the garage when you saw me, and he was driving. He said I was too excited, and I felt he was right.

"We went into the apartment and he kissed me. Then...you know the rest

"I wept and slapped him in the face.

"He simply slapped me back.

"'Get your informal clothes on,' he said. 'Let's get going.'

"I cried all the way in the car, until he drove it into the sign.

"He got a taxi and drove me to the clinic and they gave me a sedative. The next day they gave me tranquilizers and brought me up to a 'session'. It was a psychiatrist I didn't know, but he really calmed me down. I realized that my mind was a blank. I went to sessions for thirty days, and I think they hypnotized me and made sure I didn't get my memory back. I think they can do more than what ordinary shrinks can do. Regardless of what Ron said."

"The church - LOLA that is - requires that you go to 'sessions' twice a year, but Lionel had me going once a month or more frequently if necessary, and I must have had ideas implanted in me at that time as well. Also I must have been conditioned to be satisfied with my lot in life.

"Lionel hired another person to do my job in his practice, and I stayed home. I was at loose ends; I didn't know what to do. He would buy me anything I wanted, but he wanted me at home. He would come home at different times of the day and have sex. His way. And by now it didn't bother me, in fact I got to like it, because it was a kind of attention, a kind of love, I thought.

"Then one afternoon - he wasn't home - I saw a report on the Jessica Kreutz affair on television. I realized that Lionel had gotten his big promotion in the church - in LOLA - shortly after the incident. They hadn't removed my ability to think, and I got to think that indeed the 'sessions' I was going to were simply conditionings. I tried not to let myself be hypnotized, I tried to fake things, and I think I partly succeeded.

"It was when Lionel started talking in his sleep that I got really scared. I asked for a divorce. The answer was the maid and yet more sessions."

CHAPTER 13

The tyranny of the land owners and the middle classes is rapidly being destroyed, in order that we may have the dictatorship of the proletariat. A new infallibility, not of the Pope, but of the majority, has been propounded - an infallibility which we are compelled by law to believe in.
Aldous Huxley, Point Counter Point.

That night, Jon started working on the computer.
"Damn it," he said.
"What's the matter?"
"I can't get into the computer. I need a password. Please help me. Words that he might use."
"I'll write down a number of possibilities. Like my name, his mother's, psychological terms and so on."
That's what she did, and Jon started trying them one by one.
He worked on it for several hours, but with no success. This was going to be difficult. He wished Neville were there. Nev could crack it in a minute. Well, an hour maybe.
He finally went to bed. It was all he could do that night - or rather that morning. When he awoke he was in a somber mood. The problem with the password was weighing on him. She, too, seemed tense.
They kissed. That relaxed him a bit.
"Stop thinking of it for a while. Let's have a heavy breakfast. Let's get fat and lazy."
He laughed.
They were intimate as in Genesis 19 when they came back

from breakfast, but he had to admit that he was not craving it, because he was so occupied with finding the password. He caught himself thinking of it during the act.

"You lasted longer than usual," she said. "That was nice."

And he remembered once when he had asked a friend how did you 'last long', his friend had said, 'Just think of each inning of the last baseball game."

So he worked on trying to crack the password all day. It was frustrating. He was still working on it when they went out to dinner.

They made love as in Gomorrah and she went to sleep. But then he would get up in the night and work on finding the password. She would often wake up, and write something down on paper she had at the bedside. Then she would talk to him a bit and go back to sleep.

On the third night she awoke and said to him, "Let me see the book that you took from the safe."

"I have tried all kinds of combinations of words from page 74 the marked page, but I've had no success."

She looked at the marked page.

"Try aitkseot."

"Too many letters, but I'll drop the 't'." Then he said, "It doesn't work."

"Then try fesdfend."

He entered the letters, and almost yelled, "Eureka, It works. Did you write it down so we don't forget it."

"I don't have to. They are the last letters of the eight last lines on page 74. The first one I gave you were the first letters of the eight - well nine - first lines."

"You're a genius."

"Let's open it."

He punched a couple of keys, and a document came up on the screen.

"Curses," he said,"It's in code."

"Let me see," she said. And she saw and, indeed, it was a jumble of letters making no sense.

"It's a step forward," he said. "Let's celebrate."

They had a couple of glasses of wine. He fell on the bed, and she bent over him and fallated him.

"I love you," she said.

"I hope you don't feel you've been neglected the last couple of days," he said. "I have been so preoccupied with the password, and it has made me tense. What's so stupid is that there are probably people in this world who could have opened in minutes."

"You've done great," she said.

"You solved it."

"Only because you thought of bringing the book."

"I'm making progress with recovering my memory. As I remember things, I write them down. We'll share some time. You have seen me write things down. I'll tell you more of the puzzle that I've put together."

He had never tried to decode anything before. Some common sense told him that there were words like 'I' which were the only one- letter-words available. For three letter words either 'and' or 'the' would be possible. If he used 'the', the correspondence of letters would be that 'I' was 'O', 'T' was 'Y', 'H' was 'J' and 'E' was 'R'. What he got out of it, when he applied it to other words didn't really make sense.

He worked on it most of the next day. As he had said, he was not a - what are they called - cryptographer?

"Do you think it is a simple code?" he asked Nora.

"I would think so."

"I'm working on the assumption that each letter represents another letter, and if I can find the correspondence between the letters, then we can decode the whole document."

Again, he worked well into the night. Nora was sleeping quietly on the bed. She had taken to sleep in the nude, and once in a while the sheet would move on her, and he would see her breasts. Sometimes her legs would emerge, and the sheet would creep up to the magic triangle. As he worked he would look over at her, and it somehow would help him keep his sanity. But the view of the Venus mound brought back cravings he still had.

He, at a tired moment, accidentally happened to glance at the keyboard, and realized that maybe what the letter-to-letter correspondences were neighboring keys on the keyboard. In that case 'U' would be 'I' one of the one letter words, 'P' would be 'A'. That was a little trickier because 'P' was at the end of a line. He tried a couple of these possibilities out, and suddenly it was there. He had it solved. He had the correspondence of letters.

He, tediously, decoded a couple of paragraphs, and they made sense, so he now knew how to decode the whole thing, except it would take years to do it. There were well over a hundred pages.

He must have expressed his elation, because she awoke.

"I broke it," he said. "Except it is going to take eons to decipher it all."

"We'll take eons. Have you deciphered something?"

"Yes, half a page. It took me an hour." Then he added, "I know how it could be done more efficiently. The computer has a 'Find Word'-function. The alphabet has 26 letters, each of which has a code letter. I could make the correct assignment for one half of the letters, and use the 'Find'-function to change those letters into 'readable' letters. I could assign numbers and their 'shift' symbols for the other thirteen. When I had completed this, I could use the 'Find'-Function to change the numbers. But it would take a lot of time. I'll do that little by little as we drive around."

"Why do you have to do that thing with the numbers?" she asked.

"If I have changed 'A' to 'S', then the problem is that when I now come to 'Code A' it would not only change that but also the true 'A'."

"It will take a lot of time away from us. We know the essential, namely that the document is incriminating."

"You're right. I'll make a disk-copy of the entire files, and I'll also make a printout. We can do the rest of it at our leisure." He added, "I might still do a little of decoding of different sections as time allows. Sometime I'm awake when you sleep."

"I sleep more than usual. A lot of physical activity," she grinned. "The part that you decoded, what does it say?"

"This is a page I chose it at random." He handed her a page he had printed out and it read:

'We must prepare for the ice age, so we must secure property in areas around the equator. Some of our loyal flock must emigrate there, of course at great sacrifice, but it is necessary that we get a foothold. It is obvious that in that catastrophic event we can much easier accomplish our goals, since a great deal of the world's population will be dead. We must, however, expect that others will try to move or flee there as well, and we must be able to defend ourselves. This is the reason for our biological program…'

"That's potent enough," she said. "When you do a bit more - on your time, so to speak - it might be good to use your 'Find-function', or whatever it is - and get something that deals with…" She stopped mid-sentence, sat up in the bed and said, "Come over here, you lazy boy."

He was going to talk to Nev - it was Friday - and so he would ask him to get a safe deposit box. Then he thought that was silly, he could get one in the bank right there.

He took some money from the suitcase and went downtown. The place was called Lilleby. He set up a box in the name of Slowe. He placed one copy of the downloaded material, a printout of it, and the copy of the diary in it. What should he do with the key?

"What if I lose the key?" he asked the teller.

"You got two. We'll just make a copy of the other one if you lose the first."

"What if I lose both."

"Well, you come in, show identification, and we'll have it opened. But that's expensive. We have to have a locksmith come in and install another lock. My advice is not to lose the keys."

He'd just throw the keys away. That way no one, but he,

himself, could gain access to the box. There would be no room for the type of mystery where the plot hinges on what locker the key belonged to. But he couldn't get himself to throw away the keys.

He made a mental note of the box number.

He had been working on the computer for a couple of weeks. He had done most of the work at night when she was asleep. The days he preferred to be with her. He was savoring her company, and she his, they would take long walks and hold hands while strolling down the sideways to the highway. They would make love from time to time - at any time of the day - and he concluded that Ron the psychiatrist must have been right - she must be enjoying it. Little by little he had given up on the idea of normal sex and he felt fulfillment with her the way she guided him. Different, yes, but small things like her saying 'I love it when you massage my nipples from behind' or 'You are having just the right tempo' - all said before the crescendo started with the verbalization, with the Anglo-Saxon words, with the shiver.

But he found, amazingly, that he would wake up at midnight, and he would tiptoe out of bed and turn on the light in the far end of the room. She would stir a little bit, and then it was as if her dream world accustomed itself to the lumens. Maybe it casts light and shadows into the imaginary life that comes with sleep. And then there was the thought that that imaginary life was really the real life and what he was now experiencing, sitting by the soft light, was a dream. Old thoughts, thoughts that haunted him on occasion.

There were parts of the computer entries that were not in code. They were a sort of continuation of the Lionel diary where the manual journal had ceased after the wedding. It was much in the same style, but the entries about Nora concentrated rather on the delights of his physical entry into her, her anatomy. He never ceased to comment on her buttocks and the crevice that separated them. But at one point he started complaining in written word about the fact that she was often unwilling to a second - or even a third - encounter in a day. He wrote on February 19, 1997 the following:

'...She complained again today. I had come home at lunch and the act was lovely. She seemed to enjoy. But when I came back again from the clinic at seven she balked. 'I get sore,' she said. 'You must understand that.' But I had given her salves and creams that should prevent that. Maybe she isn't using them. I have my needs and I will be damned if I'm going to go to the bathroom and behave like an adolescent'

Later he wrote: 'She asked, today, if it wouldn't be better for us to get a divorce, and I told her in absolutely no uncertain terms NO. Not even discussions of it will I allow.'

Then, about a month later, with several entries of the same nature, there was the following entry which he did *not* share with Nora:

'...Back in the days when I was trying to make Nora jealous, when she worked at the old office, I had dates come late in the day and have sex with them behind closed doors. The noise must have been obvious, yet, Nora was unaffected. I touched on that in earlier diary entries. One of the girls had a special effect on me. Her name was Dolores Juanita and she was a good and willing participant in sodomic intercourse. She heaved the right way, she was quiet (and I thought I could, at a later date, teach her verbalization), and I saw her a couple of times and then she moved to Sarasota. Well, she showed up at the clinic today, and we went into my office, and we had a delightful, physical encounter. Then she said, "I need your help, doctor. I'm an illegal immigrant - I hate the word 'alien' - and I'm forever afraid that the authorities are going to catch up with me." She then paused a minute and looked at me in an uncertain way and said, "I can trust you, can't I? You won't give me away?" I assured her. I asked her how I could help her. She said that, for one, she needed money. "I hate to ask it under these circumstances. It almost sounds like prostitution, but I'm a good girl." Again I assured her that I was sure she was. Then I asked her how much she needed. It was a piddly sum. "No prostitute would ask that little," I said to her, "but I have a better idea. How would you like to come and work for me?" She told me an enthusiastic yes and then asked what the job would entail. She, curiously enough, didn't ask how much it paid. I told her that, in a sketchy fashion, I would like her to work as a maid in my home, but it was not a simple maid's job. I told her that I had possible troubles with my wife and needed her to keep an eye on her so to speak. She was excited about this. 'Sort of like the CIA,' she said. I also told her I would like us to continue our relationship and that I would arrange it so that the wife would go shopping every day at a given time of day, and during this time of day we would have time together. And of course, at night as well, and for this purpose I needed to see to it that Nora got fed all the bourbon she desired. She sleeps very well and deeply after a couple of those. Dolores Juanita then asked, 'Do you still have... you know... with your wife?' Then she rapidly said, 'I'm sorry, I shouldn't ask.' I told her it was OK, but that I did and that I would until such a day when I was ready for a divorce. That brought a smile to her face, but I, of course, do not plan on divorcing Nora. The rules are strict for LOLA. High betas and alphas do not divorce. Their wives, even though kept in the dark about many things, still pick up tidbits here and there, and publicity of the inner workings of LOLA should be avoided...'

As mentioned, Jon decided not to show this to Nora.

Even though he had the code now, decoding, even with the FIND-function, was slow. But he had hit on enough entries to deduce what the philosophy was and what their master plan was.

The entries were made in a catalogued form much like the Scriptures. It would appear, indirectly, that Joseph Helligman, was the founder, and Erasmus Helligman, or Helligman II, was the successor after the founder's death. A couple of snippets showed the general theology and sooth sayings of the cult.

Helligman II 3, 19.
19. The Earth must be saved from the onslaught of man. Pollution of air, water and minds must be fought. But what helps it if a Nation adopts a stringent policy and its neighbor

doesn't. Well, it helps, but the remedies must be as total as possible. It is necessary to have one governing council who directs the policies of the world, controls the rules of conduct, and minimizes abuses.

Helligman II, 4, 14-19

14 The Earth is dependent on the number of people inhabiting it. It stands to reason that if the population of the United States grows by 10% then so also will the consumption of gasoline, the discarding of packaging material, the use of water, the use of air.

15. Mankind is poisoning itself. Add to all of this the wholesale felling of trees, the pollution of the oceans, so that less generation of oxygen takes place. It can be extrapolated to the point where there will not be enough oxygen to sustain mankind.

16. To add to this, the warming of the Earth's atmosphere, the so-called global warming, eventually will cause an acceleration of the onset of the next ice age.

17. A policy akin to the one child policy in China will be put in effect, except a two children policy will be sufficient. The present population will then decrease, albeit more slowly. It is of import to get LOLA alphas into government positions in *all* countries, and this is one of the immediate goals of LOLA.

Helligman II, 2, 14-21

14. A wife of an alpha or a high beta must exercise absolute obedience to her husband.

15. Sodomic sex is preferred except when propagation is planned.

16. Until a World Order is in place there is no restriction on the number of children a LOLA member can have.

17. Children should be subjected to psychoanalytical sessions at an early age, so that they will become obedient LOLA members.

18. Especially the female children should be indoctrinated into absolute obedience to the male sex.

19. In the case where a female child is found to be exceptional, she should be brought up with the same guidelines as a male child

20. It is, therefore, not excluded that (some) woman may attain the status of alpha or supreme beta.

21. In no case may alphas or supreme betas leave the organization. The clandestine nature of its goals and plans are of the utmost importance. Should such attempts be made, then the perpetrator should be hunted down and eliminated as a risk.

Helligman II, 3, 29-30

29. There must be a master plan for reducing the world's population at such a future time when LOLA is in worldwide control. To this end, our laboratories are working on gene and race specific biological weapons.

30. Eventually, after several generations, a society where half of the population is created by biological intercourse and half by cloning will result. A society of alphas, betas, gammas and epsilons comparable to the writings of Huxley will be established. But this not until a World Order is achieved.

Helligman II, 60, 10

10. LOLA will establish colonies in warmer climates, e.g. Africa, so that a nucleus of alphas and beta type individuals will be present at the onset of the ice age. These may be cloned and may be cloned to DNA that will make them suitable for arctic and for tropical conditions.

Helligman II, 90, 25

25. No alpha or high beta in LOLA shall be permitted to divorce his wife. He may take on more wives if so desired, but suitable arrangements will have to be made so that all the wives have the same rights.

26. For instance at the age of sixty-two - or rather sixty-five - a wife is entitled to one half of her spouse's social security

benefits. Arrangements will be made so that all the wives obtain such an amount on the death of a LOLA alpha or high beta. At the time of death of a male LOLA member, a substitute spouse will be announced and the wife (wives) will obey this new spouse.

Anyway, he read further in the diary and decided to share some of it with Nora. There was a part, which she should certainly know about. She had been speculating about it, justifying her action by the assumptions she made, and it would be only just that she know exactly what happened.

She woke up early and they went to breakfast. Again in a secluded place, and at a secluded table. He had the manuscript in his hand.

"Let me read to you some of the things in his diary," he said.

"Why not all of it."

"In some cases I'm not quite sure of my decoding, so let me be sure first." He didn't like lying to her, but sometimes lying is better than telling the truth. He read:

Last night a supreme elder called me and asked me to fetch Jessica at her house and take her to the clinic. So I went to where she lived. Her husband is a Faithful who let me in to the apartment and he helped me put her in the car and I started driving off with her. She was wearing a nightgown - I guess the husband had been so instructed - but with the way clothes are now a days it looked more like a cocktail party dress. At a red light I noticed a police car at the opposite corner. Suddenly Jessica opened the door and jumped out and started running towards the police car. In the process she lost a shoe. I followed as rapidly as I could, and had a word with the policewoman. When she heard I was Jessica's psychiatrist, she drove to the clinic and she and Jessica followed. She then let Jessica into my custody with a warning. I got two orderlies to restrain her while we got her a gown and we forced it on her. She kept on yelling that I was abducting her, but the cop be-

lieved me, that she was an unstable patient. *I then gave her a sedative and the nurses brought her to her cell.*"

"And now some pages later," Jon said.

The Assistant Founder called. He was upset to say the least. He ordered me to 'make sure that Jessica would cause no more trouble' and told me that he was sure I knew what he meant.
'Nothing that they can pin on us, you understand' were his words. This bothers me, but for the greater good it must be done.
I ordered her kept in isolation, and told the staff that she was to have no solids and no water. I'll check in on her in three four days."

Jon skipped a couple of pages and then read further on in the diary:

She committed suicide this afternoon. We had George from the police department come. He is a Faithful as well, and we sent the body to the morgue at night, because that is when Henry, also a Faithful, is on duty and can issue a death and incineration certificate. She was sent over to the LOLA crematorium, and at the time of this writing she should be but ashes.

This was the second time Jon had read this passage, and yet he felt cold sweat running down his back as he read it. It was true. It was all true.
The police investigated the death but the case was dropped. The power these people had, and the fact that the public in general didn't know how infiltrated it was, was astonishing. If something would come up, it would always be squelched as being too incredible.
In fact it was.
No wonder Nora, who wasn't even a member, wanted out from under the influence of this evil organization.

He now read further:

The plight of the world is obvious. We are killing our planet, we are killing ourselves. There is the Green movement, which is a banner-bearer for opposition to these developments, but its leaders are weak, and many of its adherents are simply people who want to be 'different'.

It is easy to analyze the reasons for our climactic changes and our ecological disasters. Fossil fuel, one automobile in each pot, consumer society, unbridled landfills, overfishing, overhunting, overlogging.

It is talked about, and no one does anything about it. Or rather, a Band-Aid approach is taken, in most cases to appease environmentalists.

Today's world also belongs to crooks. Crooks who run big companies, big agglomerates, big banks. They milk the public without the public knowing it, unless they go bankrupt, and in such cases the crooks usually get away with just a slap on the wrist.

Democracy, and also dictatorships as they are known today, are not instruments that can solve these problems. Dictators would be able to, but are usually too egotistical to approach the problem as such. Democracies have learned that a politician must play up to the public in order to win elections; they know that by handing the populus a carrot it will be made somewhat happy. They keep the bread earner busy getting his carrot, for instance by him or her having to have two jobs and working all sorts of hours. The result is that the people running the democratic governments, and the people, who finance their campaigns, have free reign to do what they want.

The only way that the plight of the WORLD and of the ENVIRONMENT on which we depend as humans can be solved is by a dictatorship that fights for the cause, not one which functions for the benefit of the dictator.

The ideal society is really one that is structured according to Huxley's Brave New World, except some degree of randomness in procreation is preferable. You would not want a world of look-and-behave-alikes.

But the society should be run by and should be conducive to the creation of exceptional people. I guess, although I have not studied Nietzche, that it is the concept of the Uebermensch. Hitler, of course, extrapolated that to the concept of a Master race, but that is fallacious. There are geniuses in all races, and a multiracial society is to be preferred. The problem is to control it, so that there are alphas, betas, gammas and epsilons and that the members of each stratum know where they belong, what their duties are, how they can remain happy. It is the function of the alphas to create a society such as that.

In the long run population control also much be exercised. This cannot come before the concepts have been accepted by alphas in the entire world. There would then be a multinational council of alphas, and a superalpha, elected for a given period, who would be the Master of the World. But there will be wars before that can happen.

An alpha of ours erected a sort of Stonehenge in Georgia, with the credo that the world should have no more than one billion people. That means that five out of six people (even more maybe) would have to be eliminated if one wanted to do this right away. The principle, however, is patience and, the first Founder, Joseph Helligman, will be like Moses on the mountain of Nebo - he will never see the Promised Land.

The problem with democracy is, of course, that you can never, by election, tell people to do something that is for their own good, a something, which they don't want to do. It is not imaginable that someone would run for president of the United States by saying that he would prohibit families from having more than one car per family. He would be doomed to defeat, because his opponents would appeal to the worst senses of the electorate and they would not see that it would be to the benefit of society as a whole.

These are just brief outlines, but I am writing the Gospel for the present Helligman, and he is pleased with what I have written so far.

To effect all of this it is necessary to have a dedicated and loyal cadre of alphas, carefully selected. They would know the *blueprints for The New Society. A stratum of betas would then be a sort of middle management, and it would be responsible for recruiting gammas and epsilons by various means and promises. Mind enlargement, happiness and furthering of the person in society as it is today are two means by which this can be done. In other words, do like the politicians, appeal to their vanity and their pocket books. For the time being. Eventually, when Ours becomes the order of the world, every man and woman will know their place in society and will be happy.*

The problems, of course, even today, arise when someone succumbs to short term considerations, becomes affected by some type of bleeding heart liberalism. The Founder was pleased with the way I managed to keep Jessica Kreutz at the clinic, and 'made her disappear'. And there were no problems with that. It was a good thing that both the coroner and the detectives involved in this were betas and knew their job.

I felt sorry for her myself, I must admit that, when I gave her the injection and made her write and sign the suicide note. You could see she didn't want to do it, but because of the drug she was powerless. The supplemental injection, of course, made it final. It disturbed me that I was disturbed, because it was necessary for the good of the cause.

And every alpha or beta who falls away will meet a similar fate, anyone, who is a danger to our society, anyone who is trying to break and publicize the secret code of LOLA. The present Helligman, our present leader, not only agrees. He was the one who suggested it.

He was right. It is what LOLA wants.

Jon had read this out loud. Nora was white as chalk. "You are right," she said. "Both of us have no choice."

"Yes, I was planning on our having a nice dinner and making love afterwards," he said. "I didn't think I would ever say this, but now I'm not in the mood to make love."

"Nor am I," she said. "But I love you." She had regained her stamina. "We'll be all right. We have done nothing wrong. No ill will come to us."

"In many respects their goals are quite what I believe in," said Nora. "But the elimination of democracy and the ways they seem to go at it to create loyalty are wrong."

"It is the only way they could do it," said Jon. "But the frightening thing is actually that it is based on a false premise. That people of intellect can work together as a team. There will always be jealousies and power struggles. And then the second fallacy is that their people should unselfishly work for the World, its salvation. Suppose it came to pass, as a first step in our country. The alphas or one of them would get greedy and we would be back to the rule of great capital, large corporations.

"The fallacy is also that the end product is one of Goodness throughout. But there is a dichotomy in the world, namely that there is Good and Evil. And it comes from our ability to think. When God created the world, if indeed he did, he kept humans from thinking, but they ate the apple. And, as you know, I don't consider the apple just something that made Man and Woman aware of sexual instinct. It was the Tree of *Knowledge* and that is the ability to think. You can't know something if you can't think.

"And, Christianity at least, is based on the concept of Good and Evil. We say that God is almighty, but Revelations teaches us that there is a constant fight between the forces of Evil and the forces of Good.

"And the best way of weighing things in on the side of Good is to let everyone have a say. OK, so many people haven't really formed opinions when they vote. But you are not going to convince a hungry man, a man without a job, that his government is good for him. The little man has say. It's the gammas and the epsilons that have the say. They elect the alphas. OK, so there is corruption, but there has never been a less fallible system as far as the pursuit of happiness. It may take some time in the case of difficult issues, but it will get there."

She smiled at him. "I didn't know you had a soapbox. You can be quite an orator."

"Let me ask you something," he said. "It is alpha, beta, gamma and epsilon people. What happened to delta?"

She laughed. "I really don't know."

"The other question is the following: is the present Helligman the same as the one who started it all."

"No," she said. "He died somewhere along the line. I think he was a minister."

"So he should know the Greek alphabet. Maybe the Huxley concept was introduced later. There doesn't seem to be anything on the computer coming from the original founder."

"Pre-computer era, maybe."

It had taken many evenings and nights to do just this part of the translation of the coded material, but this particular morning he decided to read what he had.

He decided not to share the rest of it with Nora, simply refer to it vaguely in conversation, should it come up.

After they came back from breakfast Nora said, "You look tired. You should get some more sleep." Then she added, "It has been so nice to stay in this one place for so long. Can we stay another week?"

He went to see the manager.

"You'll have to put a deposit down, if that's the case."

"Why suddenly? I have paid promptly, so far."

"Well," the manager said, "because of the long-distance phone call last night."

Jon was taken aback but didn't show it. "Let me think about it," he said, "I'll let you know later. Of course, I'll pay for extra charges."

As he came back to the room he said to Nora, "Did you use the phone?"

"I called the lawyer. Was that wrong?"

"They may locate us. What did he say?"

"His offices are moved. So I called the new number and a secretary answered. Quite different from before."

"I think he has joined the enemy," said Jon. "I think we'd better get out of here."

"I'm sorry," she said.

"No problem, we'll just get out. It was nice being in one spot for a while."

"I'll think of it fondly," she said. "Do you think we can find another place and stay for a while?"

"That's possible."

CHAPTER 14

"Well…I think they might have waited just two minutes before they started their love making…"
D.H.Lawrence, Kangaroo

"Let's go to the 'I DO INN' and stay for a while," Nora said.

He had his reservations about the 'I DO IN'. But there was another motel he had noticed - the Carillon.

"It is not the same," said Nora.

"I don't know if we'd be safe at the 'I DO INN'," said Jon. "We could have been spotted on the way."

"We can't make our life style dependent on suspicions," said Nora. "I so wish we could stay there."

In the end they went to the Carillon. They checked in at night and turned in. She cuddled, and they made love in the dark. He was now quite accustomed to the way it was done.

They were relaxed and refreshed in the morning. They showered together - what a marvelous feeling.

They had breakfast at a place called 'Nora's'. "Most appropriate," Nora said. "So the food should be good."

They ate and exchanged sweet nothings, and then Nora said, "I've been doing a lot of telling, it is your turn to let me in on what was going on in your life - what your troubles with the big L are."

He smiled," 'Big L," he said, "That's cute." The Law by any other name is still the Law. So he started relating what had happened. He had gone through this story in his head from time to time, he had arranged the order in which to cover the events in a logical fashion.

"I'll tell this in chronological order. It will be a while before I come to the crucial points, which you'll want to know about. There may be things I tell you that you don't like, but I'll just be frank."

"That's fine. I should have told things in chronological order, too. Maybe."

"No, it was different with you. You had just remembered the most important facts." He sipped his coffee.

"Anyway, when I took the job as manager of 'Mr. Sportes' I really didn't know the first thing about retailing. I was surprised I had been able to get the job. But I fell into it OK. It wasn't that difficult. You had to find out which wholesalers you had to go to get your ware, and I could get that from old invoices.

"There were two employees there, one worked half of the week, the other worked the other half of the week. There was a cash register and at the end of the day I tallied up the money taken in and balanced the books. Sometimes they didn't balance and they were always off by a round figure, for instance ten dollars, and I was looking for addition or subtraction errors. So it occurred to me that someone was dipping into the till.

"I thought a better cash register system would be an advantage, but I didn't have too much experience in such matters.

"Shortly after I joined, one of the employees quit, and I was about to start advertising for a replacement. The other employee, Martin, was giving me trouble, and once he was the lone employee he really gave me grief. He apparently thought he should have had the managerial job.

"Luck, sometimes, comes at fortunate times. Two days after the employee had quit; a fellow walked into the store. I asked him if I could be of help and he said,

"No thanks, I just came in to window shop." He grinned and added, "Where do you keep your windows?" I remembered, I laughed.

"Then he said, all of a sudden, 'Do you have any job openings?' I asked him what type of skills he had, and he said he had never gotten a college degree, but he was knowledgeable about computers and computer science.

"'I also have customer appeal. As you see I'm both charming and humble.' We laughed again.

"Computers constitute an area I'm not all that adept in, and the thought of him helping with a better cash register system was interesting. Ordering could be streamlined, as well. Indeed, I could use someone with his talents, so I told him to come in with his CV and we settled on the next day at ten o'clock. I jotted the appointment down on the calendar. Many a moon later I realized that I didn't have the calendar on the right month. The meeting worked out fine, anyway, and I didn't bother to reenter the appointment on the right date. In fact I didn't become aware of it until much, much later.

"The guy was Neville, and it turned out to be, as you know, a lasting friendship. He was of enormous help.

"I got approval to improve the accounting system, and Neville set it up - from calling the suppliers of systems like that, to the trying out of the system on a trial basis first, and then installing it for good.

"The owner of 'Mr. Sportes' was impressed.

"One thing that bothered me was that we were overstocked on many items, particularly team T-shirts. I asked Martin why that was, and he informed me that in January you had to, in mid-month, order a sufficient supply of at least four teams' shirts, because you never knew who was going to win the superbowl.

"I asked what about the shirts from the other three teams, and he said those shirts would sell when those teams would win the superbowl. He was greatly annoyed at my asking all these questions.

"We had a 50% off sale, and got rid of a lot of the overstock. Neville told me to get rid of Martin, too. 'I think he's helping himself to cash from time to time'. I said that was my thought, too. 'But how do I get rid of him? I can't just lay him off, he has worked here for ten years.' Neville said, 'Leave it to me' and I did exactly that. Two weeks later Martin handed in his resignation. 'You'll see how you get along without me,' he said, and I spared him an answer.

"One day, much later, Neville didn't show up for work on time. That was unusual. An hour later on I got a call.

"It was Neville. He was calling from the police station. 'I'm in trouble. Can you bail me out?' Which I did. On the way back he told me that the police had come to his door and accused him of steeling a laptop computer from someone. He mentioned the day and time it was supposed to have happened. They also tried to accuse him of being involved with supplying false documents to people.

"When we got to the store, I checked the calendar and said, 'That's impossible. That is the day you were here and started working at the store.'

"'Will you testify to that?' he asked.

"'Certainly,' I said.

"And due to my testimony he was found 'not guilty'. But I realized, again much later, that I had given false information. And, in fact, Neville thought I had done it deliberately, that it was not by mistake. And I let him believe it.

"In December, Neville asked me if I'd like to know how to handle the T-shirt situation. After closing he took me out to a silk-screening place. It was sort of like a large barn with different sorts of equipment in it.

"'Hi Vivian,' he said to a gal who was obviously running the place. 'Great' she said. He asked her how fast she could produce different items, and asked her if she could work on the day of the superbowl and produce a large quantity of T-shirts. 'No hassle, man' she said, 'No hassle.'

"There was another girl there. 'Meet Helen,' said Vivian. I took to Helen at once, and she took to me."

"Not like the two of us in the coffee shop, I hope," said Nora.

"No, this was different. I was sex-starved, it was a feeling of lust, and I sensed that her glances at me were of the same nature.

"Vivian and I discussed the situation. 'There are two weeks between the semifinals - is that what they are called - and the superbowl, so I would know what T-shirt stock to order.' She showed me different grades of stock, and we decided on one. 'I can order a good quantity of both colors, and then start screen printing the winner-shirt on the Sunday of the championship. We can work - all night if necessary, can't we Helen?' Helen nodded, but she was actually looking at me; I don't know if she even heard what Vivian said.

"Vivian then said, 'Why don't you come back tomorrow and I'll have a contract. Unfortunately I have an appointment right now, and I have to go. You can ask any other questions you have of Helen. She knows the operation well.' And then she left. I was left alone with Helen. 'I have seen you before,' she said, 'At the Brown Bear Bar and Grill, I believe.'

"'Will you be there tonight?' I asked.

"'No,' she said, 'I'm working late - here - tonight.'

"'Need any help?'

"'Yeah,' she said, 'Why don't you come by and give a hand.'

"Which I did. That was the first time I had intercourse with her. Right on a large flat table where they were placing T-shirts for some reason or other. Maybe to dry or something. We managed to put spots on two of them. Afterwards she handed both of them to me and said, 'Wear them in good health' and I said, 'I'll frame them.'"

"How sweet," said Nora, in her most sarcastic voice.

"Now, now," I said. "You wanted to know."

"I wanted to know about the police."

"I'm coming to that."

But he was thinking of the clinging of Helen's limbs, how they scissored around his waist, how she undulated towards the end in a hectic, almost insane rhythm, about her sweet-smelling sweat, about her loud, uncontrolled, uncivilized screams.

"The next day," Jon said, "I went over to sign the contracts with Vivian, and she smiled at me and said, 'Hey Casanova, I guess Helen has the hotsies for you. Or has she already hotsied with you?' There was a friendly, teasing look in her eyes as she stood there, almost like a hippie from the sixties, defying society, and preaching her own delight in life.

"I looked at some of the T-shirts she had out. It was beautiful work. The designs were sharp and clear.

"'Where do you get the designs?' I asked.

" 'I do them myself. I'm an artist. Actually an oil painter, but it is hard to support yourself on just your art. This is sort of art, too.'

"She took me into another room and showed me a painting of a bar scene hanging on the wall.

"'My father was an artist who painted landscapes. There was always a road in his paintings. When people asked him why, he said that he was painting by the roadside, and the road was there to be painted. As you see, I paint bar scenes, so draw your own conclusions.'

"I remember laughing.

"The painting is actually The Brown Bear.'"

Jon reflected on that particular statement; Vivian might have spent many hours standing in the Brown Bear, but over a couple of years to come, Helen and he would have spent many hours prone underneath The Brown Bear on the wall. He chuckled a bit to himself, but didn't say anything.

"'I've never seen you there,' I said.

"'I'm banned from that place. The owner is an asshole, and I punched him in the nose one day. So I have to go elsewhere for my brews.'

"She was delightful. Just to show that a woman can be delightful and warm and good-looking without trying to be sexual about it."

"Are you accusing me of making sexual overtures?" Nora asked.

"No, sweetheart, not at all. I was contrasting her with Helen. Vivian, I think, would make you work for it if you wanted a date with her. Helen would ask *you* for a date.

"Vivian told me something else. 'One thing you don't know about Helen is that she is married to a guy named Charlie.' But I did know, she had told me. 'Her husband is a real jerk, works all the time. The only thing he does other than working is bowling, once a week.'

"I thought of the fact that he sounded like Hannah. She was investing all her time in work and then bowling once a week. I had always thought it was a strange sport - or pastime - for someone as high and mighty as Hannah. Squash or tennis - or even polo - would be more what you'd think in her style. 'So Helen and her jerk could have some togetherness if she bowled too,' I said.

"'She tried that. But she doesn't bowl well, and there was some broad on the team who she couldn't stand.'

"'Why doesn't she get a divorce?'

"'I know all about divorces,' she said. 'The rich party, mostly the man, wins out. It's all a matter of money. They can hide their holdings and cheat on their declarations of what they own, and the poor gal, or guy as the case may be, is left with pathetically little. It's a bit like table stakes poker.'

"I thought of that later on," Jon said.

"Before I go on, I should tell you a bit more about Neville and our interaction at the store. I have already told you how he got me into fishing so I could get away from home, but I made my escape route and alone-time even more practical. I suggested to the owner that we stay open late on Saturdays and Sundays. In effect I would be 'working' - in quotation marks - 'all the time'. Neville would cover for me.

"One thing that I took up due to Neville was hunting. Not that I was any good at it, but he said it would give me the opportunity to go away with Helen in the fall. And I did that one year. It worked fine.

"Even though Helen was married she had ways of getting away from home, and Vivian was only too happy to cooperate. 'I love men,' she said, 'but some of them are such horses' asses. And Helen's husband is one of those.'

"At times Helen and I would splurge and go to a motel, but most of the time we'd make use of the silk-screen shop. 'I wish we could do it in a bed all the time,' she would say, 'but don't get me wrong, I have no complaints.'

"I analyzed our relationship as one of our helping one another with our lousy marital relationships. Frustration, anger and lashing out. Our sex had a component of anger in it, like saying, 'Now take this you old stuff shirt, Charlie' or my saying 'now take this you old bitch, Hannah.' And the anger and the frustration were there and there didn't seem to be an end in sight for us. We could go on forever.

"Barring unforeseen events.

"Then, last August, Hannah was going to California for some investment seminars. I saw her to the airport, and then called Helen. Vivian had let her off for the day, and Helen arrived at my - or rather Hannah's - house shortly after I got home, and she said, 'It's going to be a treat to make out in *her* bed. One of these days we should do it in Charlie's bed.

"But in the middle of the act, the door sprang open, and there was Hannah. Her flight had been cancelled. Need I say more? 'Well, well,' she said. 'Well, well,' and then she turned around and slammed the door behind her.

"Helen had done the natural thing - sat up and covered herself with the sheet, and I was lying there on the bed in dumb nudity.

"Helen got up and got her clothes on and ran out of the house. When I talked to her next she said, 'We'd better lay low for a while. I know that broad. She and Charlie know one another; she is the one on the bowling team who gave me such trouble. Would it be all right if we didn't meet for a month?'

"I pleaded with her, but to no avail. I argued that we could just be more careful, but Helen said she was sure that Hannah would hire a detective. She just didn't want to be compromised any more than she had been already. I was obviously quite depressed.

"Right after the incident I was wondering what would happen next at home, but I decided simply go to work the next day as if nothing had happened. All that resulted from the incident was the big chill, the big silence.

"That evening I said to Hannah, 'I want you to know I'm not seeing that girl anymore.' She simply turned away from me and didn't say anything. She was doing as if I was air. And this continued the next day, and I thought, well, let it continue, see if I care. Action came a while afterwards. A man rang the doorbell and I answered. He asked me if I were John and I answered yes, and then he simply handed me an envelope, turned on his heels and left. It was separation and divorce papers.

"I'm glad I had Neville to talk to. He got hold of a divorce lawyer for me. I called him immediately and brought him the papers.

"He asked me to list the joint assets, and I had to admit that I could only list my own. He wanted me to get income tax returns for the years Hannah and I had been married, but we filed separately. He said he would try to make it so that I could stay in the house - at least for a while.

"'It is her house, isn't it?' he asked. To this I simply nodded.

"He called back in the afternoon. 'I've contacted her lawyer. From this point on you shouldn't talk to her at all. All communication should come through me. You can stay in the house for three months, then you have to leave. I can tell you, you're not going to get a penny out of this. She has made no money in the years you've been married, and your prenup states that you'd only be entitled to the gains she has enjoyed in her assets. And that's only the part which is beyond inflation.'

"'That's not possible,' I said. 'She makes lots of dough on the stock market.'

"'Not according to her financial statement which I have right in front of me, and she has no cash assets.'

"I decided to simply take it easy for a month, try not to think of all of it. I, of course, kept on talking to Neville. 'Go away for a couple of week ends,' he said. 'I can manage the store, you know that. Why don't you go hunting! I'll set up something.'"

That was in early October of last year.

"I started packing up my stuff little by little. I realized how little I really owned. Athena and I hadn't had time to accumulate furniture and the like - in fact we lived in a furnished flat. And when I married Hannah I moved in to her house and didn't have to worry about anything except clothing and whatever books and paintings I had. My paintings she hadn't liked, so they went up in the attic.

"But my wardrobe, although not extensive, still required some packing. I thought I might as well get the less used items into suitcases, and I realized I didn't have any valises. I could have gone and bought some, but when I went upstairs to get my paintings down from the attic, I realized that there were a slew of suitcases up there. So I helped myself to a few. My curiosity was peeked when one of them was fairly heavy. I tried to open it, but it was locked with one of those small locks that you find on suitcases. One of the other suitcases had a lock on it with a key, so I broke the lock on the heavy case with the intention of replacing it with the other mini padlock. When I opened the suitcase it was full of money. I don't even know how much.

"I put the suitcase back, replaced the lock and took the key with me. If Hannah came up and couldn't open the suitcase she'd simply think the lock had gone bad, shall we say. I went down to the basement level - which is where I was relegated to - and started thinking. I got out her declarations for the separation agreement. She would later have to swear under oath that they were true and correct. There was nothing there about cash. Then I went to see my lawyer, who had gotten copies of income tax returns. There was no indication there about gains; she simply showed income from dividends. That income was substantial, but there was no accumulation of cash. The dividends were cashed and simply seemed to disappear.

"'Does she live a lavish life style?' my lawyer asked, and I said No.

"'She may have been hiding money from *me*.' I said. I told him I had found some money in a suitcase upstairs.

"'It is more likely she has been hiding income from the Internal Revenue Service,' he said. 'By all rights half of what is in that suitcase should go to you. I'll follow up on it with her lawyer.'

"Then he said something bizarre. 'On second thought, let's wait until court appearance. She'll have to swear to the veracity of her statement, and if she fails to declare the cash, we can let the cat out of the bag at that time. She'll have committed perjury.'

"I rented a room in the student section of town. I gave a false name, and gave myself as a reference. The lady called that very morning and I gave myself a sterling recommendation. Then I took Hannah's suitcase to the room. I didn't see the lady at all; she had left the key to the house under the mat, and I went in. The room was nice. But I didn't quite know where to hide the money. I decided to stay until dark.

"At night I went down to the car, took the spare tire out of the well, and put the suitcase in the well."

"How much was there?" Nora asked.

"I don't know," said Jon. "I never counted it. But it is a lot. More than a million I would think."

"One night - it was in late October last year, and it was after the separation proceedings had started - I went to the Brown Bear after work. We were doing inventory, and it was about eleven o'clock at night.

"As I opened the bar door, the first thing I saw was Helen and a hunting buddy of mine, Tim, in an embrace. They were sitting at two barstools, facing one another, kissing, and his hand was down her back and virtually into her crevice.

"I got angry, seriously angry, and went over and - even though this guy was a big bruiser - I grabbed him by the shoulder and said, 'That's my girl.'

"He stood up and faced me. I realized that he was quite drunk and that Helen was quite drunk as well. He gave me a push with both his hands, and I recoiled a bit. Then I pushed him back, also with both hands, and actually not all that hard. Due to his drunken state he fell flat on his back and hit the back of his head on the floor. He was out like a light.

"There was a bald-headed guy sitting at the bar who, I thought, was paying particular attention to the incident. Why I thought that, I don't know, but it was almost as if he was taking notes.

"'My God,' Helen cried, 'You've killed him.' She went over and started to hammer her fists on my chests. I grabbed her arms and said, 'No I haven't, he is just out. I'll call you tomorrow, OK?' Without waiting for an answer, I left.

"The next day I called her and she answered politely enough, almost warmly. I got my hopes up. I didn't want to mention the previous evening; I wanted to try to get together with her again.

"'Can I come over to the shop and see you?" I asked on the phone.

"'Vivian isn't here today,' she said, 'So that would be fine.'

"At the shop we kissed and I wanted to make love to her, but she said No, that customers might be coming.

"'You know that in mid-November Charlie is going hunting,' she said. 'Aren't you going hunting too?' If you were, then you could go up to the hunting grounds and then excuse yourself and come back late in the evening. We could spend the night together.' She then said, 'I'll leave the key on the ledge above the kitchen door.' I was elated. 'What are you going to use as an excuse for going back?'

"'I'd say I wasn't feeling well and would go home,' I said. And that is exactly the way it played out. On the hunting trips we share motel rooms, and as it turned out (or was it arranged so that?) Charlie and I were to share a motel room.

"The morning after I arrived, Charlie was upset about something. 'What's the matter?' I asked. I thought that maybe he had found out about Helen and me. 'I forgot to lock the car last night. I know I put my riffle in there, but it is gone now.

I'd have to go back to Madison and get another one. That is, unless I can borrow one from one of the guys. Do you, by any chance, have two with you?'

"I saw my opportunity at this point and said, 'You know, I'm not feeling well, and I think I'll go back. You're welcome to borrow mine.'

"I knew, of course, that Tim, Helen's drunk friend, was part of the party. So I left and went back to Madison.

"I went over to Helen's and Charlie's house, let myself in, and waited. It was evening by then. I left the lights out as much as I could. I drew the curtains in the rumpus room and started watching television. It became eleven o'clock, twelve o'clock, and no Helen. Something must have happened. The natural thing would be to go home, but I somehow remained hopeful

"I fell asleep on the sofa, and woke up at seven in the morning. I shaved with some of Charlie's stuff, and I called Neville at the store and said I'd be back in two hours. I did just that - went in to work. The district manager was there, and Neville was standing, looking somewhat sheepish.

"'I have two envelopes, one for each of you,' he said. "Each contains a pink slip. Let me explain. Neville, on his application, said he had never been arrested. That is not true. What is worse is that you knew about it,' he said facing me. 'I'm sorry, but that is inexcusable.'

"Neville was taking it fairly well, but he must have been suspecting what was coming since it is unusual to see your rarely seen boss in the store early in the morning. I was still dumbfounded. Neville suggested we go and have a beer. The Brown Bear wasn't open yet, but the bartender - not the owner - was there. He let us in the back door and drew us a couple of beers.

"'Remember that guy, Tim?' he said to me. 'Awful what happened to him.'

"'What happened?'

"'He was shot dead last night on a hunting trip.'

"'Glad you weren't there?' said Neville. 'At least you

didn't do it.'

"I looked worried, all of a sudden, I guess. 'You were home, weren't you?'

"'Well,' I said, 'I was at Helen's. But she never showed up.'

"Now he looked pensive. 'Got to go,' he said. 'I'll call Celli. I need to talk to her.'

"He left, and I had one more beer and then left and went home. The front door in the house leads into a hallway that backtracks into the kitchen, and there is a window there, which allows you to see who is ringing the doorbell.

"Hannah was in the kitchen, as I entered, and she was silent as usual. I had bought some Bratwurst on the way home, and started to fix it in a pan. Then the doorbell rang, and I - and Hannah - turned to see who it was. It was Charlie, and Hannah went out to open the door. Then she stuck her head in the kitchen and waved me out there. Not a word, just a hand motion. Grave face as usual.

"I went out. Charlie was standing there with the riffle. He had put it in a canvas riffle case, and he handed it to me. 'Thanks for loaning it to me. Do you know that the sight is not adjusted? Take it out and see for yourself.'

"I removed the riffle from the case and placed it on my shoulder and looked through the sight. It looked OK to me. I then placed it on the gun rack. I gave Charlie back the gun case and he thanked me for the help I'd been and left.

"I went back to my cooking, and took my meal downstairs. As I mentioned, that's where I was relegated to for the time where I could stay in the house.

"In the afternoon I went for a walk. While I was coming home there was a squad car in front of the house, and it bothered me. My own car was parked a distance away, and I simply went to it and drove to the room I had rented.

"My cell phone rang and it was Neville. 'Where did you say you rented a room?' I gave him the address. 'Can we meet there?' I gathered it was urgent.

"We met and Neville said, 'You know that Celli and me

have become an item. So much so that we got married yesterday evening. It was just the ceremony, we'll have a reception later. You also know she is a lawyer.' I nodded. 'She has friends in the police department and some on the district attorney's staff. They say you're in trouble. The police have interrogated Hannah and Charlie. Hannah says you didn't come home until the day after the shooting, Charlie said you stayed at the motel until the morning after the shooting. They both deny that Charlie brought back the riffle.

"I said, 'and it now has my fingerprints on it.'

"'I am in the process of moving my stuff over to Celli's,' he said. 'But you know where my old room is. Why don't you come there tonight! I'll bring Celli along.'

"We met and they suggested that I make myself scarce. Neville provided me with fake papers. I pulled a name out of a list he gave me, but he didn't want to know which name I had used, and where I went. We arranged to meet in Paducah at some future date. In the meantime he suggested a complicated system where I call from a pay phone to a pay phone in Madison every Friday, and he would keep me up on developments. You didn't know that I had a full beard at the time. I shaved it off that night. The landlady still hadn't seen me. I never watched the news on TV, but I know the police wanted me to report to them."

"But you are innocent, so why not go back?" Nora asked.

"I'll be able to assess whether that is feasible when Neville has good news. So far it doesn't look encouraging.

"In a nutshell, I am accused of killing a man, I think. I don't know for sure. What I know for sure is that I didn't kill anybody."

"Then why don't you go to the police and tell them just that?"

"Because I think they have an airtight case against me. Celli, the lawyer thinks so as well. I took off when I realized what was happening."

"All I need to know, I know. You didn't do anything wrong. You have never done anything wrong." She looked at him deeply and assuringly.

"I have," he said, "and you may as well know that. I was drunk when Althea was killed in the crash…"

"And you were driving?"

"No," he said. "But it was my fault she was driving. She wouldn't have been driving if I had been sober. It is almost like *The Postman Always Rings Twice*."

"Not quite," she said. "You really have not committed a crime. An error, maybe, but not a crime. There is a difference, you know."

"I thought I ought to tell you. You might as well know that it could be that I am different from what you think."

She looked at him, and he looked at her. "No," she said, "You're not different from what I think or thought. Did it help to start talking about it?"

"Yes," he said. "That sounds like something Lionel would say to a patient."

"Yes," she said." But I am not like Lionel." Then she added, "I still think you should give yourself up. We have a system of justice, and if you're innocent you cannot be found guilty."

"I have to disagree with you."

CHAPTER 15

An unbidden guest is worse than a Tatar
A. Pushkin, The Captain's Daughter

Nora was set on staying at the motel. Mostly because she wanted to stay put for a while.
He had brought in the computers and the printer. He had wanted to start working a bit more on the decoding.
"Why don't we just relax!" said Nora.
Afterwards they decided to watch television. The post-coital silver screen. They both lay in the bed in the altogether, and she was clicking the remote.
"I always wanted to see that film," she said. "Can we?"
"Sure."
The film rolled on. It was a detective flick.
"This is fun," she said, and cuddled up to him. He was enjoying it, too.
At one point someone hits the detective over the head with a bottle, and the detective is knocked out.
"That's ridiculous," Jon said. "A light tap like that won't knock anybody out."
"Maybe he's a delicate Private Dick," she said. "I have heard of delicate dicks." She giggled. "I'm being naughty."
"I'd never have expected it of you. We are getting very comfortable with another."
"We are and that's good. But the love is there, isn't it."

He kissed her. It was a good, long kiss. "Does this convince you?"

She shut off the TV and said, "Let me convince you."

Some nights are so beautiful.

She asked again how long they could stay. She was obviously tired of the constant packing and unpacking.

"I'll go down to the lobby and see the manager."

The manager was there, at the counter. There were no guests around.

"This morning there was a private detective here looking for a lady. He held out a photo and gave me a copy. Said, 'If you see her or know where she is, give me a call.' He left his card with a telephone number."

The manager showed Jon the photo. It was Nora.

"Why did he say he was looking for the lady?"

"Her father is rich and she went and married and eloped with someone who isn't of their class. That was the word he used. But I suspect that it wasn't true."

"Why?"

"Well, he offered a reward. But he also looked unreliable."

"How much did he offer you?"

The man mentioned a figure, and Jon wrote out a check and said to manager, "This should cover our stay and then some. We'll be checking out shortly."

The guy would probably collect from the detective as well, but he had a head start.

Should he tell Nora? She'd probably figure it out anyway. He really didn't want the days of bliss to end, but things were getting uncomfortable.

They drove to a remote motel called 'The Tradewinds'. He somehow always associated that name with water, but this place was arid. As he checked in he was watching the manager carefully. Had LOLA been here too?

But the manager was natural enough.

He checked in as a single. Safer that way, he thought. The manager hadn't seen him pull into the parking lot and he had parked at the end.

He thought, before they would get settled in the room they'd go to dinner and then come back. The parking lot was empty at this point in time, and this way he could see, when they were back, if there was any sign of suspicious cars. Although, how would he know if a car was 'suspicious'?

They had an adequate meal and as they came back from their dinner there were no cars at all at the motel, and he felt good about things. In spite of his worry, both of them felt happy and warm and he felt like holding her, making love to her, right in the car.

"No," she said, "Let's go to the room. Let's unpack afterwards."

The room was on the second floor, and they went up the outside stairs. She first, and he was holding his hands on her waist and squeezing it lightly as they went up. She made some coy movements with her behind, and he relished. He already felt her nude and naked, he already held her in his arms and felt her nipples

They entered the room. They undressed hurriedly, messily, simply throwing pieces of clothing on the chest of drawers in the middle of the wall opposite the bed.

They fumbled in the dark and met by the bed and he pulled her to him, and they virtually fell on the bed, kissing, embracing.

"No," she said, "Tonight let me turn around, you know like the first time. There's something sentimental about it."

An acquired taste, he thought. In general he'd prefer her lying on her back as she had done the last couple of times. It was the same entry, in either case. He wondered if the conventional sex would ever come.

The room had been warm as they came in, and it was like a tropical night, and indeed in the rhythm of their bodies he forgot where he was, who he was, the fact that they were two not one. He thought at first how wonderful this all was and she, too, got drawn into this nocturnal rite of everlasting love. They moved, first slowly in cadence with their thoughts, but then thoughts disappeared, and he felt an overwhelming power had possessed him, he felt that he had never been in such unison with the world - Nay, with the earth - as now. And then as he came to climax there was this enormous flash of light.

He felt her push him back and loosen herself from him, and he realized that the light really *was* on in the room. He turned around and saw two men, one holding a key in his hand. The man behind him was the manager or, in any event, the person he had checked in with in the lobby.

The man with the key handed it to the manager and said, "Wait for me in the lobby. Keep the car running so it stays warm. You can take us back to the airstrip when I'm through here." The voice was powerful. He had only had a short glimpse of the man with Nora in the church parking lot, but it would appear that the man was Lionel.

He felt there was an extraordinary power present, a power he wanted to resist. It was like hanging on to a tree in a hurricane, with the wind drawing you. Maybe it was like that between Carybdis and Scylla or with the Ehrlkonig.

Jon, to some extent, regained control of himself. 'Us', he thought. Was he going to take them with him? Or only Nora?

"What do you mean coming in here like that!" Jon said. "This is a rented room, and we have privacy rights. I'm going to call the police."

"Go ahead," the man said. "But first of all you have a nerve talking about privacy, you who have emptied my safe. You ask me what I'm doing here. I have come to take back what's mine." So, indeed, he was face to face with Lionel. Lionel turned to Nora.

She had gotten to her feet; she was motionless, as in a trance. "Don't dress yet," Lionel said. "Turn around, let me see you from the back."

Jon had expected her to be defiant, to refuse, to start getting her clothes on, but she was mesmerized. She did as she was told.

He felt humiliated standing there naked, and he asked himself, why couldn't he just dress? What power did this man have? Yet, he could not, and he understood the spell she was under.

"Stand behind me," said Jon.

"It won't help," said Lionel. He laughed a short laugh.

Nora simply stood frozen with her back to Lionel. She was half in front of Jon, and he could see her face. It wasn't fright he saw in it, it was submission.

"Tell me, Leonora, what do you see in this little boy here, this epsilon. No, not even an epsilon. Don't you realize what you have with me...?" He obviously meant himself. "Weren't we a team on our way to save the earth from the onslaught of people like the man you were just cavorting with. I see you have taught him the enlightened way of intercourse. Did you do that so he and you could re-enter LOLA as common members of the Love of Life Assembly? How silly. Here you were, by my side, aiding me in the greatest undertaking the world has ever seen. Restoring the earth to an ecologically sound planet, with a size population it can sustain. Possibly preventing the new ice age, making the world a place of harmony, with no strife between the races, with no insecurity. You're part of that team. I am on the next highest stage of that organization, and I will, I will become the next Helligman. You'll be like a queen. But not the type of queen, who raises her hand in superiority to the masses, but a compassionate queen, who helps husband a world that needs the attention of men and women with foresight. Don't you understand that?" He paused. Jon was amazed at the electricity that filled the room with his booming voice, his presence, his personality. He had to keep on telling himself not to fall under the spell of this man. But what about Nora? She still stood there, motionless, showing her beautiful hindquarters to this lunatic. Was he a madman? Did he really have a grip on what he was undertaking?

"You know," he said to Jon, "The trouble with people like you, with most people, with people that aren't LOLA, is that they have no vision. They wander around on the earth, using up its resources, ruining it in the process. What do people accomplish in a lifetime? They consume. They think of their comfort. They drink, they eat, they go to the movies, they do things where the structure of society does things for them, not the other way around. Kennedy had that right. 'Ask not what your country can do for you...'. Or maybe you don't even remember, maybe you have not even heard of that."

"It is interesting you should quote a man whose vice president was the author of the Great Society."

"But Kennedy had vision. He was the last of our presidents who had vision. After all, he put a man - an American - on the moon."

"And what worldly good did that do?"

"Worldly is a good word. Has it ever occurred to you that the world may get in such a bad shape that we may have to go elsewhere in the universe to be able to live?"

Jon realized that he was doing what had to be done. If he could get Lionel into a discussion, then maybe he would be less able to mesmerize Nora.

"Had Kennedy lived," said Lionel, "He might have seen things our way. Anyway, we are having our people in government and in the political parties now. And in the next four generation we'll further our plans. You see - we are not planning to reach our goals tomorrow. No, it will take generations. But we are patient."

Jon thought, 'I've got to keep Lionel talking and discussing.'

Lionel stopped talking for a short bit, as if he was savoring the silence. "Don't you see, Lenonora, that Christ saved mankind, and he is revered and worshipped the world over today. But without Earth, there will be no mankind, so we are the superstars that will be revered and worshipped in future centuries. The betas, the gammas and the epsilons will fall to their knees and say, Holy Leonora, full of grace..."

"You're blasphemous," said Jon. "And you would have to kill a lot of people to reduce the world's population by eighty percent."

"I don't know where you come up with the notion that

we're going to kill off people," Lionel said, "Leonora must have been feeding you wrong information."

Jon looked at Nora, but she was standing there motionless.

"You were going to cut the population in half every generation."

"Easily accomplished," said Lionel. "After a woman has her baby, you have her tubes tied. The problem is that you have to do it all over the world. Otherwise one nation or one race will take advantage of it."

"And how are you going to accomplish this type of world domination?"

"Some force will be necessary," he said. "And we'll have an army of epsilons that are programmed to be even more dedicated than extreme Muslims."

"Ever read Karel Capek? The War of the Salamanders?" Jon said.

"Yes, I know. – The salamanders take over the world. There have been a lot of trashy sci-fi movies about that in recent years, but God, how you sound like Leonora. Tossing out these literary references. You're people who live in books and think that what you read is reality. Let me quote something back to you. 'If you see it in black and white is must be true.' I think it is Goethe, and it is said in a sarcastic vein. But you little, intellectual nincompoops have never woken up to that. Anyway, Yes, the army of epsilons is one reason we're working on cloning. And we'll accomplish that in less than a decade. Once again, ours is not a program that'll be accomplished in a hurry. Although the sooner it can be done the better. Better for the Earth." He stopped for a minute, and Jon was trying to find ways of keeping him talking. Maybe Nora would sort of wake up if this guy got too interested in talking about his plans, but so far she showed no sign of coming out of her trance-like state.

"Your math is over-simplified," said Jon. "The true situation is the opposite of a Fibbionaci number."

"I know all about that," said Lionel, "But to someone like you, I thought I'd make it a little simpler." He paused again.

He seemed to have some trouble catching his breath. Was he talked out? Jon figured he had to keep him talking.

"And this new society you are working towards, is that going to be maintained by cloning or by natural processes?"

"Once the population size is down to less than two billion," Lionel said, "We'll have each family have one cloned and one natural child. We may have to adjust this somewhat to keep the balance of genders."

"Of sexes," Jon corrected. "Gender is a grammatical term."

"Modern language," said Lionel. "The word 'gay' had quite a different meaning at one time than it has now a days. But you have to move with the time, don't you now? And you seem to be stuck in some very antiquated morass. You'd never be able to handle Leonora. She needs a firm hand, not some intellectual garbage, some one-sided ecology, which simply targets problems but not solutions. You'd be sitting in a home where nothing would be done, the newspapers would pile up, and you'd be like the Collier brothers when you died. You'd suffocate in a huge stack of papers, quoting opinions to one another but never taking action. You would be the cheap ones who simply object but are never constructive. We have a society full of people like that. You disgust me..."

The man took one step forward, as if he was going to go to Nora and touch her. Was he going to have sex with her right then and there? Jon's blood rose. Then, of the sudden, the man held his chest. He staggered, started wheezing. He was still close by the chair, and then he sank back into it. His gaze was fixed on Nora. At first Jon didn't realize it, but then - of course - Lionel was just out of the hospital. He had probably had a relapse of what put him there in the first place.

Lionel's voice waned as he spoke. "Don't worry, I'm not going to die on you." You could almost see in his face that he regretted having sent the manager away.

"Get your clothes on, Nora," Jon said. "We're out of here right now."

"You can't keep on running," Lionel said. His voice was now a whisper, almost.

But Nora was still as if frozen. Jon shook her, and she seemed to come to.

"Is it right what we are doing?" she said.

"Come on, little Nora, don't start doubting now. We are One, remember, we belong together. All right, so we are little epsilons, but we are epsilons in pursuit of our happiness. That's what this country is about. There are other ways of reaching the goals than what this madman thinks. He wants to kill 80 per cent of all people. I think overpopulation can be handled in different ways. If need be, let the ice age come, let it be a horrible, but divine way of eliminating 80 per cent of the population, but when the sun shines again in two thousand years, it will be a new beginning for mankind. Like Phoenix, mankind will rise again."

"And make the same mistakes," It came as a whisper from the man in the chair. But his voice was gaining strength as he said; "You just don't know what you're doing."

"Yes we do," Jon said. He had dressed. Nora was still standing naked. He gathered up her clothes, put them under his arm, took her by the arm.

"Open the door," he said to her. She did, almost like a robot. They walked out in the cold night air, and suddenly her naked body shivered, as they descended the stairs and went through the light snow cover to the car.

They got in the car, and she tried to put her slip on. "Never mind that," he said. The car was cold already, then heated up slowly. She sat with her arms over her breasts and kept on shivering. He drove down the road and found an entrance, a type of gravel road into a field, where he stopped. The car had warmed up nicely by then and her shivers had stopped.

She looked at him and said, "I have never needed anyone as much as I needed you in there," she said. "You were wonderful. I love you. I did pretty badly, didn't I?"

"You did just fine," he said.

She kissed him. "I can't get my clothes on in here. Can I go outside? It will be cold."

She opened the door and picked up pieces of clothing, one

by one. She kept on laughing and started shivering again.

She got into the car when she was dressed. He was thinking that even in the cold, dark evening, she dressed meticulously.

Then he put the car in gear and they were on their way to - who knows where - just out of there. .

Down the road a bit he stopped the car.

"I need some fresh air," he said.

She automatically followed him and they stood outside. He held his arm around her shoulders.

Then they heard the roar of a small engine. He looked forward to see up.

The small plane was going south.

She had fallen asleep for a while, in fact for quite a while

"In the old days they used to call guys like Lionel 'alienists'. He is so out of touch with decency and reason."

"I never heard the term before," she said.

"I read it in Heart of Darkness," he said.

"Oh, that one." She didn't seem enthusiastic about Joseph Conrad.

"I think it is a good term. It is an old term for 'psychiatrist', but it lends an aura of mysticism to it. Maybe madness is a better word than mysticism."

"Lionel is an idealist; you can't blame him for that," Nora said. Now, of the sudden, she seemed defensive.

"He's an apostle of darkness." Jon said. "True, he is an idealist as regards the Eco, the Earth, but the Devil has tempted him into a dogma of zealous ideology - No, a zealous means to an end. In many ways I agree with his goals but how do you get there? Not the way he - or rather LOLA - is thinking."

She wasn't saying anything. He had better drop the subject.

"You must have control of the world," she said. "He used to say that often…"

"OK, I agree, but you don't have to out-Hitler Hitler in racial cleansing."

"He isn't thinking of racial purging."

"He wants quotas."

"But that makes sense."

"How are you going to do that without killing or sterilizing a lot of people?"

"He talks about doing like the Chinese, that is to allow only one child per family. He says that it would halve the population in one generation, bring it down to one quarter in two, and down to one eighth in three. A goal of, say, two billion people on Earth could easily be reached."

"But how are you going to make people abide by that? He'd still be faced with using forced sterilization after the birth of one child and abortions by the truck load?"

She sat still. She had beaten the fear but now it had been replaced with anger - he saw that. Then he said to himself, that was probably not a bad turn of events. How to get back on track? He was concerned because they were talking about Lionel in the present tense. Lionel should be out of their lives - if he was ever there it should be in form of a foe. They should be in a post-Lionel phase of their lives; yet, Lionel seemed very much part of hers, still. Lionel still seemed to have the control he had before.

"Let's not let it - let him - throw a shadow on our love."

She still didn't say anything.

He continued, "I thought the other night, as we were driving around at random, that he, in effect, had sent us on an Odyssey to Nowhere, but he actually sent us on a mission to Somewhere."

"How so?"

"To a place in Georgia where we will be legally married."

She suddenly smiled, and tears came to her eyes. Then she was silent, and her joy was being felt, like a vibration. "Maybe this whole episode - this whole flight from Lionel -was all an act of goodness, and God forbid, should he die, his last act of goodness. It might get him into Heaven, although the good act was done unbeknownst to himself."

"Heaven," Jon said - he was feeling bitter again, "He might

sit at the right hand of the Helligman."

"Stop it Jon. It isn't fair, and it's blasphemous."

Her sudden persistence in defending Lionel made him think again that maybe the Manchurian Candidate was not as fictional as all that. Ron wasn't necessarily right.

She fell asleep again. When she awoke she had completely regained her composure. "I'm sorry about our conversation before. You must realize that I, too, am an ardent ecologist. Are you? I have never really asked you."

"I'm an ecologist. But I have accepted that the world is as it is, and that one can only do so much. I am - correction, I was a member of the Sierra Club."

"That's OK. I think I'm slowly moving in that direction too. There's only so much we can do. But what we can do, we should do."

Good, Jon thought. That's all I can hope for. The topic of Lionel will probably come up from time to time in their - hopefully long - lives, and he would have to find a way of dealing with it whenever that happened. The best thing to say would be, "Yes, dear," if she ever - or when she would talk about her former husband in positive terms. And then he thought - former husband. Lionel was still her husband. Her handling of her planned bigamy - and his own - was an enigma.

"You know," she said, "When we 'hit the road', as you call it, one of the great feelings I had was one of liberation. You're my liberator, my knight in shining armor. But please forgive me, sweetheart, I have just refound my memory, I have regained a long part of my life. You can't expect me to discard another long part as well, to discard the period when I was married to Lionel."

There was a short silence. He didn't really know what to say.

"I got my faith back," she said suddenly. "That started with saying grace before meals. And thank you. I don't think it means as much to you as it does to me, but you're handling it well. You're handling everything well. Stop here," she said suddenly.

They stopped. She had tears in her eyes. "I just have to kiss you."

They sat in each other's embrace in a no-parking zone in a small town not too far from Macon.

"It's Wednesday tomorrow," she said. "They sometimes have services on Wednesday. Can we go to church tomorrow?"

He smiled.

"You don't think the walls will come tumbling down when I enter?" he said. She kissed him again.

"That's a Yes, isn't it?" She kissed him again, and he kissed her back.

"What are our plans right now?" she asked.

"It's late and I don't really want to check into a motel at this hour. I think we'll head for Macon. I'll take my time, drive around a bit. Could you drive from time to time? I could snooze in the car. Tomorrow morning we'll get the papers - you know the marriage application - at Macon, and then we'll find a motel."

"Why not a motel now?"

"The last manager was obvious LOLA. He must have been the one, who alerted LOLA to where we were. I want to find an out-of-the-way place where we can stay for a little while again. Then we'll get married."

"I won't be Mrs. Slowe," she said. "I'm a bit sorry about that. But I'll be Ms. Kristina. That has a good ring to it. Better than Miss Kristina. It is a step up in the world to graduate from Miss to Ms."

"Better than from Miss to Mrs?"

"In a sense of independence, Yes. But I'll think of myself as Mrs. Slowe and I'll love you. I just wish we could marry under your real name."

"Too dangerous," he said. "I'll tell you some day when we're safe somewhere far away from here."

"Why can't we go there now?"

"We could. If you want to, we'll do that just after we're married."

She kissed him again.

"Remind me to call Nev on Friday," he said. It was the second time he had been afraid of forgetting to call Nev at the appointed time. He thought right then and there that by now, by *now*, he was really getting to *be* Jonathan Slowe, not the old John from Wisconsin.

They found a motel in a small village in northern Georgia - again one of those Bates-type motels that have been forgotten by the advent of the Interstate highways. He went into an office, which was a long counter with a coffeepot at the end of it. There was a bell, which he rang, and several minutes later a middle-aged woman in a shabby robe came out and he checked in. He figured he could renew the lease, so to speak, on a daily basis. There didn't seem to be a rush on accommodations right now and right here.

"We won't need housekeeping," he said.

She looked at him. He thought that maybe he had said the wrong thing. Maybe they didn't clean the rooms?

"OK," she said. She gave him a key with a huge, wooden tag on it. "You know there are cooking facilities in the room, if you'd like to prepare your own meals. We don't have continental breakfast."

"Great," Jon said. "That's some mammoth tag you have on your keys."

"That way we don't lose them," she said. "They don't fit well in pockets."

"Any churches around here? Protestant ones?"

"There's Bethel. About a mile out of town. Mostly Catholics around here," she said. "We're an old community. We don't really take to new-fangled ideas like Lutheranism."

"I didn't mean to offend you."

"You didn't," she said. "But these new things that comes up, you know, Seventh Dayers, the Clocktower people, they're run out of town. *We* don't mind ordinary Protestants though. They've been here a while."

He was reassured. Apparently LOLA was not in the vicinity. At least not directly.

Jon had been thinking about the fact that they'd now know his car. They'd settle in, and he would look around and see what could be done about the car.

"I don't want to sell Hakon," Nora said, when he mentioned it.

"Hakon?"

"That's what I call our wagon. He is wonderful."

"Hakon is Norwegian. It's a Swedish car."

"Don't let a little geography come between us, dear," she said.

After they had settled in, Nora wanted to take a bath and while she did he drove up to the service station.

"Sure, I can," the mechanic said. "We have spray equipment in the back. What color do you want it?"

The station was only three blocks from the motel, so he left the car there and told the man he would call back and tell him what color. He'd better consult with Nora.

Blue it was. He picked it up at night. He changed the plates and put his legitimate plates on. That should cover their tracks. At least somewhat.

Then the mechanic said something startling. "I found this little device underneath the car." He handed him a small magnetic object.

"What is it?"

"It's a tracking device. Do you want me to put it back?"

"No, thank you."

So that was how they had followed them. Well, informers too. But when had they put it in? Maybe the night when Harry's car was at the motel parking lot. Harry probably still wasn't sure at that point whether he had the right car and that Nora was in it, but he put in the device, anyway. Once, later, when he had passed them on the right he had seen her. And then the 'accident'.

Nora was singing as she prepared breakfast. 'My funny Valentine'. She had a nice voice. Not dramatic, but nice. It was a vision into the future - their life. He liked it right now -

sort of. But how would he cope with it in the long run? It was like the old advice, 'Never to marry a widow'.

A widower too. You would always be reminded of the things that the departed did better. Because, Athena had - had had a really great voice and he was reminded of her cheerful notes.

Because Athena sang a lot, and much of her singing - and that had surprised him at the onset - was Country Westerns. It was, in a way, incongruous with her whole personality, but then again, as time went by, he realized that her voice and her rendition gave a special meaning to what she was singing. As he was listening to Nora, a scene came back to him from four years earlier.

That particular morning he had gone for a walk and had stopped at a MacDonald's for coffee on the way. He had brought half of the cup back with him and had finished it before Athena got up. He threw the empty cup in the garbage. Again it was during breakfast preparation that Athena was singing
'Get along, little dogey, get along, get along
It's your misfortune and none of my own...'
Then she said, changing her voice an octave deeper, 'That brings me back to my days at the OK Coral. When I was cooking for all them cowhands...'
Just to be safe he asked, "You really did that?"
"Don't be silly - I'm just so happy. Be happy you have a forgiving wife. You stopped at a MacDonald's this morning. And so why didn't you bring me back a blueberry muffin!" She was now talking in a discant voice, an octave higher than her normal tone.
"Do they have them?"
"I don't know. I'm just giving you a hard time. A wife is permitted to do that, isn't she?"

"Don't you ever sing Country Western?" he asked.
"I guess you're kidding."

"No, in fact I wasn't. They can be pleasing to the ear."

"I think they are frivolous. Just think of the titles. 'I would give my right arm to be in your arms,' 'If you were me you'd leave me alone. Billy broke my heart at Walgreens', 'I don't know whether to kill myself or to go bowling.'"

"You really can rattle off a few," he said. "But most of those are parodies of Country Western. There is some very good material to be sung. 'I will always love you,' comes to mind. And, incidentally, I will."

She smiled. But she didn't really get it.

Never marry a married woman - a slightly revised thought. But he was not sorry he had done just that or was going to do just that. Small differences that had to be ironed out or lived with.

He could live with that, he chuckled to himself.

So they headed for Macon. It was Tuesday and as they passed a church in a small town near to Macon she said, "They have Wednesday services here. Can we go?"

He nodded.

They checked in to a motel as man and wife - he used the name Chuck Dickens and paid with cash on a daily basis.

The owner was a lady in her late fifties. She had a wart on her nose, and she talked with a lisp.

"We close on the twenty-ninth" she said. "Me and my husband go to Marco Island for a family reunion. But you can pay by the day until then," she said. "As long as you pay ahead of time."

Afterwards Nora said, "It doesn't really matter, we could take care of the license and then arrange the twenty-ninth to be our wedding day. We could get married and then just drive on."

They were just tired of running. It was as if they were saying to themselves, 'If LOLA wants to do away with us, let them. We love each other, and if we have to die in the midst of a love, then so be it.'

They went to services the next morning in the little church nearby. She had put on her best conservative dress, and she looked wonderful. It was a different picture than the one he remembered so often - when she was sitting in the coffee shop.

During the service, Jon looked at her. She had tears in her eyes, and she closed them and you could see her lips move in cadence with the prayer. It was as if she were shaking, then she unfolded her hands and put her right hand in his left and squeezed it and whispered, "I thank God and Jesus for having found you."

They filed out last, and the pastor was standing by the door and shaking the hands of people as they left.

"It's good to see you young people here," he said. "We will see you again, won't we?"

"Sure," Nora said, "Although we're just passing through." Jon was surprised she'd take the initiative like that. Then she said, "Could you marry the two of us?"

"Oh, certainly, and bless you. Let's go in the office and talk about details."

"I hope that the 29th is OK with you."

The pastor smiled. "You always live on a tight schedule like that?"

They got the license taken care of. She looked at him with joy as he gave his real name to the clerk.

"So your name is Jantzen." Again she had tears in her eyes. "I'll still be Ms. Kristina. OK?"

"You know it is.

They went to service the next Sunday and Nora was full of joy, a different type of elation he had not seen in her before. It was as if the chains of Lionel had finally been completely broken. Jon wondered how Lionel was faring, but he didn't bring it up. Then he thought of Athena.

"We should be able to say anything on our minds out loud," she would say. *"Even if it were to cause strife. There shouldn't be taboos."*

That was one time when he hadn't wanted to hurt her feelings for some reason or another.

"Hurt feelings are walls that keep people from being close."

And they had never kept anything from one another. At times he might have forgotten to tell her something, or vice versa, but that wasn't a wall.

They would drive in the countryside in their - now blue - 91 Volvo. They would eat at quaint places. They would go home and make love. It was as if life had decided to stand still, like the sun over Gideon, and the walls would come tumbling down whenever they were in each other's embrace.

Too soon the day came when they had to leave. Yet, it was long awaited, a truly joyous day - they would be wed.

"I wish it were farther away from Palm Harbor - like, not within driving distance," she said, "The memory of my first wedding seems to have some geographic power."

The manager and her husband were packed up - for Marco Island. They stood by their car, somewhat impatiently, waiting for the keys. Once handed over, they waved and took off.

It was an odd feeling, standing in front of the empty motel. A bit like a ghost town.

They drove the short stretch north to the little church. The pastor came in - not in his usual flashy garb, but in a black get-up with a white collar. His wife and seventeen-year-old son were witnesses. The wife was all spiffed up, hair just made and in place, lipstick - the whole nine yards. The boy was pimply, awkward, but seemed to enjoy the ceremony.

"It's early in the day for a wedding," the wife said.

The pastor didn't respond.

"Have you ever been married before?" he asked Jon.

"My wife died," Jon said. "I have the death certificate with me." He managed to answer without lying.

"It wasn't recently?" the Pastor asked.

"I didn't jump from my late wife's deathbed into the arms of my wife-to-be. It was five years ago."

"Don't get defensive," said the pastor.

"In any event Nora is the woman in my life."

"Well, your mother too, maybe," the pastor said. "Or, again, that of course is not a given." He laughed - a hearty laugh that seemed to come from way down in his substantial stomach.

The pastor, somehow, never got around to asking Nora.

"You may now kiss the bride," the pastor said at the end of the ceremony. Then, relaxed, he said, "Why don't you come over to the house and we'll have a glass of Mogen David."

It was a delightful house, with bookshelves, full of books. The wife was still all spiffed up and sat on her chair with the air of wanting these two intruders out as fast as possible so she could get on with whatever she was doing. Not chores, for sure.

Afterwards Nora said, "It would be wonderful to have a simple house like that with books and Mogen David. Those are the real values in life. Not success like Lionel's."

She was over Lionel. He hoped.

Once outside he said, "Do you want to stop somewhere and check in to a motel."

"What I'd really like is to go back to the area in Tennessee where we were a while back. I know it is quite a ways. It would be a good place for a honeymoon. We can celebrate up there."

As they drove through Northern Georgia, into Tennessee and then into the mountains the snow started falling again. They stopped at a rest stop, and as she stepped out of the car she would shiver. "It's nice to look at, but it so *cold*."

They drove on and reached the top of the mountain and drove off on the side road they had been on when they were there before.

It was a winter wonderland, a purity of air framed in falling snowflakes. As they drove she grabbed his arm and squeezed it.

"It's perfect for a honeymoon. Let's find a motel, check in, and then let's us tease ourselves a bit," she said, "And go have dinner first and then proceed to the nuptial bed."

He smiled. "You know, when I saw you first I was lusting

after you, and I had this fantasy that you wore a short black dress, and that it was buttoned up all the way on the back. You would sit on the bed with your back to me and I would unhook the hundreds of buttons, one at a time."

"*Quel raffinement.* Well, I guess I'm wearing the wrong dress."

But he realized that the time of 'love' versus 'being in love' seemed to have come. The act of lovemaking was quieter, more serene, as were it something holy, something ordained. In spite of Genesis 11.

They came to a motel, and she said, "Are we close to the restaurant where we had dinner a couple of weeks ago?"

He said yes and did the checking in. "Let's go find the place where we ate before, and then…"

They had dinner in the restaurant they had been at once before. It looked quaint on the outside, but the interior was quite elegant.

They were led to a table and the server came over and said, "My name is Jusuf. I am your server."

It must have shown in their attitude that they were pleased with him because he seemed to be pleased himself.

"Nice," he said, "Many people hostile because I'm Arab."

"Don't bother us none," said Nora, tongue in cheek. "I usually never talk slang, but I am just in such a liberated mood." To Jusuf she said, "You don't mind my talking slang?"

"Don't bother me none," he said and laughed.

"Here are menus and wine list," he said.

"We'll order some wine right off," Jon said. He pointed at an entry and said, "Where does the wine come from?"

"From the grape," said Jusuf.

Jon laughed, then said, "Where does the grape come from - and please don't say the vine. What country?"

"Yes," Jusuf said, "It comes from the country, from the vineyard."

"Why isn't it the 'wineyard'?" mused Nora.

"I often wonder," Jusuf said. "English most mysterious."

He served them well. Both wine and food were good.

"Your chef is excellent," Jon said.

"I haven't tasted her," said Nora.

"Don't compete with Jusuf, please." They both chuckled. It was an excellent meal, and an excellent idea.

"Can we take the empty wine bottle with us?" Nora asked. And she put it in her bag.

No one else had come to the restaurant. They had had the place all to themselves.

"There is a scene like that in 'La desobeiance'" said Nora.

"Name dropper," Jon said teasingly. "The book is actually in Italian."

Jon tipped Jusuf well. He bowed and said, "Most generously."

"I forgot my watch," Jon said, actually addressing Nora, "What time is it?" But Jusuf answered, "It is 20:29 on the 29[th.]

"You always give the time that exactly?"

"Always," he said. "Must be accurate and complete. And I'm off for the day in 31 minutes."

They smiled and waved as they left. The maitre'd apologized for the missing crowd. "Wish I could say, 'See you again,'" He looked sad.

So did they.

"Did you take the bottle as a memento?" asked Jon. "I, incidentally, have a bottle of brandy in the trunk of the car."

"Right," she said, "We didn't have an after-dinner treat, and I'm in need of just that." She added, "But I yearn for more than what just comes in a bottle."

"We'll take the brandy with us too," he said.

"For 'Afterwards'."

Outside, it was dark. The night was still with a little snow in the air. They kissed, and intertwined as they went to the car and took off.

Her wedding night had arrived in pure, white beauty.

CHAPTER 16

I don't know what happened. There was all the blood, and Harold opened his eyes. He died almost at once. He never spoke, but he gave a sort of gasp.
W.Somerset Maugham, Before the Party

He stepped out of the car but she was already out of the car, waiting for him. In spite of the cold. She had the cognac bottle from the trunk in one hand, her handbag in the other.

He grabbed her in his arms and carried her over the threshold. Once inside he let her down, and she put down the bottle. She took out a candle and a book of matches from her bag. She placed the candle in the empty bottle.

He helped her. The candle filled the room with a weak, soft light - a bit like the time when they were 'married' before.

"Light onto our castle," he said, and she smiled.

"It is that," she said.

Even in the soft light the room was stark, unwelcoming, the host to many trysts, too many weary traveling couples arguing about mundane things.

He embraced her and pulled down the zipper in the back of her skirt.

He had a hard time finding the bed and was going to put on the light, but she said, "Not with the light on tonight. In the dark."

Odd he thought. Maybe it was the dismal locale. He turned out the light again and opened the curtains. It had gotten dark, and the light from the parking lot lamp right outside gave the room an eerie ambiance. So he closed them again.

She sat on the bed and he stood in front of her. She started undressing him - one piece of clothing at a time, and when he was completely naked, she placed him in her mouth, but just for a short while, and then she said, "Now you."

So he sat down, and she stood up. He first drew down her skirt. She wiggled to help him, but he sensed the movement as a sensuous shadow in the soft back lighting.

Then he stood up and she sat down on the edge of the bed. Was this the moment he had been waiting for? He helped her off with her blouse, then her bra. What marvelous breasts. In the semidarkness they stood out like a beacon guiding ships at sea. He reached down and grabbed the elastic about her panties and she lifted herself so he could ease them down her legs to the floor.

His head cast a shadow on her Venus mound, but as he stood back, and as she moved back and lay down, the hill was exquisite in the candlelight. This *was* the moment he had been waiting for, desiring. At times he had wondered if it would ever arrive. He was sure now.

He kissed her nipples; he kissed the pubic hair. He was aroused. He placed his hand on her left breast. She lifted her hand and held his. Was she going to move it away as in the past? Instead she moved it downward towards the hill in her center.

And, indeed, she led him to her Venus mound, to the enchanted lips. His heart jumped with joy. He felt wetness in the magic moss there; he was impatient - no time for preliminaries. It was as if he was saying to himself, 'Don't let this slip away, smythe while the iron is hot."

She spread her legs, lifted her legs high and his hope soared. But what he had thought would be an easy entry became more difficult than he had thought. His erectness waned as he tried, then she sat up again, and massaged him with her hands and her mouth. He tried again.

As he finally managed to enter her completely there was a

small shriek from her, and in the beginning the expression in her face was almost one of pain. It showed even in the faint light. He was strangely conscious of all the things that were happening.

She followed his movements, almost with hesitation, then in an accelerated fashion. Then he really started feeling her movements and they became hectic, and she moaned,

It became passionate, wild. He felt the rhythm like an African drumbeat go through his whole body, he sensed her hard breathing, he felt her perspiration. Her moaning became louder, uncontrolled and, at the point when he was at his climax, he felt the tremor in her whole body and then she shook with convulsion after convulsion. She grabbed him about his neck and drew him down and kissed him, bit his lip. She was as if in a trance.

Then, slowly, as if she woke up, she looked at him. She closed her legs around him, and scissored his phallus inbetween her limbs, and as he waned he was kept inside her.

But the convulsions continued, at longer and longer intervals. Then finally they abated and she said,

"I'll let you go now."

He turned over and they lay, side by side. He reached for her hand, and she squeezed it.

He could feel her falling asleep, and half in a dream state he heard her whisper, "I love my husband." Then her lids closed, her breathing became regular - a sound of bliss.

They slept a short while and as she stirred he woke up. He went to the bathroom. He felt as if transformed. For the first time - since Athena - he felt pure after an act of love.

As he put on the light, the fan came on, as well. It was a hellish noise. Always something to mar the bliss. He looked at his torso in the mirror, as if it had been sanctified, then he looked down at himself. To his surprise he noticed some blood on his groin and member. 'Bad luck' he thought, 'but it worked out OK. Then he heard her say, "Can't you turn off the fan. It sounds like a panzer-battalion."

"Only if I turn off the light. It's OK, I'm finished anyway.

Incidentally," he added (and in the process wondered if he should say it at all),"You're getting your menstruation."

"No, I'm not," she answered.

She'd know better in the morning.

He came back to the bed and lay down again, next to her. Then she sat up.

"I want to pour us a glass of cognac," she said, "The 'Afterwards' has come." And he thought with relish that there would be more and different 'Afterwards' to come in future days.

She got up, tiptoed around the bed, took the bottle and went over towards the bathroom. She had to feel her way in the faint light of the candles. She ran into the wall before she found the door. She opened it; she didn't put on the light. Her aversion for the sound of the fan.

He felt relaxed. He almost smiled as thoughts of the past came into his mind. The accident with the green car was long ago, it was forgotten, all was restful. Lionel was a thing of the past. Everything was good. He had enjoyed this traditional sex as much as he had the sins of Sodom.

"It may be a bit," she said, "I want to wash up some."

He thought, 'Was the fire still in her so she needed to cool off?' She apparently figured that it was too dark as it was, but as she put on the light the fan came on again with a horrible, screeching noise.

"I hate it," she said, "When you can't turn on the light without the fan going on. I'll turn the light off again, and work in the dark. Anyway, I like the idea of us having the 'Afterwards' without artificial illumination. I can still see from the candlelight in there."

He was marveling at her skill to work without light, then thought - well, all she actually had to know was where the soap was.

"Are there glasses out there?" he asked.

"Yes," she said, "unless you want to call them plastics."

He laughed. She could just see his outline as he lay on the bed.

She had put the bottle on the floor, and was going to run

the water, when all of a sudden the light came on in the room. Why would Jon put on the light, after what they had just said, she thought. Then she heard a voice, as out of nowhere. "Better say your prayers, punk."

She stiffened in fright, then looked out.

She saw the outline of a man standing - with his back to her - with a long pistol in his hand - pointing it at Jon. Strange thoughts - irrelevant ones - entered her mind. Why was the pistol so long? She saw Jon's face and body past the man's silhouette. He was sitting up in the bed, stark naked. He was frightened. His skin was pale, and he looked as stiff as a board. She noticed he had lost his erection. There was still some blood on his member. Why did she notice things like that? Then suddenly the reality came to her - was this the end?

The man lifted the revolver a bit and fired. There must have been a silencer on it, because it was just a small, insignificant popping sound. A bullet hit the frame of the picture above the bed and a big crack appeared in the glass, but it didn't shatter. Again irrelevant thoughts passed through her mind - it was such a schmaltzy print. Then she thought, 'a reproduction, not a print. A print is drawn.' Why these fleeting thoughts? Motel art. Mortal art. It was as if she was just an observer to a bad movie.

Then she got to her senses.

"You know what I've come for," the man said, "And if I don't get Dr. Ondmand's computer right now, you're dead."

The man stepped back from the bed, and his back was only a couple of feet from the bathroom. He lifted the revolver and this time took aim. She could see he wasn't going to miss. The first shot had been a warning - she knew that now. Why didn't Jon say something? Like, "Sure, I'll give it to you." It wasn't worth his life to keep it, was it? Furthermore he had secured the copies.

Through the corner of her eye she saw the shadow of the cognac bottle. She took it in her hands, carefully so as not to make noise. The man was virtually in front of her with his back to her. He was still, in a position of concentration, his arms outstretched with both hands on the handle of the revolver, aiming at Jon's body. She stepped out into the half-opened doorway with the bottle over her head and she swung it down on the man's skull with all her force.

It was as if he became compressed a very small bit, as if he was stagnated for a fraction of a second, and then he felt forwards like a dead weight. In the fall, the front of his head hit the corner of the bed and it got turned around in a grotesque way. His eyes were as if fixed directly at her in a cold, blinkless stare of both surprise and reproach.

Then there was a silence, a deep, odd silence - for just a fraction of a second - and then in a gush, blood started streaming out of the side and of the back of the man's head. The pistol had fallen loosely out of his hand in the fall.

Jon sat on the bed, motionless. His face was white.

She had hit the man so hard that the bottle had broken. Again obscure, meaningless observations froze in her mind - the bottom of the bottle had landed in an improbable manner right side up on the floor. She stood with the ragged top of the bottle in her hand as if she was going to start a bar fight in a Western saloon.

She had been calm and collected for the last seconds, but now she started shaking. She had totally lost a feel for reality.

"I think he's dead?" said Jon. He was getting out of his trance. He looked at her. "You saved my life. - You saved *us*." Was there amazement, admiration in his eyes?

He got up. He put on his pants and fastened his belt and went over, and felt the throat of the man. "He *is* dead. We've got to do something."

She was still standing there, motionless.

"He may be dead, but you didn't kill him. The hit he took against the corner of the bed killed him."

He went over to her and embraced her and kissed her. "I love you," he said. "But let's get out of here. First..." Even in the kiss, she seemed as if she belonged in some other world.

He went through the man's pockets. He covered his own

hands with a paper napkin and took out the billfold and removed all identification. He left the money in. He took out two sets of keys.

"Give me the plastic bag in the waste paper basket," he said. She obeyed mechanically.

What was he doing? She thought.

He removed a piece of tissue from the bathroom and took the revolver making sure not to leave prints on it. Then he placed it in the plastic bag.

She followed it all as if simply a bystander on a dark street. It was as if she couldn't see Jon and the man, as if there were a bubble around her and nothing existed outside the bubble. Then in her mind she heard the sound again, the horrible sound, of glass hitting the skull and the world stood still. There was the silence, a deadening silence in a literal sense, and then there was the sight of the blood.

"Can you pull yourself together and get dressed?" he asked.

She automatically started putting on her clothes. He had his on already and said, "We've got to get out of here

"What do you plan to do?"

"I'd like to make it look as if he was the guy who was registered and was staying in the room. That'll give us some time."

She felt Jon taking her by the hand and led her out the door. She felt the cold air on her and the bubble expanded and she sensed the lights in the parking lot, and then she felt she was standing by the car, while Jon opened the door and helped her and the bubble inside and once inside the sense of the bubble disappeared. She was cold and she felt Jon kiss her on the cheek and close the door and go around the car and enter the driver's side. She was shivering and it was waking her up, she was regaining a full consciousness she seemed to have lost for a spell.

He started the car and put on the heater. "It will be just a minute and it will warm up. Try to sleep," she heard him say. She didn't answer. Good council, she thought, but how do you do it? Or will it come by itself? She didn't really know if she was awake or if she was asleep.

There were no lights on in the other rooms. There was one car parked away from the lamplights.

"Must be his," said Jon. "A rent-a-car, I guess." He went over to it, tried one set of the man's keys in it. The larger key opened the door and he ascertained that, indeed, it was rented. There was nothing in there other than the contract papers. First he was in doubt then he decided to remove them.

Once back in the Volvo, he said to Nora, "The gal at the counter wouldn't recognize me. This way it will be difficult to identify the fellow. It will give us a head start."

"Try to sleep," she heard him say again.

"It's past midnight," she heard him say. "Not by much, but we'll arouse suspicion if we check into a motel this time of night, so I'll just drive around."

She could feel the warmth from the heater a little, then a little more, and it was as if she were an ice cube thawing out. He had the heat up high, and soon it was toasty. She felt sleep coming over her and then she slept. She'd wake up now and again and look to her left and see his somber profile, concentrating on the road.

Then she woke up completely and the car was stopped. He was sitting there staring out, and she asked him where they were. Then she thought it was silly to ask, because he had said he'd just drive around.

They were at a rest stop. "I have to go pipi," she said.

"I'll follow you to the rest room," he said.

That was nice, she thought. A sense of humor returned to her. How many beaus offer to walk their belles to the toilet? There was a slight smile on her face.

"What are you smiling at?" Jon asked. Why ask, he thought, he should just be happy she wasn't weeping.

"Just you," she said. She squeezed his arm and said, "You're wonderful."

The night was warmer now; they must be further south, she thought. Or maybe on lower ground. The rest stop was empty save for a couple of cars. There was a surly woman in the rest room mopping the floor.

'A grandes eaux' she thought. Where did that come from? *'la parure.* Maupassant.' Or did she remember it wrong?

"You're not supposed to be in here while I'm mopping? Didn't you read the sign?" The woman was even surlier when she spoke. Well, she couldn't have an easy life.

"I didn't see any sign."

"I must have forgotten to put it out," the woman said. "Go ahead and use one of the stalls."

When Nora got out the floor was wet over to the sinks.

"You shouldn't step there," the woman said.

"I want to wash my hands."

"Hoyty toy," the woman said, "I want to wash my hands. What's the matter, afraid of a little piss?"

Nora went out and Jon was waiting. The conversation had done her good; she was back in real life.

Jon kissed her again, and she kissed him back, then as he finished the kiss, she puckered her lips and he kissed her once again. Then she hugged him close to her and then for some reason she started crying.

"Now, now," he said, and she said, "I'm all right. Really, I'm all right."

In the car he pulled some tissues from the glove compartment and dried off whatever tears were left.

"Can you stay awake for about five minutes?" he asked. "I just need a little shuteye."

She almost right away heard his regular breathing. She realized, then, how tired *she* was

Thoughts kept drifting into her mind. At one time the horrible noise banged in her head, and she held her hands to her ears. That just made it worse, then it ebbed away, little by little. But she saw the scene, she saw the man fall, again, the head turn, she felt the horrible silence, she saw the blood.

Then Jon woke up. She felt for his hand, and he squeezed hers affectionately. She was not alone again. She realized how much she needed him. Not for reasons of love, yes for reasons of love, too, but for reasons of support.

He had slept for fifteen minutes.

"My batteries are charged again," he said. "Ready to roll."

As he put on the headlights, they saw a man come over towards the car, but the minute the lights went on he changed directions.

Jon looked worried.

"I wonder what that was about," he said. "Probably just nerves on my part." He drove off. She started getting drowsy again. She heard him say, "At least we're not being tailed, and I don't think he got our license plate number, if he was snooping on us. But why would he be...?"

And at this point she fell into a deep sleep. She awoke once when he was getting gas somewhere.

Then suddenly it was light. He had stopped the car. They were in a sterile parking lot, parked behind a square, one-story building. She noticed the garbage bins.

"Ready to have some breakfast?" she heard him ask. And she was suddenly quite awake.

"I must look a fright," she said. "Can I go to their bathroom and freshen up in there?"

She took out her toiletry bag and they went into the restaurant. She went to the ladies' room.

He sat down at a table and was sitting there as she came out and went back to the car to put the toiletry bag into the back seat. He watched the sexiness of her gait, and again he was reminded of the wonderful forms the clothes concealed.

She came into the diner and sat across from him. She placed her hands on the table and reached over to him and he took her hands.

They'd get through this all right.

"We'll linger here until ten o'clock, then we'll go on and find a motel, and get some sleep," he said. She smiled demurely, thankfully. That was a Yes. "The sleep in the car isn't restful. Maybe with a real good sleep I can forget all of this. It is funny, for years I was trying to remember; now I'm trying to forget."

CHAPTER 17

> Not one returns to tell us of the Road
> Which to discover we must travel too
> Edward Fitzgerald, Omar Khayyam.

Celli was not the type of woman who would catch your attention right away. You had to see her several times and in several situations in order to appreciate her physical qualities.

Jon thought it was like beer - you had to acquire a taste for it.

What caught the eye immediately were her breasts. She was a slight woman, but her breasts were large and protruded in an almost provocative fashion. All this without the air of sexiness.

In fact her general comportment was one of her always being businesslike, serious almost somber, and the color of her skin was not the stuff that beauty-cream ads were made of. It had a gray hue to it. Her eyes were grayish as well, fairly large, wide-set.

As you saw more and more of her it was as if you got to appreciate more and more of her appearance. But it was almost piecemeal, one day one might notice how flat her stomach was, the next maybe how well-shaped her legs, then her shoulders. It was almost like taking a course and having a lecture a day. Maybe it was due to her no-nonsense attitude, the fact that she didn't flaunt her good features, but made the beholder work for it, so to speak.

Her eyes were mostly cold, even when she smiled, which was not that often. One exception was with Neville. When they were together she would occasionally kiss him and her eyes would light up. She really loved that guy. It was obvious.

The day they had met John, now Jon, at Neville's old room she had been as businesslike as usual. She thought John's actions were dumb, to be blunt, that he had bargained for trouble when he took the infidelity route. Even if Hannah were a bad bargain, he should have found other ways of handling it. Yet, she had seen many situations at the law firm she worked at, which were similar to John's.

When Neville had mentioned the computer disk John had sent him, she had told him to open it. You never could know what was on it. When it arrived, enveloped in plastic, she had been alert and told him to preserve fingerprints, just in case. However, there obviously was no need for that. But she also told him to make a copy of the disk.

"I have deciphered the password, but the rest is in code. Do you want me to try to decode it?"

She had said, "Sure," and he had said it would take a bit of time. But in less than two days he was back with it. He had figured out the code (as had Jon), and he had simply applied the Find and Change functions to the whole document and transferred it to another document. He had then printed it out.

The contents startled her - even *she* showed physical signs of surprise, at times anger, as she was reading it. Part of it was that portion that Jon had read the week he and Nora had been whiling away the time, waiting for the marriage to be officiated.

But due to events, and the longing for the physical touch of Nora, he had never finished reading it completely. Celli, however, a fast reader had completed the reading in one evening.

"Have you read it, honey?" she asked, and Nev shook his head. "Only decoded it. Well, I picked up bits here and there."

While reading it - because he was present as she did so - she showed more emotion than he had ever seen her display.

"It is very, very interesting," she said, "They advocate sodomy as the preferable sexual practice, you must have seen that?" she said that - more to herself than to Neville. "I guess they hypnotize the women into liking that. Hard to imagine."

At another point, she said, "It's also interesting that they enlist preferably physicians, biological scientists and lawyers for their high betas. They plan on perfecting human cloning and they have already produced apparently healthy babies. They are doing the cloning in a manner that will preserve certain 'genius' characteristics of the donor. It isn't the master race theories of Hitler, though; they seem to want to maintain the racial balance of the world. I have to say that for them."

Then a little later: "They have total disregard for women. They are actually talking about the Taliban in great praise. They don't dismember, but they submit their woman to obedience by hypnosis. The woman goes to 'sessions' every six months or even more frequently. I guess to get an obedience booster.

"They want to reduce the world's population to a small fraction of what it is now, and they are, when their day comes in a couple of generations, going to effectuate a policy where a couple can have only two children. One child is cloned. They are going to have enclaves where the 'natural' fruitful multiplication occurs, but they'll keep those enclaves in control, number-wise, and it is all a bit like Huxley. The writer seems to be an assistant to the Founder who was documenting their 'Gospel' and also keeping a diary of daily or long-term decisions. It's all quite diabolic.

"But I don't know, and I assume you don't know…" she was addressing Neville rather than herself at this point,"How your friend laid hands on this document. He obviously stole it, and it must be a powder keg to sit on, sweetheart. I can see where it could be dangerous for you. They, the so-called LOLA, seem to have a substantial network already, and they seem to be quite ruthless. I don't want to find you dead some morning."

Neville laughed. "This is the first time I've ever seen you

lose your sense of what's rational. This could just be a manuscript that someone is using for a book. John always wanted to be a writer, and maybe he is going to transcribe this into a bestseller."

Celli drove west on the shores of Lake Mendota, up to the law office of the firm where she was working. The day was a sunny winter's day. The snow was glistening on the lawns, the students, all bundled up, were walking on the sidewalks in the direction of the University, and the lakes were frozen from shore to shore. Except where the power plant was located.

There, there was a spot that never froze over, and it was occupied perennially by ducks. They seemed to enjoy the weather as much as she did.

She had hardly sat down at her desk when the receptionist announced on her intercom that a man from the police department wanted to see her. There was nothing unusual in that. She handled many criminal cases. In fact that is how she had met Neville at first. "Do you know a man named Ronald Jones?" the detective asked her.

"It's the first time I hear the name," she said.

"Well, but do you know a man of that name?"

"How could I when I don't know the name."

The detective looked sheepish.

"He said he contacted you to meet someone named Nevada."

"I don't know anyone named Nevada. What is all this about anyway?"

"Well," said the detective, "Jones was arrested for impersonation and fraudulent misrepresentation. He had fake papers, attesting that he was a psychiatrist who had graduated from Harvard."

"And I suppose he hadn't."

The detective was a bit taken back.

"How did you find all of this out?" she asked.

"He had a curriculum vitae that didn't jive with that on record. The course numbers were incorrect."

Then the detective said, "I'm really the one who is asking questions."

"Not unless I'm being interrogated. I presume that this was just a friendly conversation. If there is nothing more, then I wish you good luck on your investigation. Although you have your man - Jones, was that his name?"

"Well, we don't have the contact. We're interested in the party who is supplying the fake papers. But thanks for your time."

She went to a nearby pay phone and called Nev. They got together at a coffee shop shortly thereafter.

"How did this thing with the psychiatrist Ron come about?" she asked. "Was it your friend, John, again?"

"He just told me on the phone that someone was coming who'd need our help. I took care of the paperwork."

"You messed up on the CV," she said. "No matter how, the point is, I want you to start - *no,* get started and not stop until you're finished - destroying all evidence you have about our - your operation."

"The computer, too? If so, how do you get rid of a computer?"

"You're usually resourceful. How about walking out on the ice on Lake Monona over to the point at the power station. There is always a thawed-out spot there. Just throw it in. But erase all files first." She looked angry. Then she said, "This is serious. When will you talk to John again?"

"Tomorrow noon."

"Set up the meeting with him. You had an arrangement like that, didn't you."

"Sure, in Paducah."

"How far is that from here?"

"Six hundred miles, I'd think."

"Tell him we'll meet him in say four to six days. In the meantime, I'll turn in my resignation here. It won't be difficult - I was just passed over for partner."

She added, "We'll be pulling up stakes. We're moving. In four days. Hope there is enough of a window of opportunity.

In the meantime can you make yourself scarce? Go home to mother, for instance?" Her voice dripped with sarcasm.
Then she added, "We'll meet at home in four days."

Jon and Nora had checked into a new motel. It was trying, this moving.
It was Friday, and he said, "I have to call Madison today. Would you like to come along to the phone? I can't call from here."
They left the motel, and drove 30 miles down the road.
At twelve he called Nev.
"Hi," Neville said, "I'm glad you called. I'll do the talking first. First of all your divorce went through the twenty-eighth."
He was not a bigamist, he thought.
"Secondly, we'd like to meet with you. It is just a matter of deciding on a place we can meet. Do you remember when you once told me about your first roll in the hay?"
"Sure," Jon said.
"You mentioned a motel, remember that?" Jon nodded, and then realized he had to say,"Yes".
"Meet me there in three or four days. Just check the motel daily to see if we have arrived. I'm sorry I can't be more specific, but my wife has said that there are some things here that have to be straightened out first." Then he added,
"You are...?"
"Slowe."
"What?" then after a pause, "I get it."
"OK, see you then. You can be there, right?"
"Sure."
"But I have no news on the other front. My wife is coming as well."
So Celli was coming as well. Good.
"OK, I'll be seeing you."
Then he hung up.
Jon was wondering what had happened that they wanted to come and meet in person. Maybe it was simply that it would make conversation easier, but it was a lot for them to do. OK,

so he was a friend, but to drive - what, seven hundred miles to do a friend a favor - it seemed too good to be true.

He went back to the car and said to Nora, "Nev and Celli are coming to Paducah and want to meet with us."

He went over and kissed her.

Her kisses were absent-minded at first. She was thinking of other things. Then it suddenly dawned on her what he had said, and she said, "That's great." It cheered her up. "They may help me out of my dilemma. Help me make up my mind. You know I've taken a life. I need to know where to go from here."

'My mind,' he thought. Again, it was no longer plural.

"We'll see our way through this," he said.

"It's more what I'll decide," she said. "That's why it'll be good to talk to them." She sat and looked in front of herself, as if she was looking into a vacuum.

"I killed a man," she said. "I have to pay the consequences. The thief next to Christ wouldn't have gotten into Heaven had he not been on the cross, himself."

He didn't say anything. He'd try to influence her later on, when she could think more coolly, when she was further removed from the events. He decided not to tell her anything about the fact that his divorce had gone through.

He sat right next to her and kissed her again. She cuddled up to him, put her head in the cup of his shoulders. She was weeping a bit.

"Thank you for just being there," she said.

After a while he said, "There is always one way out."

"And that is…?"

"For you to change identity. Neville can do it when we see him in Paducah."

She looked bothered. Then she said, "I like my name. I want to be Nora Kristina. I don't think I could live, now, trying to be someone else. My name, particularly now, is a badge of happiness."

"Well, you wouldn't be what you aren't. You would be like a brand name suit with the label torn out…"

"And sold at a discount price."

Bad comparison, he thought.

"As a last resort." Then she added, with an ironic look, "We talked about it earlier. I guess I'd have to change my hair color, use eye make up, get some phony glasses and wear cheap-girl clothes."

Was she mocking him? No, she was complaining. He had been earnest in his proposal.

"I must admit I like the suit with the name label," he said.

"It will probably wear better," she said. "I am glad we *are* legally married. I was thinking before about my mother who gave up her Catholicism to marry my father and her not living in grace!"

Her mother had often talked about the state of grace, how she had given it up when she married a Lutheran. The veiled words had come back to Nora the day before. Was her mother saying that whenever she and her dad made love that she was in mortal sin? Maybe that is a thing she, Nora, had felt it would be as well. Maybe that is why she had insisted, as a teenager, on having some sort of church blessing before letting a man into her. But was the way she hung on to her boyfriends, in actuality, not 'letting a man into her?' Maybe that is where it all started, the misery with Lionel, with her refusing to accept the LOLA as a church.

"But there are practical reasons too. For instance I couldn't be made to testify against you, or the other way around, should that ever come up," she said. "Our marriage has helped me get through what we have just gone through. The way fate has been throwing us curves, I think of our marriage as being a safe harbor in a hostile sea. You must forgive me for being so terribly and totally uncertain. To me it is a terrible struggle to decide what to do about all of this."

Then, strangely, she looked a little happier.

But he thought she had to make *right* decision. The one that was right for *them*, not just for her. Even if it was her future, mostly, that was at stake.

They checked into a motel and he fell asleep and slept for

a couple of hours.

When he woke up she was already up. She had brought some coffee and some rolls from the lobby.

"I feel I have aged ten years. Will you love me when I'm old?" she asked. Then she added, "How silly I am, that's a question I'm sure has been asked a million times."

She bent over him, and he drew her to him. And she found herself, all clothed except for panties, under the sheets with him. Afterwards she said, "I guess that's what they call a quickie. And your dress gets all crumpled up." She smiled. Was she settled down? Was the seesaw at an equilibrium point? Had she made up her mind? It could be jail time. He shuddered.

"What will the future bring? I still don't know." They were lying on the bed, resting.

"Let's wait and see what Neville and Celli have to say."

"You have a lot of faith in him," she said, "And in his lawyer-wife. I guess it helps me, too, to know that we can get some outside advice."

The room in the motel they had checked in to had cooking facilities, so they ate in. Nora relished her role as a cook, finding out what Jon liked, finding out how to cook for him and it kept her mind off the events.

"I like being a real wife," she said. She was somewhat more cheerful. Then she got pensive again. It was a constant up-and-down battle. He had to keep her mind off the events.

Their room - as do most motel rooms, had a TV. He was actually sorry it did. It had been nice to be out of the reach of the news. News was like the long arm of society, reaching in and telling you things you didn't want to know. When there was no interesting news, the media would stir up something to talk about. It was all business. Get customers, keep the customers. He recalled the CEO of the sporting goods store. That was what he said all the time. And, 'Keep the cost down.' He thought of Neville for a spell, then he drifted back to reality.

But TV might keep her occupied for a spell. It was as if he had a sole purpose right now - that of keeping her calm.

"I think we should use our time to enjoy each other. Maybe watch TV. Maybe do other things."

They did the other things first.

Afterwards, she seemed happy again. They lay naked on the bed and he clicked on the TV.

He put on the local channel.

There were some ads playing, then the announcer came on. Nothing about a killed man.

"Maybe they haven't found him yet," Jon said.

She looked anxious again.

Then the announcer broke in. 'We have breaking news.'

They showed a reporter talking to a member of the police force. The sign said, 'Clearwater Police.'

"The murdered man," said the announcer, "Is a well-known psychiatrist, Lionel Ondmand. All the evidence points to his wife. The poker with which he was bludgeoned has her fingerprints on it. She was known to be in the house the night of the twenty-ninth, and she has several motives. Her husband wanted to divorce her. There was a one million-dollar insurance policy that she could cash in on. And she has totally disappeared..."

They had brought him back alive just so they could kill him. Now they'd pin it on her.

She shot off the TV. She was trembling.

"They can't do that to me, can they?" she asked. Then she started shaking and crying. "What do I do?"

"What do *we* do, you mean." He held her tight. She was sobbing. "Those son-of-bitches. They killed him and are putting it on me."

"Take it easy. Let's think this over, calmly, if we can. There is a way out." It had come to him right away. The only thing to do.

"Once again, let me suggest that you simply change identity and we'll skip to somewhere where there is no LOLA."

"Yes," she sobbed. "But I've told you I don't like it."

She looked up at him, smiled through her tears. "And I'm afraid."

"We are both afraid, but it is the only thing to do. To run away from it."

"But it isn't just LOLA. Now we also - both of us - have to be afraid of the police," she said. She was sobbing again.

"You don't have to worry. Lionel's murder took place while we were at the motel after the wedding."

"How did you sign in, there?"

"As a single. Fake name and license plate number. They never check the number."

"And here?"

"Mr. and Mrs. Jantzen. I felt good about it, now I don't know."

"But can't we undo that?" she asked, "We could check out right now and I can check in as myself at another motel. That way we can substantiate my not being in Palm Harbor." After a bit she said, "We could just check out together. That way she'll see me. I'll say something that will make her remember me. That way they'll know I wasn't in Palm Harbor."

He said, "But that doesn't cover - how do they put it - 'the night of the twenty-ninth?' You could have been in Palm Harbor and driven all night, and presented yourself here."

He added, "It seems to me there are quite a few things that would put you some place which was not Palm Harbor. Why don't we just get going, and think of something."

He was pensive. Just to be on the safe side, they checked out again and both checked in as two singles at another motel. The personnel would remember them, but would it do any good?

In the morning they went over to the car, and drove off. Nora had started crying again. "I'm sorry, but this is awful. What should I do? I should probably give myself up."

"Don't be silly. What would you tell the police?"

She looked out in the air.

"Don't ask that," she said. "Show some compassion. I did it for us."

'*Us*' was right. He pulled into a rest stop and put his arms around her and said.

"Whatever is in the future, we're together. That's what counts. I love you."

Her crying subsided. "Thank you," she said, and she turned and kissed him hard. "Be at my side all our lives, say you will."

"I'll be there. There at your side, all our living lives," he said. And he meant it. He didn't relish the thought that now she was in the same situation he was in. He wondered how long it would take for the police to catch up with them. How they could avoid them.

If they caught up, then would they find out about him?

"The police must have found the man in our motel room by now. The first thing they'll ask is if someone checked into a motel in this area very late. That is if they figure out that the dead man in the motel is not the man who checked into the room. Think of it this way: when checking around at other motels they'll be looking for a single man, not a couple, and certainly not a single woman. As I said, I gave a false name on our wedding night, and a false vehicle description."

"But the crime is there - the man I killed - whether they find us or not. I have to live with that."

"Once again, *you* didn't kill him, the fall unto the corner of the bed did - at worst it was self-defense," Jon said. "Pure and simple."

They drove up to Murphysboro and checked into a motel there. They put the TV on right away.

The local station continued their coverage of the Ondman killing, but had nothing on the man who had died on their wedding night.

Then the announcer said, "We are continuing our coverage of the murder of the famous psychiatrist, Lionel Ondmand, who was found dead in his house. The exact time of death hasn't been established but it is sometime in the time frame of the 29th. The fingerprints on the poker that killed him have been identified as those of Mrs. Ondman. There is an All Points out on her. Any information..."

Jon had turned off the TV.

Nora looked aghast. "Who do you think killed him?" she asked, as if she was asking herself the question.

"LOLA," was Jon's spontaneous answer.

"But why? He was high up in the organization. He would be the supreme Helligman in a couple of years."

"They found out what had happened with the diary and the computer. They are aware that news will leak out about their organization from time to time. Right now they have satisfied low betas and gammas who can testify to how good and great LOLA is, but if some of the truth comes out, what do they say then? They could drag Ondmand into court and he would have to say, under oath, that he had not produced the document that compromised LOLA. To say that they're really fake. A better way of answering charges to the public is to say that 'it isn't so at all,' and if you do away with the fellow who owns and has written the stuff he can't be asked about it." Then he added. "But I don't think it will fly."

"Really: who did it, who in the organization? It wasn't Harry; he's dead. Who in LOLA would resort to killing like that."

"Well, they sent someone who was willing to kill us. So they have, shall we say, executioners."

"But what do we do?" She was close to tears. "Poor Lionel."

Come on, he thought, what is this 'poor Lionel' stuff! Again, can't she see that he was an evil man?

"I still think the best course for both of us would be to give ourselves up. You haven't committed any crime, so you shouldn't have to worry." He all of a sudden remembered the conversation he had had with Celli that night in Nev's old room. "The truth doesn't matter," he said, "Only what appears to be the truth. I know I'm in the same situation with Tim's murder as you are in Lionel's death. Both are frame-ups. But that does not help us." Maybe he shouldn't have said that.

She stiffened. "If Lionel had been alive, he would never have allowed this to happen."

Then all of sudden she seemed almost angry.

"You should never have taken Lionel's computer," she said.

"What do you mean? I said Yes when you used me as a coin to flip, and I did what you wanted me to."

"I told you to take the book, not the computer."

'Not true,' he thought.

"You wanted to have something that would make Lionel agree to a divorce. There was nothing in the book that you could use."

"My life would have been simpler if you hadn't taken the computer."

"So would mine." Were all thoughts of love suddenly gone?

"Right. Then you could have continued to spend your nights with Shirley What's-Her-Name. You could turn on the light and look at all her freckles and her red pubic hair. Or did she shave herself down there. There are women who do that, you know."

Her tears were gone.

"She was not my girlfriend or anything like that." He was annoyed.

"Come on, now. She stood there, with her hand on your shoulder and looked at me and said, 'So this is your new girlfriend'. The word 'new' certainly implies that she had been your girlfriend before."

"But she didn't say 'new'."

"Yes, she did."

Suddenly Nora started crying again. "I'm so sorry," she said. She looked up at him and said, "Come over here." He did, and she pulled him down to her and kissed him. On the lips, on the neck, on his chest. "I love you," she sobbed. "It's just that it's all getting to be a bit much for me."

Things can be tragic-comic. Her statement about Lionel before she started crying was a bit like the title of one of those Country-Western tunes she had cited earlier. But once again there was this latent loyalty to Lionel. He had to convince her to let go of her loyalty to this madman. It was time for some stronger words.

"Let's be practical," he said. "LOLA may still be after us. Actually," he added, "It's time you take a look at the diary. Have you had a chance to at all?"

"Only four pages," she said. "But my eyes are worn out." All the weeping, he thought, he could understand that. "Maybe you could read out loud to me some of the stuff you haven't had a chance to read to me. The diary may throw more light on why LOLA is so anxious to get it back. Do we have a copy handy?"

And he read, and she almost gasped at times.

He read the portion dealing with the employment of Dolores Juanita. A couple of lines he had further deciphered during a spare moment in the past days read,

When Nora dies, Dolores can step right into her shoes. Some day soon.

He now saw anger in Nora's eyes. Perhaps no more see-saw.

"You were right before," she said. "None of us have a choice."

"Exactly," he said. "I was planning on our having a nice dinner, but now I'm not in the mood for anything – eating, lovemaking."

"Nor am I," she said. "But I love you." She had regained her stamina. "We'll be all right. We have done nothing wrong. No ill will come to us."

"But I think it would be wisest to get new identities, and Neville is our man."

"We'd better discuss that some more," she said.

She still had her reservations.

The next morning they went on their way to Paducah. It wasn't all that far - about a hundred miles he estimated.

CHAPTER 18

Hanging and wiving goes by destiny.
William Shakespeare, The Merchant of Venice.

Jon - we'll keep on calling him Jon - and Nora had checked in at the motel in Paducah twice, without success. Nev simply wasn't there yet.

In the meantime they found other accommodations.

Their third try worked out.

It had been late as they rolled into Paducah and Jon stopped at the entrance to the motel. He didn't like the fact that he had been there twice before and asked for Neville, so he said to the girl at the counter, "Any vacancies?"

"I'm afraid not, not tonight. I can have you booked somewhere else." She was pleasant.

Then he felt a tap on his shoulder. It was Neville.

"This is Mr. Slowe," he said to the receptionist.

"Oh, I didn't know. You should have said so."

Jon laughed silently, and accepted the key.

"The room is right next to ours." Then, as if to explain, "As I told you on the phone, Celli is along. You might need her."

"More than you know," said Jon.

"Why don't you get settled in your room. I'll come and knock on your door in half an hour. We have a lot to talk about."

"Do you want me to bring Nora?" Jon said, then added hurriedly, "That's my wife's name."

"Let me check with Celli. I'll knock on your door in about five minutes and tell you whether you should come alone or with...what's her name."

"Nora."

"Yes."

They walked out to the parking lot in silence. They stopped at the car, and he motioned to Nora to step out. Neville extended his hand.

"What does one say to the bride, 'Much happiness'?"

"Definitely not 'congratulation' if there is anything to conventional custom."

They parted at their door, and went in.

"He didn't really seem to be pleased. Do we have to see them right now?" she asked. "I'd like to rest a bit first."

"Go ahead," said Jon. "I'll stave him off for half an hour when he knocks."

"Love you," she said.

As Neville came back to his own room Celli said, "So I guess Jon arrived."

"Well, sort of. They arrived."

"What do you mean 'they'?"

"He's got himself married. Nice girl. A bit older than he is."

Celli looked at him in disbelief.

"The fool. He hardly learns he is divorced and he goes and marries again. He didn't know the latest developments in Madison. He could really have spoiled everything. Didn't he understand any of the spiel we gave him about how to stay out of sight."

"He didn't even know about the divorce when he got married."

"But he *does* know that the divorce went through?"

"Yes, I told him that when I talked to him last. I think there are even worse things that have happened than their marriage - we'll find out when he comes in here. Do you want to see only him or see both of them?"

"That is not an easy question," she said. "I presume he wanted me as his attorney - but at some future time he may not need one in Madison. We'll see. You said they thought they needed my help. Maybe it has become more complicated with her in the picture. What's her name?"

"Nora or something."

"How's that for precision," she scolded. "Well we'll find out."

And ten minutes later he phoned their room. Better than knocking, he thought. Then there was a knock on their door. Neville opened up and they were both standing outside. He looked over at Celli, and she nodded, so they entered.

"My best wishes," she said. She took out a manila envelope from her attaché case and gave it to Jon. These are your divorce papers. But before we go on, do you and or your wife want to be represented in anything by an attorney?"

They both nodded.

"Would you consider me your attorney?"

They both nodded.

"We'll agree to that temporarily. Note that I'll charge you for my time and effort. Incidentally, I have passed the bar in Florida. I'm from there originally and always wanted to go back."

"We'd love to have you represent us." said Jon.

"There are other things that may come up that may prevent me from being an attorney for both of you, and in that case one of you may have to find someone else to represent you. But now, to the business at hand," Celli said. She brought out a legal size, yellow pad. Addressing Nora she said, "What's your name?"

"Leonora Kristina," said Nora. "I kept my maiden name."

"And yours?" she asked of Jon. He seemed to be startled then realized that she had only known him under his real name.

"Jonathan Slowe. But I married under my real name."

"Jonathan Slowe. You must be kidding." She was sharp, he thought, she got it right away. She then added, "I, of course, have not met you before, although you look a bit like one of Neville's friends. But he had a full beard."

Playing lawyer games, Jon thought.

"Why don't we start from the beginning, and you start, Jon, then Nora can go on. And correct each other only if you think something is grossly wrong in your spouse's account."

So they spent most of two hours going through all the events that had taken place since Jon left Madison and since Nora got married to Lionel and then later to Jon.

Celli was taking notes copiously as the talking progressed. She looked serious, very serious.

"On what day did you kill the intruder - in self-defense that is - in the motel room up the road?"

"The twenty-ninth," said Nora.

"It may have been after midnight," said Jon.

"No..."

"Yes..."

"Hold it a minute," Celli said. "It's important."

They talked amongst themselves and Jon gave way. Yes, it was before midnight.

"When did you see the report on the TV that Nora's husband - Lionel, is that it? - was killed. And was that reported on the day it happened.

"According to the reports it occurred on the twenty-ninth." They both agreed.

"Well, I'll check on it. But it is obvious that Nora couldn't have been in two places at the same time. The question is, could she have killed her husband, driven or flown to where she says she was in time to establish an apparent alibi? That is what a DA would ask the police to establish. Now, where did the... death... of the intruder happen - in what town, at what motel?"

"Not too far from Clarksville," Jon said, "About five maybe ten miles out of Clarksville." He gave the room number.

"You've sure gotten around, haven't you? Clarksville is not too far from here?"

"I don't know," Jon said, "Maybe eighty miles, maybe even less."

"So I could drive there and back in a day's time?"
"Certainly."
"What else happened on that day?"
"We got married."
Jon thought all of a sudden that by chance he was now not a bigamist. The divorce was on the twenty-eighth. Nora must have thought the same. She smiled at Jon. The first smile she had produced during the half-hour they had been there.
"Did you get married in Clarksville?"
"No, in Macon."
"I know where that is," said Celli. "That's no good. You would have had time to go to Palm Harbor and do your deed there and then gone back. But Clarksville - that would have been hard to do. Anything in Clarksville that can be established would clear you of anything that happened in Palm Harbor on that day. So tell me!"
"Jusuf." They almost said it in unison.
They told her the story of the dinner, and Jon gave her the details about how to get to the restaurant.
"But it may not be in existence anymore," said Nora.
Celli looked puzzled. Jon told her that the maitre d' had mentioned that the restaurant was in financial trouble.
"Of course," said Celli, "the most obvious and important alibi would come from a police report about the dead Mr. John Doe in your motel room in Clarksville. So if Nora is also accused of the demise of Mr. Doe, then she couldn't have killed her husband. I would rather not touch that, because it would mean that you, Nora, would have to stand trial."
"That's perfectly all right," said Nora.
Celli, once more, looked puzzled. Most people would try to avoid an involuntary manslaughter charge.
"OK, if you say so. I need to know what name you checked in under. Because you said earlier that you never used the Slowe name."
"I used the name Joe E. Brown."
Celli laughed, a cold, calculated laugh, and said, "Some people have a way with words. You have a way with names."

But I don't think many people now a days know who Joe E. Brown is. Do you have anything else linking you to the location or to the...event?"

"I carefully picked up his gun and put it in a plastic bag and it should have John Doe's fingerprints on it."

"And not yours?"

"And not mine."

"It is not advisable to drive around with it. Supposed you were stopped by the police for some reason or another. Can you deposit it somewhere?"

Jon said, "Lilleby. I have a safety deposit box there."

"They don't check for weapons there?"

"I think you could walk in with a bazooka, and they wouldn't mind. I'll go to Lilleby at the first convenient moment. It's not too long a drive."

"This is where I have to tell you the reason for my not being able to represent both of you, maybe. In a defense of Nora in Tampa it would be in Nora's interest to have Jon testify on her behalf. That would be one witness that would put her well out of reach of her husband on the twenty-ninth. But in representing Jon in Madison, I could hardly, unless he asked me to help him give himself up, use him in any overt situation. So there's the conflict. My sense is, anyway, that his testimony wouldn't help - it would not be credible. Too many people claimed to have seen Nora on the twenty-ninth in Tampa. Furthermore, if Jon testified it would fuel the old theory of a conspiracy. And Jon would be in the same boat you're in." She was addressing Nora.

"Jon is fairly safe at the present," she said. "LOLA probably doesn't have a fix on him, yet. Ondmand may have had, but I think it was just people from his inner circle that were on the track. And his two henchmen are dead. Regarding a police search for you, Jon, you've made a couple of mistakes. Using your real name once when you signed in to a motel and, of course, when you got married. But for the time being you're probably safe.

Nora interrupted. "But I would have to go through with a

trial down in Tampa. I would plead not guilty. I didn't do it."

"You are *very likely - no with absolute certainty* facing at least life in prison. It could be the death penalty," Celli said.

Nora was pale. "So what do I do?"

"We scram," said Jon.

"I didn't hear what you said," said Celli,"but don't repeat it." She looked over her notes. "Let's discuss it further when I get back from Clarksville."

"Am I going with you?" asked Nev.

"Yes, honey," she said to Nev, "We have our work cut out for us tomorrow."

She pulled out a bottle of bourbon from her suitcase. Let's relax with a drink. Incidentally, Jon, I hope you have gone easy on the drinking while you have been down here, as we advised. It may be advisable to maintain moderation."

Always giving legal advice thought Jon.

Celli and Nev found the motel without too much trouble. The East Indian girl behind the counter was easily swayed by the fact that Celli - with her business card - showed that she was a lawyer. "I'm an officer of the court," she said, and that had a visible impression on the girl.

And it was the twenty-ninth.

"But he died, you know," she said. "He was nice man, but fell and broke his head."

"I had heard that," said Celli. "Is there any coffee left from the continental breakfast?" she asked.

"Oh, we only serve tea," said the girl. "I can make you a cup."

"You're very nice," said Celli. And she had a cup of tea with honey. She was sitting in the breakfast alcove, and watched the television. And there was a piece on the killing in Palm Harbor. It happened on the twenty-ninth and it was reported to have happened between eight and eleven at night.

Neville checked on the restaurant, and sure enough, it was boarded up. The maitre d', whose name no one seemed to know, had already moved elsewhere, whereto no one knew.

Jusuf, well people knew Jusuf, but they also knew him to be an illegal alien.

She stopped at the police station. She talked to the police chief and to the sheriff. They told her that no so-called death had been reported. But she was insistent, so she and a detective went to the motel and to the room. There was no bullet hole in the picture; the room had been newly carpeted.

"The rugs wear out," said the owner. He was Indian, like the girl at the counter. "But no one died here," he said.

"The girl told me someone actually did."

"She was talking about something that happened last year. Someone fell and hurt their head. He wasn't dead."

So, empty-handed, she and Nev drove back to Paducah. It was a dilemma. She would want to clear Nora of having caused the death of her husband even if that would complicate her in the case in Clarksville, should it ever come up. But apparently LOLA had been there already. John Doe must have been LOLA, she had gathered that already, and maybe their network reached even up here, and maybe they were making the killing go away altogether because they wanted her charged in Palm harbor. With new - but uncertain - information she had from Madison, it might be that she had only the Florida case to worry about. The word 'only' was poorly chosen.

Then suddenly a thought occurred to her. This affair with Ron Jones, the psychiatrist, could that have been LOLA as well? Jon had mentioned that the man had had trouble with LOLA. Could his arrest have had something to do with that? Then she postponed the thought to a later time, stored it somewhere in her brain. Better stick to the task at hand.

It was late as they drove back into the motel in Paducah. Celli was pensive, "I'll have to go to Florida, but right now I'm tired," she said. "In the morning we'll talk a bit more."

Neville came and talked to Jon and Celli. "We'll stay here while Celli goes to Florida," he said. "She'll look at the lay of the land there."

The next morning they had breakfast at a nearby diner and

before anyone had even come close to finishing their meal Celli said her goodbye. A warm kiss to Nev. Strong woman, Jon thought. "She's a strange one," Nora said when they were alone.

"She's a good lawyer," said Jon.

No answer. A bit of jealousy?

CHAPTER 19

O conspiracy!
Sham'st thou to show thy dangerous brow by night, when evils are most free?
Shakespeare, Julius Cesar.

Celli went to Westlake Wetlands first and saw the realtress. Jon's description had been exact; she had no problem identifying the gal. Celli knew she had to find a place to live, anyway, so she asked the gal to show her a couple of places that were for rent. She was driven around to several, but was waiting for an opportunity to see the place where Jon lived.

And it happened rather rapidly. The third place was in the association where Jon lived. But to Celli's amazement she was shown a unit, which she was pretty sure was Jon's.

"Do you know Jon Slowe?" she asked the realtress.

"No," she said, "Can't say that I do."

Celli thought she could check with Jon later, but she rented the unit for three months.

"Has it been unoccupied for a long time?" asked Celli.

"In fact it has," said the realtress, "But it is in perfect order. The last occupants were the owners. They stayed here during the summer months. A bit the reverse of what people do - the so-called snowbirds - but I guess they need the money."

When she signed the lease she noticed that the gal signed with her right hand.

No doubt about it. LOLA had gotten to her or maybe she

had simply pocketed the cash she had gotten.
After having settled in - it didn't take long, she only had two suitcases - she went in search of the divorce lawyer. She first called, and the phone was answered by a receptionist.
"Is your address the one shown in the phone book?"
"No, we're at a new address," said the female voice, and she gave it, and gave Nora directions. When she got there she found an elegant office in a good section of town.
"I'm a lawyer," she said, "And I would like to see your boss on a private matter. He can be of help to me."
She was led into the office, which was as nice as the anteroom. There were signs that its occupant wasn't quite moved in. She was offered a seat in a comfortable chair, which faced his desk.
"It's my intention to start a law practice here," she said, "And I was told by a colleague up North that there was an organization called LOLA, which I absolutely must join."
The lawyer smiled. "Oh yes, most definitely. They can be of great help to you. I'll make some contacts for you."
He made a phone call, and it ended with him giving his name and telephone number. "Not there," he said. "But he'll call back."
"Incidentally," Celli said, "do you know someone by the name of Nora Ondman?"
The lawyers smiling, yet unattractive features froze into a configuration of even less attractiveness.
"Why are you asking?"
"I'm thinking of representing her."
"Do you know where she is?"
"No."
"Then how can you represent her?"
"Someone has been calling me. He doesn't give his name."
"She's a fugitive, you know," he said. "She committed a murder."
"Well, my contact said she was in trouble with the law, but didn't specify the nature of the crime. Maybe I should go see the police."

"No," the lawyer said. It surprised her, then on second thought she knew why. He'd be on the phone with LOLA right away. She'd be tailed.

"Incidentally what's your name and how can I contact you?"

But she had already got on her feet.

"You have been most useful," she said. And he had.

She was admitted into the district attorney's office. The man was tall, meat-less and bald. He had cold eyes, and a business-like attitude. But his eyes lit up when he saw the woman enter the office, and Celli was acutely aware that she had attracted him sexually. She sat down in the seat offered her, fronting the large desk at which the man was seated. She pulled back her skirt a bit, crossed her legs and made sure it rose a bit on her legs.

She stated her business and he said, "She, obviously, must give herself up."

"I can make her do that, through the contact, but only if there is some light at the end of the tunnel."

"Which tunnel and which light are your referring to?"

"What kind of charge are we talking about?"

"First degree murder."

"That is not getting her to waltz into your office, with or without a book and a computer."

His gaze switched from sexual curiosity to intense attention.

"Are we talking about a laptop and what kind of journal...or literature are we talking about?"

"How can I tell, if I don't know your literary taste?" she asked. "And your musical one, for that matter. Do you like the fifties music, such as 'Whatever Lola Wants'?"

"I play it every day."

"Then," she said, "You know what literature I'm referring to. But let's stop beating around the bush, do you speak for LOLA."

"I speak for the citizenry of Pinnelboro," he said.

"Come on, now, this is not a re-election matter. I need to know."

"We never reveal that we are," he said.

"Good enough. What about the judge who is likely to preside? Is he LOLA as well?"

"He, too, is serving the public. He, too, can't tell."

"All right, then, what's your best offer if the book is included?"

He thought a bit.

"You are going to deliver both her and the book?"

"If the offer is satisfactory."

"The case has been widely publicized. The evidence is overwhelming, believe me. Before a jury she wouldn't stand a chance."

"I've heard that speech by prosecutors again and again," she said. "Be serious and answer my question. I accept that you have some, on the surface, real good evidence. My client - if I can call her that - claims she is innocent and she has been framed."

"And that is one speech I have heard from multitudes of defendants."

"But LOLA's involved."

He thought a bit. The woman was sharp. She had edged her way into being in a bargaining position and she had the LOLA information she needed.

"With satisfactory literary delivery, we could go for involuntary man slaughter, although it is going to be difficult to present in that light. After all, Dr. Ondmand was hit in the back of the head. She would have to plead Guilty, of course, and would be asked to describe how it took place. The judge is bound to ask that question at sentencing time."

"Therein" said Celli, "lies the difference between a Guilty plea on her part vis-à-vis a Not Guilty plea. In the latter case she wouldn't be obliged to describe something she hadn't done. But let me take the proposal back to her contact and play it from there. Do I have your promise that I'll not be followed or tailed?"

"As much as I can give it. Someone contacted the police and told them you were coming here. Some loose gun may take it upon himself. But I'll try." He was starting to stand up to indicate to her that the interview was over when she said,

"Can we have a talk with the judge. Sometimes judges renege on promises made by DAs."

"It's rather an irregular procedure - beforehand, you know, but I'll see what I can do. Where can I reach you?"

"*You* can't," she said. "I'll contact you. As the French don't say, *cherchez l'homme*."

The remark made the otherwise gray man smile. Probably the closest he had come to a laugh since he was in his teens

She and the district attorney saw Judge Dommeren in chambers. He was a man of about sixty. He had a round face and a belly to match, but he actually cut a fairly impressive figure.

He had a kind smile as he smiled at Celli, and she was reminded of something that happened in her childhood. And that put her on guard. Her father had had frequent arguments with the neighbor three houses down. She, therefore, disliked the man as well. He was having a barbecue one late afternoon and was grilling in a round-bottomed Weber grill. He had started the charcoal and then gone into the house. She stole into the property and poured water on the starting fire. She hid in the bushes and saw the man curse, dry everything out and start again. After a while she repeated the procedure. But the wife of the man had been on the lookout, and came out. Celli started running, and could easily have outrun the woman. She turned around to see how far ahead she was; the woman had a kind and inviting smile on her face. So Celli stopped running.

Not a good move. But she remembered, and it came back to her in a flash as the judge smiled at her. Judges usually don't smile.

"I've been briefed about this, Miss," he said.

"My name is Celeste Sagfor. And it is Ms."

"Yes, naturally."

"This is a little unusual, but there are some important cir-

cumstances so I have allowed it. First let me ask you Ms. Sagfor, what made you so interested in this case?"
She hadn't expected this question. She thought fast. She didn't want to tell him about Neville being her husband and of Jon, other than indirectly. She rapidly thought that she could feign interest in joining LOLA. She had already floated that point earlier in other connections.
"I heard about it from a friend of Mrs. Ondmand. He knew I was thinking of joining LOLA, and asked me if I could help in any way. I got the lady's side of the story from her friend, and I was asking myself if there wasn't a better way of doing all of this than the plan that seemed to have been pursued. I believe strongly in the mission of LOLA, and as I said - or maybe I didn't get that far - I intend to get membership in LOLA. It seemed to me from what I heard that this - shall we call it a book? - was essential to LOLA and that it was important to get it back. I don't know if Mrs. Ondmand is innocent and didn't kill her husband as she claims, but from my point of view it is important that the documents be returned to their rightful owners. Taking those items was, if I understand all of this correctly, a bit like stealing the Ark of the Covenant."
"Well put," said the judge. He looked at the district attorney in an approving way. "And you know what the minimum sentence is that one could give in such a case? You think that might entice Mrs. Ondmand to give up the documents. Then, of course, if she doesn't feel so inclined you could tell her what the worst case scenario would be: the death penalty."
"Correct."
"I take it you have heard what you came to hear," the judge said. She took this as a signal for her to leave, and she rose and extended her hand. But he didn't get up.
"See you in court, one way or the other," he said.
"Have a good day," she said, and she gave a slight wave to the district attorney who looked fairly satisfied with himself. But what did he actually do? These men who take credit wherever they can.
Celli had said she would be gone two weeks, probably.

She would call on Nev's cell phone from time to time, so they should be available.

Nora had suddenly become calm. No more seesaw, just on an even keel. Whenever Jon tried to broach the subject of fleeing it all, she simply put her index finger vertically on his lips and said, "It's all decided. I'm going to love you with all my body and all my soul these last days we're together."

And they made love. The way God had ordained it. And he realized how much it meant to both of them.

"Why should our love story have such a grim interlude?" he asked. He had chosen the word carefully. He had not said 'end'. But she used words of finality in her next sentence.

"Don't you know that all haunting and real love stories are tragic. There are never happy endings. And the reason is that intense love can have no other ending in literary terms. Look at 'Romeo and Juliet', 'A Farewell to Arms', Eric Knight's 'This Above All.' You have the intense love in print. It just can't last forever. The reason is that what is described is 'being in love', not loving. And love is much more difficult to make, shall we say 'interesting' to the reader."

"You think we are back to 'being in love again?"

"In a way, Yes. But only because we have to compress many years into a few weeks. And so let's do that, as we have these last days."

And they did just that.

Four days later she said, "Can we do it the LOLA way?"

"You really like it that way?" He was thinking of Ron the Psychiatrist at that very moment.

"Oh, yes, and you like it, too. I know that. It is Oneness of a kind. And I have my menstruation."

He suddenly remembered what she had said on the twenty-ninth when she had said 'No I don't.' He realized with elation, of a sudden, what it meant. He had been her first man.

Celli came back from Palm Harbor much sooner than expected. But she just came back for a conference with Nora and Jon. Nothing definite yet.

"My old law firm has an affiliate or a sister firm down here. Madison helps Florida if they need help up there and vice versa. So I got the legal scoop on all of this." Celli looked very serious. She looked at Nora. "I talked to the district attorney who, of course, said you should give yourself up. I told him I'd try to persuade you to do that, but there were probably loose ends that had to be tied up before it could be done."

"I'm in favor of doing that," said Nora.

"Please, Nora," Jon said. "You don't know what you're saying."

"Stop arguing," Celli said. "The complication here is LOLA. The other complication is that the case is classified as a murder case, and that the number of witnesses - all LOLA to be sure - putting you on the scene of the crime is long and impressive. Your fingerprints on the poker could maybe be explained away, but if you were there you'd have the opportunity and the means. And they have the motive, namely that the beneficiary in his will and his million dollar life insurance policy were the Church of LOLA up until two days before his death at which point you were made the beneficiary."

"In a way I'm rich," she said bitterly.

"Only if you were cleared, and I might as well make it very clear to you, there is no way you'll be cleared. You are looking at life in prison, maybe even the death penalty."

Nora got white.

"I can advise you in legal matters," Celli said, "But I cannot aid and abet you in any shape or form. So why don't you think it over? Neville will come and see you in your room at about eleven, and you can talk, and we can all go out for lunch."

And Neville came to the room and said, "Change your identities and take off. Well, you can remain Mr. Slowe, but you, Nora, would have to get a new name. Maybe change your appearance a bit."

"Is that what Celli suggests?" asked Nora

"You're missing the point. That is what I suggest. You

must be able to figure all of this out."

"Of course," she said. "I'm sorry."

They talked to Celli again. "The judge, who would probably be presiding is Judge Dommeren. I think that both he and the DA are LOLA."

"That's not so good," Nora said.

"Well, it may work to our advantage. The DA was talking to me in veiled tongue. But I got the feeling that in return for the diary or book or whatever you'd call it, they could go for a reduced charge. For instance involuntary manslaughter and you would look at the most eight years, probably with four years off for good behavior. I understand from Neville that you would like to stand trial and have it taken care of in the open."

"But I'd have to admit to something I didn't do."

"But in trying you they couldn't pin the John Doe event on you. The timing element."

"But this is a land of justice. How can they do this?"

"Well," Celli said, "as a general question that is not a given. There are many people on death row who later are found to be innocent. Particularly now with DNA evidence. That shows the fallacy of the system."

"The way the system was, but with DNA evidence isn't it now more foolproof?"

"I was using it as an example only. DNA evidence would play no part in this trial, should there be a trial before a jury, of your involvement in your husband's death. I forgot to mention the other day that at the time you married, legally, you were probably a widow. No problem of that kind for you."

Nora smiled sarcastically. "Thank God for small favors. I get away with murder in Clarksville and then later am convicted of a murder in Florida I didn't commit. But at least I'm not a bigamist."

"Exactly. And you must look at the end result. You'd go to jail, in reality for four years, maybe, whereas you might spend your life in prison otherwise."

Nora had tears in her eyes. She looked at Jon. He looked

as if he was going to cry, as well.
"Well," Celli said, "talk it over and let me know tomorrow. If you decide to go with a reduced sentence we should all go to Pinnelboro. You, incidentally, don't have the apartment there, Jon."
"How is that, I paid for three months, if I remember correctly."
"I saw the realtress. I could recognize her by your description. She said the unit had been vacant for six months. I checked with the neighbor, the only one you actually talked to, and he denies ever having seen anyone in the unit. I think she simply pocketed the money - you gave her cash, right?"
"I have a receipt."
"Is she right or left handed?"
"Left handed, definitely, I was wondering about how odd she was when she signed for the money and the lease."
"Well, she is right handed and there is nothing odd about the way she writes."
"Is she LOLA too?"
"There could be involvement, but I don't think so. I think the DA was working on a theory at one time - and maybe still is - that you, Nora, had someone working with you. From that point of view it is good that the association with Jon is not generally known." She was quiet for a spell, then said. "Run along you two love birds and enjoy one another. Come back and let's decide how to play it from here on in. If you decide to go with a plea, then I'll go back to Pinnelboro and call you from there.
And Nora had decided. Yes, a plea.
"It may be a couple of weeks. Let's say I'll be back here in two weeks after I've laid the groundwork. Then we'll all go to Florida. Use the time well, you two," she said. She had a, for her, unusually tender facial expression as she said this.
There were calls in the two weeks from Celli, but otherwise it was bliss with a haunting backdrop. Except the last two days. The events to come started weighing on Nora.
Understandably so.

Celli went back to Westlake Wetlands. She didn't want to call on her cell phone or from a phone in Palm Harbor, so she drove north. In Land O' Lakes, just before the entry to I-75 she bought a telephone card and phoned Paducah on his cell phone from a pay phone. She told Neville about what had taken place.

"Talk to Nora about it, see what she says. I'll talk to you tomorrow. I'll call from some place where the call can't be traced, like right now."

"You're not in…" he asked. She interrupted.

"No, but I'm going right back."

When she called back the next morning he had talked to Nora and Jon.

"She has the problem of how to plead guilty to something she hasn't done, but she has come up with an idea. Is it all right if she talks to you directly about it?"

"I don't like it, but I'm representing her, so I might as well talk to her at some point."

Nora got on the phone. Her voice was trembling a bit. She was constantly feeling the pressure.

"I've been thinking things over," Nora said to Celli. "When I swung the bottle that night at what you call the John Doe, I didn't know who he was, and I still don't. It was semi-darkness, and even if it were a relative of mine, for instance my late husband, I wouldn't necessarily have known it was he. How is the judge going to charge me? With what words?"

"I see what you're driving at," said Celli. "He would ordinarily say something like this, 'Leonora Ondmand, you are charged with the killing of your husband, Lionel Ondmand. I'm not too sure about the word 'killing'. It may be 'murder' or it may be 'involuntary manslaughter'. But something to that effect."

"Could he avoid using the name 'Lionel Ondmand'?"

"I don't think you can dictate to a judge the words he uses to charge you."

"Well," Nora said, "Without that concession it's no deal."

"And if it's no deal, what then?"

"Then I take off with Jon to places unknown."

"That's what Nev has been suggesting all the time," Celli said. "Why should the judge let you dictate the choice of words he uses?"

There was silence on the phone, then suddenly Nora said, "Is it possible to say the following: 'If someone swings a poker at someone in the dark and then flees, how does she know whom she has killed?'"

"The judge will simply say that it is reasonable to assume that it was Dr. Ondmand."

"And can't you say that it could have been someone else lying dead and that Dr. Ondmand had fled to other venues. Wouldn't it be embarrassing for the court if Dr. Ondmand was found alive after sentence had been handed down?"

"Well they know it was Dr. Ondmand. Positive identification has been made. But the argument," Celli said, "might possibly fly, after all they are getting the book back. The argument I have to make is that although identification has been made, it is not really identification of the person who swung the poker - pardon me the hard object."

Celli little by little sounded convinced.

"Anyway, work on it some more. I don't want you back in Florida yet, so stay there. I'll be in touch with you in a couple of days. Have you been waiting at the phone all day?"

"Yes, we have." It was Neville's voice. He had been on the other phone all the while. "We didn't want to chance your calling without us being here."

"You mean to tell me you haven't had anything to eat all that time. You must be hungry."

"I brought in some rolls this morning, but otherwise you're right. And we are hungry."

"Tell the two lovebirds to go eat something."

"Aren't you and me lovebirds?" Neville teased.

Celli smiled. Again one of those rare occasions where her face lit up into a genuine smile, except there was no one there to appreciate it. In her mind she had gone over to where Neville was and had given him a kiss. Actually this last trip had been the first time they had been separated since they had married.

"You bet we are," she said. "Let's go prove it when I'm back in Paducah."

The judge looked pensive.
"I really can't do that."
"Then no book."
He looked pensive again.
"I'll need to think it over. Where can I reach you?"
"I'll call you tomorrow at ten, or any convenient time thereafter," she said.
And the interview was over.

She was thinking of what wording Nora could use in her pleas so that it would apply to John Doe as well as to her ill-fated, late husband.

Nora, herself, had tried out a couple of wordings and thought the following to be the best. 'On the night of the twenty-ninth in the semidarkness I saw a figure close to me in a threatening posture, and I panicked. If you bring a hard object down with too much force on someone's head you might kill that someone, but that was not my intention. I brought the object down on the head, I heard the cracking of the skull, and I apparently had applied too much force. I became panic-stricken and left the room and went into hiding. I didn't mean to kill. I am sorry that Dr. Ondman is dead.'

This way she would be confessing to John Doe's death in her own mind and the court, essentially, could interpret it as answering the allocution charge. In any event, if the John Doe problem should arise, there would be a good case for double jeopardy.

CHAPTER 20

You'll earn me the rewards of…
Distorted judgments, noise and blame
Alexander Pushkin, Eugene Onegin

They met in Celli and Neville's room.

"It's all set then?" said Celli. No one said No, so she continued. "First of all, Jon and Nora, I want the copy you have of the 'book'. In return I'll give you this."

She handed Jon a package. "It's the decoded version. When we get to Florida I want you, Jon, to get a motel room in the Blue Motel in Palm Harbor. A single room. After the surrender of Nora, there will be no direct contact between you and her. The conspiracy theory may not be on the table, but I don't want it to resurface."

"What about Nora."

"She'll be in County Jail until the preliminary hearing. Bail will be set there. Do you have enough money for a substantial bail?"

"I'm sure I do," said Jon.

"But when Nora is released on bail, I still don't want you to see one another. At least not overtly. You could meet in the coffee shop where you met first, but don't sit at the same table."

Nora looked at Jon. "I don't think I can stand it."

"You'd better learn to live with it," Celli said. "Because after sentencing you'll be separated for a long time." She paused, then said, "After the surrender, Jon, I want to talk to you on the phone. But I want you to call me. Again, call from a pay phone. I don't want you to have my cell phone number. It may be tapped. So give me three rings in the condo, and I'll go down to a pay phone and call you back. Then you should be at the payphone in the coffee shop - I know the number. Call me about two hours after the surrender…"

Such a terrible word.

"And always call from a payphone," she repeated.

Grayness set in. Nora and Jon felt miserable.

"We should leave about four o'clock tomorrow morning," said Celli. "You may not have much time together, so make use of the night as much as you can."

Then she did something quite out of character for her. She went over and patted Nora on the head, and then she kissed her on the forehead. It was quite touching.

When they were back in their room, Jon said, "You should think this over one more time,"

"You know I have made up my mind." She added, "One aspect we have not touched on is that they killed. You might be in danger, too. You know, after I go to prison."

An even more horrible thought was that they might kill her. He would ask Celli to arrange for solitary confinement for her. That would not be pleasant, but it would be safer.

"If they try to hypnotize you in prison, just gaze at the bridge of their noses. I hate to admit it at a time like this, but I'm a bit scared for myself as well."

"They could make me talk about you?"

"Well, I guess so."

"Let's not talk about it," Nora said. "I've made up my mind and that's it." Her voice was trembling. Then she went over to Jon and said, "Please, make love to me."

"Wrong words," he said, "let *us* make love."

He held her and kissed her, and in the night they forgot the terrible future that lay ahead. But the morning was gray again. He put the television on, more to distract her than to watch the news. They were discussing the upcoming campaign and the

Republican preliminaries.

A strategist for George Bush was being interviewed.

"Oh, my Lord," Nora said. "I know him. He used to come to the house. I'm sure he's LOLA. They're everywhere."

"Don't worry," Jon said, "Bush won't have a chance." But quietly he was wondering.

They walked over and knocked on Celli and Neville's door.

They headed out for Florida in the early morning. They drove over to Celli's car and surveyed the lot. Was there someone on the look-out?

"We'll meet at the courthouse," Celli said. "I'll stop at the first rest stop in Georgia and the first rest stop in Florida. Just in case we need to be in touch for some reason. Otherwise, there will be no contact until we get to Pinnelboro. We'll rendezvous there and then we'll go to the judge's chamber. I'd like the surrender to take place there."

Nora looked worried. She had been aware of the gravity of the situation all along, but it seemed to come home to her with heart-wrenching force now.

Celli said to Jon," When we get to the courthouse, try to park close to where I park. I'll try to park so that there is an empty spot nearby. When you arrive, I'll get out of the car and you, Nora, will then come over to me. Alone. Jon, you simply drive off. Just to be on the safe side, you and Nora make the best of the trip. It may be the last time you have a chance to touch one another for a long time."

Nora was definitely crying now.

Celli and Neville got out of Jon's car and walked in the shadows, away from the parking lot lights, until they got to their car. Jon and Nora saw them leave. They waited a couple of minutes. There seemed to be no car following them.

"You still want to go through with it?"

She simply nodded. Were there tears in her eyes again?

They caught up with Celli's car about half an hour later, and followed it at a good distance. They stopped at the rest stops, but nothing untoward happened.

They stopped the car at the courthouse. It was dark by

now. Celli was already parked, and as they pulled up and they saw her get out of the car and walk slowly across the street. She motioned for Nora to follow.

Nora kissed Jon. She was shaking.

"You'll wait for me - always. Right?"

"Right," he said. "But you'll be out on parole until the sentencing."

"I know, but say it anyway."

"I'll say it and I mean it, I'll wait for you."

He could almost see her sob as she left the car. Then she straightened up and walked with resolute steps over to Celli, and he saw them disappear into the building.

When the judge got the telephone call that Celli and Nora were there, he interrupted what he was doing and drove over there directly.

The two women were standing in the hallway, and the police were already there.

The judge nodded to one of the officers. He handcuffed Nora. She looked at Celli, frightened. Celli said," Just be calm. It's a difficult time that lies ahead. Just be strong."

The police led her away. Her head was bowed and Celli watched her as the party turned a corner and was then out of sight.

Celli and the judge went to his chambers and Celli handed him the 'book' and the one copy she had. The judge opened it up, looked at it and carefully accounted for all the pages being there.

"Have you read it?" he asked Celli.

"No, your honor."

"Well," he said. "The computer is the important thing, and that's in code, anyway. But a code can be broken."

"My client has no such talents, I can assure you, and I, overnight, could certainly not do it either."

"Good enough," said the judge. "The hearing will be behind closed doors tomorrow morning at seven o'clock. I want no publicity about this. I'll gag you too, in the sense that I don't want you to talk to anyone about the matter. Have you talked to anyone yet."

"No, your honor."

"Good. Then don't."

"Now for the computer."

Celli showed him her car key. "Would you and a police officer escort me to my car. I have it there."

The judge made a call and an officer came in.

"He can follow you and me and can give you a receipt for it," the judge said.

The policeman looked at the judge.

"Do as she says."

Down at the car she opened the well and took out the computer. She handed it to the officer and they went inside. They had just booked Nora. The officer wrote out a receipt and handed it to her.

Then he shook his head and said, "See you at seven."

"Before we leave," said Celli. "I'm concerned about my client's safety. There have been nasty rumors - I realize they are just rumors - about, for instance..."

The judge didn't look pleased.

"Our penal system will protect her, rest assured."

"Like solitary?"

"If she so wishes."

Jon talked to Celli as planned. "The preliminary hearing is at seven tomorrow morning. The same arrangement. Call me again at, say, eleven. Use another payphone. And do *not* talk to anyone about anything relating to the case. Even in idle conversation."

When he called, the news was bad.

"She is being held without bail." Celli said. "I didn't count on that. That's my mistake. I'm sorry." She continued, "Go back to your room."

Back in the motel room he felt depressed. He needed to see Nora, talk to her. He wanted them to discuss what they should do, how they should stay in contact when she was incarcerated. He didn't often cry, but suddenly, as he sat on his bed, the tears started flowing.

There was a knock on the door. It was Neville.

"Celli feels awful about the bail thing," he said." But more to the point, there are a couple of things you need to consider. Celli wants you *not* to contact Nora for at least three months."

Jon's jaws dropped. Why?

"It's too dangerous for you. You have to look at the final outcome, four years - maybe more - from now. Do you love her enough to wait for her."

"Of course."

"Well, Celli will convey that to her and explain the same thing I'll explain to you. You want to stay away from the Law. You don't want to arouse suspicions. So far everything has gone fairly well, but you - both you and Nora - should be able to see that this is by no means over."

"That means I can't see her in jail. God, this is awful. Why can't I just say I'm her husband and I want - what do you call it, visitation rights."

"The problem is that you got married so shortly after - or maybe even before - Ondmand was killed. That fuels the accomplice theory. What you could do, however, to diffuse that, is to do as if you aren't married, and write her a letter and saying things like, 'Well, I don't know you but I admire you,' or something like that. You'll see her at sentencing, and you could have gotten fascinated with her at that point. You're a good writer; you have good imagination, you can figure out something to say. And she'll get a lot of letters like that. There will be nothing suspicious about it. The point is that it will appear that you don't know one another, and then later you can petition to be married to her."

"Even while she is in jail. And even if we're already married. They'll know, won't they?"

"She was charged as Leonora Ondman. The Court simply accepted her as such."

"So we'd remarry with exactly the same names that we married under in Macon."

"Not really in your case. Unless you're cleared in Madison

in the meantime. It's the only way I can think that it could be done. One more thing is that if your are married, or even if you aren't, once you have established yourself as a legitimate visitor - shall we say - you'll know the time when she is actually released. That way you can wait for her outside the prison gate."

Jon thought that was quite clear thinking on the part of Celli. Because the words spoken by Neville were Celli's.

Neville left. He had left addresses for the correctional institutions of Florida, so that a letter addressed to Nora c/o those institutions should reach her.

He lay on the bed for quite a while. Then he went to a liquor store and bought a bottle of Jack Daniels. In the morning when he awoke, the bottle was empty.

The gal at the reception counter said to him," A lady came to see you. She said for you to call her at this number." She handed him a slip of paper.

"Thanks."

Then he had four cups of coffee.

Celli had told him he could come to the sentencing. There would be enough people there so that he could get lost in the crowd.

Again it was announced for a week hence, but Celli said that the actual sentencing date was one day earlier. The judge simply didn't want the media interfering too much. That is what she surmised. There would still be leaks, so the courtroom would not be empty.

Jon was restless. Would she be desolate? Of course. Would she wonder if he would be thinking of her, loving her? He visualized the terror of isolation and got to think of John the Baptist. Please, Nora, don't doubt me, I'll be there. I'll be there when you get out from under the yoke of your confinement. It may seem a long time, but four years are not an eternity.

There was a small group of people congregated outside the courtroom door. One was a girl - twenty years old maybe. It was obvious that she was there to be judged in some way.

The door opened, and the crowd filed in.

It became apparent from the initial interchange between the judge and the lawyer that the girl had been the get-a-way driver in a failed bank robbery.

The girl's lawyer stood up and asked for a postponement of sentencing and the judge asked "Why?"

"She is pregnant, your honor. She would very much wish that the child not be born in prison."

The judge got angry. "Did she get pregnant just so she could postpone sentencing. I could sentence her anyway, you know."

"No," the girl's lawyer said. "She was pregnant at the time of the crime."

So the judge postponed the sentencing until the birth of the child had taken place.

Jon, suddenly, thought that Nora might be pregnant. It was two weeks since she had her period. It was possible, maybe.

He noticed Celli enter, and bailiffs entered with Nora from a side door. They got seated at the table that the other lawyer and the girl were vacating.

Jon marveled at the fact that the press had been kept out of all of this. LOLA network, undoubtedly. Keep it all a low profile, and simply come out with everything after the fact.

Nora looked around and saw Jon. There was a sad smile in her eyes. Recognition. Support in a distant way. Knowing he was there.

The sentencing played out as planned at the onset. The judge asked for an explanation, without mentioning the name of Ondmand, and Nora delivered her statement with shivering voice, but verbatim as she had composed it.

"On the night of the twenty-ninth in the semidarkness I saw a figure close to me in a threatening posture, and I panicked. If you bring a hard object down with too much force on someone's head you kill, but that was not my intention. I brought the object down on the head, I heard the cracking of the skull, and I apparently had applied too much force. I became panic-stricken and left the room and went into hiding. I didn't mean to kill. I am sorry that Dr. Ondman is dead."

The judge banged his gavel. His countenance was one of anger, all of a sudden.

"This is a heinous crime," he said," And I sentence you to life in prison without parole."

Celli was at her feet in an instant. "Your honor, there was a plea bargain. You and the D.A."

"One more word out of you and I'll hold you in contempt, although that would be superfluous."

Celli looked puzzled.

"I'll appeal, you can be sure of that," she said defiantly.

Nora looked as if she was going to faint. She looked back and sought Jon's eyes. He looked lost, shrugged his shoulders in the saddest way. Then she looked ahead of herself again.

They walked her out, and she looked around again. It was as if she, hungrily, soaked in the last glance they exchanged, and then she disappeared behind the door.

Then something strange happened. Two police officers entered the courtroom and went up to Celli, and there was an exchange of words. Then they handcuffed her and let her out by the side door as well.

What was going on?

Out in the hallway, the press had finally arrived. They were interviewing the district attorney.

Yes, it had been a plea-bargain but not the way the lawyer, Ms. Sagfor, had implied. The judge was fully justified in what had been done. There had been several witnesses present during the plea-bargaining session

Why the arrest of Celli Sagfor? Well, she was wanted for fraud in Wisconsin. It had just come to the attention of the district attorney's office. Extradition was not challenged.

"Timing is everything," someone said.

LOLA is everywhere, thought Jon.

What about Neville, he thought? On the way home he called the motel where he and Celli were - or in her case had been - staying.

"Sorry, sir," the voice said. "He was arrested just an hour

ago. Are you a friend? Could you take care of the bill?" Then she added, "He left a message. He said you'd been cleared in Madison, Morrison, or something."

He hung up. He felt all alone. He bought a bottle of Bourbon and went back to the motel room. Was he next? He fell asleep again, and woke up in the late afternoon - again facing an empty bottle. He thought he would go some place to eat, but then thought that the place that might give him some peace of mind was the coffee shop.

Then he went to the payphone and called Shirley Shelly.

ABOUT THE AUTHOR

J.T.Carstensen spent part of his life as a scientist until he broke away from this during a sabbatical in Paris in 1977. Here he started plein air painting and is by now well known in the Midwest for his oil paintings. He has written ten single-author technical books, and hence is familiar with composing in words, but his literary writings have mostly stayed under wraps. Aside from this volume he has written another novel and a collection of short stories to be published. He is philosophical but likes to interweave his concepts of society and mankind into dramatic situations that depict people caught up in webs of intrigue.